Forever Bound

*Susan
&
Randy
Best Wishes*

J. B. MILLHOLLIN

Fulton Books, Inc.
Meadville, PA

Published by Fulton Books 2017

ISBN 978-1-63338-336-4 (Paperback)
ISBN 978-1-63338-337-1 (Digital)

Printed in the United States of America

PROLOGUE

Webber's Furniture Store

Nashville, Tennessee
September 29, 2014

*E*ach and every day, he would keep his eyes locked on that front door. He would appear busy, doing those mundane, daily duties furniture store managers must do, but all the while he kept his eyes glued on each and every potential customer that walked through the door. From the moment he opened the front door of Webber's Furniture, until he locked it at night, that particular element of his managerial responsibilities had become the most important part of his daily existence.

He didn't give a shit about the dowdy, middle-aged housewife who was price shopping for a cheap chair to place in her basement. He had learned well how to spot those customers from a mile away. He waited only for the wealthy, the big spender, those that would make his week, his month, his year. Dear old Mrs. Johnston was certainly one of those customers, and she was just walking in the door.

"Mr. Harris, Mr. Harris, I need some assistance please. Did you hear me, Mr. Harris? I need some help over here."

Her thick Southern drawl cut through Chuck's early morning daze, and effectively brought him back to his purpose for being there. "Yes, Mrs. Johnston, I'm coming. I'll be right there. You just keep looking around, and I'll be right there."

She had been coming to the store for as long as he could remember. He had waited on her for almost twenty years, and she had been a patron prior to the time he was first employed.

She needed your attention—she needed all your attention every time she came in. But in return, she was also a very good customer. She seldom left the store without a purchase of some type. Hopefully, today would be no exception.

"Mr. Harris, I love this table. I really believe it would just be a wonderful fit on my patio. What do you think? Do you think it would be a wonderful fit on my patio?"

"Well, you know I've only seen your patio twice, but from what I remember, yes, it would be perfect."

"How long you worked here, Mr. Harris? How long?"

"Been here twenty years. Been right here helping you for twenty years now."

"In all those years, you've only seen my patio twice? I just couldn't remember. My memory's really not so good anymore. Well, I'm sure it's all changed since you last saw it. If I purchase this, why don't you come over, and just look around. That way you'll have a better idea what I want and need, so whatever I do buy fits with the rest of the house."

She was at least eighty years old, but she was also the store's best customer. It wasn't unusual for her to spend up to three or four thousand a month, and that was every month of the year. She might buy an item one week, then replace it with a new item the next. She had the money—she used it to scratch her itch. Who could blame her?

"Mr. Harris, not to change the subject, but how's that pretty little thing Katy getting along? I just love her. You two been married, what now, twenty years?"

"Yes. I married her right before I started work here at the store."

"And your children, they're both off to college now, aren't they? I think I remember you telling me they were both away at school."

He needed to keep her appropriately focused on the issue at hand. He needed the sale and the money the sale would generate. He was a little short this week. "Yes, they are. Now, what do you think about the table? Does it suit your purpose, or do we need to look elsewhere?"

Both kids were away at school all right, and the cost was killing him. His father-in-law hadn't raised his pay in over two years. Angelo's theory was that Chuck and his wife, Katy, would eventually inherit the store once he was dead anyway. So, he concluded, Chuck could just suffer now and enjoy the true monetary benefit once he was dead.

Angelo Bonaventura had purchased Webber's Furniture Store almost a quarter of a century ago. Pursuant to the terms of the deal, he was allowed to retain the name given the business by its former owner. Angelo did not want his name associated with the business, feeling perhaps there could be a few that might not walk through the front door because of it. His theory had worked well. Few knew of the sale, and business remained constant.

Chuck thought back to those early years, the years Angelo basically starved both his daughter and himself. Eventually, he did what he needed to do to get ahead and stay ahead. Once again, Mrs. Johnston would be part of that scenario if he could just get her to bite on a piece of furniture, rather than continuing to waste his time wandering throughout the store.

"Maybe my purchase, if I do buy something today, will provide a nice big commission for you, Mr. Harris. You know, help you educate those fine children of yours. What do y'all say 'bout that?"

"Sounds like a plan to me. Now, let's find that special something so we can set it up on that patio of yours, how 'bout that?"

Commission my fat ass. Angelo didn't know the meaning of the word. He paid straight salary, and it had taken his *own* ingenuity to figure out how to come up with the rest of the funds he needed to breakeven, and possibly get a little ahead each month—the cheap fucker.

Angelo initially purchased the store for a specific purpose. Of course, his father-in-law knew nothing about furniture. But the true purpose became apparent not long after Chuck became employed. Once a week, a certified letter would arrive from the Bahamas. The envelope contained two checks, always in differing amounts. After a few years, he, rather than Angelo, was allowed to make it part of the regular deposits of the store, using fictitious names on the deposit slip. After the first year of those continuing deposits, it became clear that the store was being used to launder money. He was sure there were other businesses in the area, most likely owned by associates of Angelo that were doing the same thing. Even though they all weren't actually business partners, they did assist each other in some of their money-laundering efforts.

"Mr. Harris, I know the table is marked at thirty-two hundred dollars, but I also know you can do better than that." She turned and smiled at him, placing her eighty-year-old withered hand on his sleeve. "Now, you can do better than that, can't you?"

"I sure can, but I need to know you're really interested. Is that the one you want? You've been looking around for over two hours now, are you sure that's the one you want?"

"Oh yes, that's the one."

"Okay, I can reduce the price to twenty-nine hundred for you, Mrs. Johnston, but no further. It's already marked as reduced, but this price would reduce it almost ten percent more."

She thought for another moment, turned to him, and said, "How soon can it be delivered, Mr. Harris? And can you bring it yourself? I want you to see the rest of my home."

"I can have it delivered later this week. I'll be glad to come with the delivery crew and look over the rest of your home. How does that suit you?"

"Perfect." Every wrinkle in her face moved as she smiled from ear to ear. "Let's go finish this up. I play cards in an hour, and mustn't be late."

As they walked back to the counter to finish the transaction, Chuck reviewed the finances involving this transaction. He would deposit the check in his own cleverly titled account, very similar to the business name, order a replacement piece at wholesale cost, paying for it out of the money she paid him, and keep the balance. He had to carefully pick appropriate clients, clients that would have no contact with his father-in-law, but that had not been hard to do. He would follow the same process three or four times a month. No one had any idea what he was doing. The money never went through the office account, and all the items he sold in this manner were still in inventory—a perfect plan resulting in thousands of untaxed dollars each year. Not once had he been questioned by his father-in-law. Easy money and an absolute necessity as concerned his family's day-to-day existence.

"How should I make this check out?"

"I'll fill that in, Mrs. Johnston, you just fill in the amount and sign it."

After she left, the day remained relatively simple. There were no more transactions that presented any additional, profit-making opportunities.

Later that day, he performed his normal store-closing procedure, finishing up near nine fifteen. He locked the door, and as he
turned to walk to his car, he noticed two men approaching.

"Sorry, gentlemen, we're closed for the day. We open at nine in
the morning."

Just before he felt an incredible pain in the back of his head, he
heard one say, "You're closed forever, asshole."

As he slowly came to, he tried to move his arms, but was unable
to do so. They were tied to the armrests of the desk chair he used in
his office on a daily basis. He opened his eyes and looked up to find
Angelo and two of his men, Billy Martin and Rocco Nelson, standing next to him. He had water dripping off his face, and the rest of
his body was soaked.

"Takes a lot of fucking water to wake you up. Used three buck-
ets on you. You're a deep sleeper." Billy flashed a toothless smile as he
finished his sentence.

"What's going on? What the hell's going on, Angelo? Why are
you here? You're never in the store. Why am I tied up?"

Anglo was standing beyond the glare of the single desk lamp
that illuminated Chuck's office. He walked out of the shadows and
said, "Do you honestly think I didn't know what you were doing—
how much you were stealing from me? I was just hoping you would
stop on your own. But you never did. You just kept taking and taking
and taking. You've gone as far as your gonna go, Chuck."

"What the hell are you talkin' about? I haven't taken anything
from you. *Ever*."

"Seriously? I mean, seriously? You surely, in your current position, aren't going to deny you've been stealing from me for years, are
you? I think it would be in your best interest at this point in time,
Chucky, to just come clean and admit it. Maybe we can work something out. I mean, seriously, do you think I would be going to this
extreme if I didn't already know what you've done?"

"Honestly, Angelo, I've done nothing. Check the books. I've done nothing."

"That's not what Mrs. Harris says. She tells me she gave you a check for twenty-nine hundred dollars today, but you know, the deposit didn't reflect anything of that nature. And this isn't the first time I've checked on transactions, Chuck. There have been many, many times. I knew what you done, but I just hoped you would quit. Finish him, boys."

"Wait, wait. What about Katy? What about the kids?"

"Fuck, I can support them a hell of a lot better than you ever could—and I can be a better role model than you would ever be. Pop him, boys."

Three shots echoed loudly throughout the building. Once they were sure he was dead, they untied him and left him lying on the office floor. They rifled through drawers and cash registers throughout the building. Angelo knew the location of each security camera; and he had made sure that the night before, the boys had spray painted the lens of the one covering the parking lot. Once inside the darkened building, they wore masks until they sprayed the one in the office. They then removed the masks while handling Chuck's "issue" and put them back on while rifling through the store.

Later that night, after Katy had called law enforcement, concerned her husband hadn't come home, they found the dead body of her husband, obviously a victim of a robbery gone bad. It was months before Billy got drunk, and spilled the beans to his live-in girlfriend. During that time, Angelo's prophecy proved extremely accurate. He was, indeed, a better financial provider *and* a better role model than Mr. Harris ever was. Chuck's funeral was poorly attended. Only his immediate family and poor old Mrs. Harris were in attendance.

CHAPTER 1

Downtown Nashville
March 16, 2015

She raised her head off the pillow in an effort to help her determine where the hell she was. The room was dark, but she could tell it was day—there was a thin sliver of light entering the room from around the edges of the window curtains.

Rosa Norway looked down at the man sleeping next to her. As she continued to awaken, she finally remembered the party at Nicki's house that went well into the night. When the party seemed to be dying down, most of the participants moved downtown, to a bar called the Stage, and remained until they closed down. By then, she was pretty well wasted, and as a result of a breakdown in intellectual processing, she decided to go home with David—David of all people.

They had tried a romantic relationship before, but it had failed, and failed miserably. She hadn't even seen him in months. But for some reason, they concluded sleeping together, and trying to rekindle a dead relationship last night was logical and appropriate. Now, here she was, naked in his bed, trying to figure out how to get out of his house without waking him.

She quietly moved away from him and closer to the edge of the bed. Slowly she slid her slight 5'8" frame off the side of the bed and got down on her hands and knees, moving around the floor in an effort to find all her clothes. It was too dark in the room to find them by vision alone, so locating by "feel" was the only other available option. She finally found her bra and panties near the bedroom door, and the rest of her clothing was strung out between the door and the bed.

She put on her clothes while he continued sleeping, removed the car keys from her purse, quietly walked out the bedroom door, down the hallway, and into the living room. The room was full of light from a mid-March sun, which was just breaking over the horizon. She hurriedly opened the front door and started toward her car. About halfway there, she noticed she had pulled into the driveway first last night and was now blocked by his piece-of-shit 2008 Ford, which she soon determined was locked up tight as a drum.

Rosa looked at her watch and knew getting to court on time was going to be an issue if she didn't get this vehicle "problem" resolved quickly. And she knew, after practicing now for almost ten years, she absolutely could not be late for court. The judge presiding over this trial was a great guy, a good judge, but none of the judges would tolerate an attorney being late on the day you selected a jury—just too many people were inconvenienced.

She not only needed to get David's ass out of bed so he could move his car, but she needed to drive from east Nashville to Mount Juliet, get herself cleaned up, pick up all her files at the office in Mount Juliet, and return to the courthouse in Nashville. That all needed to be done in ninety minutes. Difficult, but not impossible. At least for the first portion of her trip, the flow of early morning traffic would be toward Nashville and not toward Mount Juliet, which would be an immense benefit.

She walked back in the house, shook him, and made him get up. He bitched and moaned, as he had most of the time during their relationship, but he finally found the keys and moved his car.

As she drove toward Mount Juliet, *now* she remembered what she hated about him. He could be so much fun when the times were fun, and such a complete prick when the going got rough. This morning, with a hangover, with no sleep last night, and with the car issue, his prick side showed up. Good thing. She needed to see that side one more time. The next time she encountered him at a party or bar, she would avoid him *before* she started drinking or just leave when she determined he was there. Nashville was certainly big enough for the two of them. She just needed to use a little common sense the next time they encountered each other.

Once she arrived home, Rosa still had a little over an hour before she needed to appear before Judge Beason. She hurried through the door of her small, two-bedroom bungalow, which she had purchased during the past year, and walked to the bathroom. From there, it was straight to her walk-in closet, pulling out an appropriate dark, business suit.

As she started to pull on her skirt, she looked at herself in the full-length mirror and immediately stopped what she was doing. As she evaluated her slight 135-pound frame, was she starting to put on a little weight? She dropped her skirt and unsnapped her bra. What the hell! Was she starting to droop? Were her girls starting to settle! She really needed to pay more attention to herself. But more importantly, where had those lines emanating from the corners of her eyes come from? Was she going to need a little work done in the near future? She didn't want to look old before it was her time to look old.

This was insane! She had no time to assess herself. Rosa quickly finished dressing. She was back in her vehicle and on her way to the office with forty-five minutes to spare.

She ran through the front door and never said a word to her secretary, June. She rushed past the open door of Bill Stone's office, the private investigator who shared the building with her, and her former lover, hearing him yell, "Morning," but never acknowledged his existence as she grabbed her files.

"Hey, what's the rush?" he yelled at her, as she again ran past his door.

She stopped, backed up, peeked her head around his doorframe, and said, "Sorry, Stoney, morning to you too. I'm in a hurry. I can't be late to court. I only have about forty minutes. I'll see you when I get out of court and back here. Everything okay?"

He smiled as he said, "Yes, everything's fine. Go, go, take off. I'll see you later this afternoon."

She waved a hurried good-bye, walked out the door, and started her journey to the Davidson County courthouse in Nashville. Traffic on I-40 was heavy, but moving at eighty miles an hour. Only an accident involving vehicles somewhere in front of her would cause her to be late. That was the only problem living in Mount Juliet. It wasn't the county seat, and as a result, she had to leave town to attend court concerning every case she tried. But the change in her routine, her weekly and monthly routine, was so much easier than what she had to endure while living and working in Nashville, she gladly accepted the fact she needed to drive a few more miles to get to court.

Stoney—so handsome—such a great guy. But they had tried making it work. They tried for months, to make not only a great working relationship thrive, but to make it work romantically. They had failed miserably.

The events surrounding the trial of their client Jake McKay, and all the issues involving his subsequent murder, had pulled the two of them together; but without that common thread, those common issues holding them together, their relationship started to falter a short six weeks later, and before long, they decided it would be best for both to continue only their business relationship. That, at first, was difficult, but it wasn't long before Stoney had some blond bimbo show up at the office wondering if he had made it to work yet, expressing her concern the prior evening might have killed him off. That in and of itself had helped her move on.

Stoney noticed the look in her eyes after the bimbo had left the office and had tried to explain it all away. But she just told him to forget it—that they both needed to move on. She told him obviously he had moved on, and she was doing the same.

Luckily, they were still able to work together. At least that part of the relationship had been salvaged. They were both busy day and night, and continuing to feed each other business when the services were needed.

She had mentioned nothing to Stoney, but she was going to say something to him, when the time was right, about his selection in women. He seemed to have a taste for the seedy side of life when it came to his relationships, and as a friend, she was about to point that out. Her taste in men certainly wasn't much better, but some of the women she knew Stoney had been with appeared to be nothing short of streetwalkers. He could listen to her or just tell her to go to hell, but she still cared too much for him to let it remain unsaid. She just needed the right time and place. Maybe tonight, if she remembered, and if the timing was right, she would again bring it up.

Her thoughts ultimately turned to her client, Angelo Bonaventura. He would be waiting for her in the courthouse. They would need to find a conference room and go through the jury list one more time before they started jury selection.

She was having trouble getting away from a group of clients she hated to represent. They wouldn't let her go. First there was Jake McKay. His trial had ended tragically with his murder, but the group was happy with how she had represented him, so they sent her Rico Montago. He had been charged with murder. Rico skipped town

15

before she ever met him, and hadn't been seen since. Then along came Angelo. He had been charged with murdering his son-in-law, and his trial was set to commence this morning.

She finally found a spot in the parking garage and hurried across the street to the courthouse. Once inside, she found Judge Beason, who was still in the clerk's office prior to walking back to the judge's chambers to review the court file.

"I'm running a little late, judge. Can I have an additional fifteen minutes before we meet in chambers?"

"Morning, Rosa. Sure. I'm running a little behind today anyway. Not a problem. I'll see you in fifteen."

Rosa walked quickly down the hallway and through the door entering the courtroom. She saw Angelo along with his entourage seated near the back and motioned for him to follow her. She walked across the hallway, opened the door into a conference room, then motioned for them to follow her into the room.

She laid her files down on the table and waited for them. The first one in was Angelo, who looked at her and said, "Where the fuck you been? I been here almost an hour waiting for you. You think I have time to simply sit and wait on you? Now, where the fuck you been?"

She turned away and mumbled, "I wonder. Could today get any better? Could today *possibly* get any better?"

CHAPTER 2

*M*eeting with Angelo Bonaventura, Rosa concluded, was worse than sleeping with David. Both situations were worse than death itself, but meeting with Angelo was as day-altering as it gets.

He was now seated at the conference table, waiting for her to say something to get this party started so the jury could eventually find him not guilty of a crime "he never committed." With him was his closest cohort, Rocco Nelson; Angelo's woman, Gail Harper; and his daughter, Katy Harris. Rosa had met all of them and discussed Angelo's "situation" numerous times since he had been charged.

"So what's going on? Is this circus gonna continue, or are you gonna get it dismissed before it starts? Where the fuck are we, Rosa?"

Angelo was an average man in most every respect. He was average height, brown hair, brown eyes, average in looks, average in most every way—with the exception of his incredible temper. She had never witnessed anyone lose it so quickly. And when he did, she could never be sure which direction he would take. She had been with him preparing for trial, in his home, and while there, she had watched as he threw chairs, threw his drink against the wall, and kicked the dog all in the same night. When he lost his temper, he was uncontrollable like no one she had ever witnessed. At least until now, she had been able to contain her response, and simply shut up until his rant was over.

"No, Angelo, we're moving ahead. I went through the process of explaining the selection of a jury with you. You've had the jury list for over a week now. I've asked you to review it more than once so we can make sure we can strike anyone that might have some type of personal issue with you. Have you reviewed it? Are there people on the list we need to remove?"

"You mean *this* list?"

He removed the folded list from his inside coat pocket, looked at Rosa, and smiled, while he tore it into a thousand pieces, throwing them in the air, littering the area where they were seated.

"Now, that's what I think of this stupid trumped-up proceeding. Sure. I looked the piece of shit over. There was no one on there that was a problem. What a waste of time this is. What a complete waste of time."

Rosa looked around the floor now covered with small pieces of paper that was once a useful list of names, a list she had intended to use while the prospective jurors' names were being called to proceed to the jury box to be questioned. "You know, that wasn't very smart, Angelo. I needed that list."

"Get another one. For what I'm paying you, surely you can take a few minutes of your precious time and dig up another copy of that list. Now, what's gonna happen today? Tell me that if you know, will you?"

She should have stayed in bed with David and just skipped the whole day. The day would have truly been more fun being screwed repeatedly by a man she didn't love, than getting fucked over by this son of a bitch in court.

"We've discussed the process, Angelo, and you know how the selection of a jury works. It's vitally important that we seat the appropriate jurors on the panel. It literally could mean the difference between success and failure. So I'm going to take my time with this. Don't even think about pushing me through the process. By the way, the chief prosecutor, John Winstrom, decided he had more important things to do than try this case, so he's named his assistant Marvin Johnston to try it, and he's as slow as I am."

Rosa was somewhat concerned about John's decision not to try the case. She had dealt with him a number of times and enjoyed confronting him in court. He was fair, thorough, and honest, along with good-looking, tall, and well-dressed. In addition, he treated her like a lady should be treated, and most importantly, *soon he would be single*. But he had opted out, for reasons of his own, assigning Marvin to the case. Marvin was a good prosecutor and easy to deal with—he just wasn't John.

"So this Marvin what's-his-name, what's his story? Can he be bought off or threatened or something like that? What's his story here, Rosa?"

"Don't go there with me, Angelo. No to all of those questions. He's a good prosecutor, and he'll do all he can to put you away. Hopefully we can win the case on its own merits, and not through some type of intimidation. I realize that may not be your style, but maybe we can just get it done the legal way."

While Rocco smiled in the background, Angelo turned a shade of red and said, "Whatever you say, Rosa. You just need to be right. You need to get me off this trumped-up charge. It would not be good if I get convicted."

"Do you mind if we just move on? Would that be okay with you? Have you reviewed your answers to the questions I'm going to ask you? Are you ready to review those with me one more time? Because it won't be long, and you're going to need to be prepared to answer each and every one of them in front of the jury. I fully intend on you testifying. If they get all of Billy's testimony into evidence, you and you alone are going to need to offset it, along, of course, with Gail's testimony, that you were with her the night Chuck was murdered."

She sat quietly while all the conversation swirled around her, but Gail Harper never sat anywhere without being noticed.

She was an incredibly beautiful woman with a striking figure to match. She said little. She stayed out of the way. Other than a run-through of questions and her responding answers with Rosa, she had never spoken a word during the many times they had all been together. It was always Angelo's show. That's the way he wanted it, that's the way it was. She was clearly bought and paid for, and from all Rosa could discern, that was exactly the way she liked it.

"Gail, are you ready to testify when we need you?"

"Yes."

Rosa would need to, again, instruct her to speak above a whisper and to refrain from looking down every time she spoke, lessons she clearly had learned from Angelo.

"Gail, you and Angelo were together traveling to Knoxville the night Chuck was murdered, correct?"

"Yes."

"So basically the most important testimony concerning Chuck's murder centers around Billy Martin, is that correct?" Angelo, again, diverted the conversation in his direction, a trait he had learned to master well.

"Yes," Rosa responded. "Without his testimony, their case falls apart. With it, the jury will need to decide who to believe, Billy or Gail. It's really just that simple."

"Have you heard what they offered Billy in return for his testimony?"

"No, but I do know they got the upper hand when it comes to his future. They not only have the murder charge involving Chuck's death, but when the cops arrested him, he was armed. That pistol has been tied in to a couple of other shootings in Nashville. They have him right where they want him."

"I assume you'll get him to testify as to the bargain the prosecutor made with him when he testifies, won't you, Rosa?"

"Sure. That will all be part of my cross-examination."

"If he testifies, that is," Angelo said, with an accompanying condescending smile.

"Oh, he'll testify. They have nothing without him." She thought for a second as Angelo continued to smile without saying a word. "Why do you say that? Is there something I don't know about him testifying?"

"No, no, not at all. We would all hope he makes it to the courthouse and can testify as he wishes. That's certainly all our hope."

This conversation was headed down a road Rosa had no desire to travel. She decided it was time to leave this group to themselves and visit with the judge about today's activities.

"I have no idea what that means, and I really don't wanna know. I need to visit with the judge for a moment. When we're finished, I'll check with the clerk and make sure all the prospective jurors are accounted for."

"We'll wait patiently for your return," Angelo replied sarcastically.

Rosa picked up her files and walked out the door. As she walked toward chambers, she had no doubt she had chosen the wrong profession. She should have shined shoes, trained birds, anything other than having to deal with assholes like this. What a way to make a living!

She walked in the chambers door as Judge Beason was closing the court file, his review completed. Marvin Jackson was seated in front of the judge's desk, and he stood as she walked in.

"Marv, how are you?"

Rosa shook his hand when it was offered as he said, "Good, Rosa. All is well. And how's the practice in Mount Juliet? Is it working out as well as you had hoped?"

"Not enough hours in the day. Yes, I've been busy, and I really do enjoy life outside Nashville." As she took a chair next to him, she said, "Any changes concerning the trial we need to discuss before we pick a jury?"

"No, none that I know of. Judge, are there any issues you have that need to be discussed before we walk in the courtroom?"

"No. It appears to me the state is going to call this Billy Martin. Has he been offered a deal, or why is he coming forward with this testimony?"

"Yes, he has. The deal will all be disclosed when he testifies," Marvin responded.

"Great. Knowing this defendant as we do, I'm assuming this witness is in protective custody?"

"Yes, he is. He has a couple of cops with him, and he's in a motel room to be transported here when we need him. He's an important witness. Without him, we would have a problem."

The judge looked at Rosa and said, "You ready to proceed?"

"I am, judge."

"I'll see both of you in the courtroom in just a minute or two, and we'll get started."

Rosa stood, then walked down the hallway to gather up her client and his entourage. But as she did, she considered the smile on Angelo's face when discussing the prosecution's chief witness. Was her imagination just a little too active, or did that smile indicate he really did know way more about these proceedings than she did? If it was anyone else, Rosa wouldn't have thought anything about it, but this guy was dangerous. She needed to watch her every move with him. She wondered how much money she could make as a waitress.

CHAPTER 3

Rosa finished jury selection at four thirty and started her journey home shortly thereafter. The drive toward Mount Juliet out of Nashville at rush hour was never a drive she enjoyed. Negotiating I-40 at that time of day was always bumper-to-bumper at breakneck speed. One mistake by the guy ahead of you, and you were toast. That was the one disadvantage with living twenty miles out of Nashville, but the benefits of living there far outweighed the disadvantages. So she accepted her punishment at rush hour, and appreciated her life in Mount Juliet the rest of the time.

She walked in the office at five, just as her secretary was walking out the door.

June walked right on by toward her car, and as she was walking away, she said, "Hi, Rosa. Your messages are on your desk. You may want to return a few of those calls yet today, but basically there were no emergencies. Stoney is still in his office. Give me a call if you have any questions. See you tomorrow morning." She gave Rosa a wave of her hand as she continued on to her vehicle.

"Well, okay then. Thanks. I'll be in for a few minutes tomorrow morning before I leave for Nashville. See you then."

June shut the car door as Rosa ended her sentence.

She walked through the reception area and down the hallway, shutting off lights as she walked. She could see the lights in Stoney's office were still burning. She walked in her office, turned on the lights, laid her files on her desk, and walked across the hall into Stoney's office.

His office was decorated in early medieval. He had no pictures on the walls, no lamps or pictures on his desk, and his office furniture looked like he had just confiscated it from a landfill. When someone hired Stoney to investigate, that was exactly what you got—Stoney and an investigation—nothing more, nothing less.

"Hey, stranger," Rosa said as she plopped down in one of four chairs situated around the front of Stoney's desk.

"Well, Rosa, how the hell are you? Been a while."

"I know, I know. I've been so damn busy I haven't had time for anything but work. What about you? I haven't seen you in your office for a couple of weeks. What's going on?"

He was almost too good-looking. Dark brown hair, a knockout physique, and piercing blue eyes caught a woman's attention quickly. Even now, when she knew it was over between the two of them, there still remained that desire to grab him, throw him to the floor, and make love, one more time, for old time's sake.

"Just business. Had a number of domestics that needed some work the last few weeks. I've been really busy. It doesn't seem like there are enough hours in the day. Leaving the force and going into investigating was the best move I've made in a long time. I owe that significant change all to you. Thanks for letting me tag along, and leave the city behind."

She thought for a moment, and then said, "Guess everything worked out except our relationship. I'm really sorry we didn't make it as a couple, Stoney. I thought you and I would last forever, I really did. I'm just sorry—"

He put his hand up to stop the conversation before it proceeded any further. "Forget it. The one good thing that did come out of it is that we're great business partners, and still the best of friends. We were able to work together, put that Jake McKay mess behind us, and here we are today, friends and partners. I'm just thankful for that. Neither of us have ever been the best at picking the right lover, and we each fell victim to our own weakness I guess. Let's not speak of it again. Let's just move on with what we have. How was your weekend?"

"Good, until I got drunk and ended up with that idiot David Goodson." She looked down and just shook her head. "Like you say, we both have a hell of time picking our lovers. What a waste—spending time with him."

Stoney laughed and said, "David Goodson? Spending time with him is about as bad as it gets. Been there, done that. Not the way *you* spent your time with him of course, but I too learned the hard way. I've spent the last second with him I'm going to, at least in this lifetime. How did today go? I understand you started that Bonaventura trial today."

"Yes, I did. We just got started picking a jury. It'll probably take a couple of days to pick it. I'm trying to be really careful. This asshole is well-known in Nashville, but for all the wrong reasons, so I just want to make certain nobody on the jury knows him—or particularly, knows *about* him. So far, I haven't found anyone that presents a problem, but we've a long way to go yet."

"What's he like to work with?"

"He's a fucking prick. Excuse my terminology, but in this instance, that term describes him perfectly. Everything has to be done his way. He has, in his own subtle way, threatened me that this trial better end up the way he wants it, 'or else.' I'm not sure exactly what that means, but I got a pretty good idea."

"Sounds like you're playing with fire to me."

"Unfortunately, you're probably correct."

"What's the evidence show? Who are their witnesses? Is there anything I can do to help?"

"No, I don't think so. The evidence really isn't that complicated. The state has the usual crew testifying as to cause of death and the type of weapon used. They have a couple of people who will testify they saw a car like his driving away from the furniture store about the time the medical examiner indicates his son-in-law was murdered. But the real problem is this guy Billy Martin, who claims he was with Angelo at the time it happened. His testimony is crucial to their case. Marvin's handling it, and he told me today that without his testimony, they would have no case at all."

"They got something on this Billy what's-his-name? Why is he testifying?"

"Oh, sure, they got plenty, and I know without a doubt they're offering him a deal in return for his testimony. So it's all going to come down to whether they believe him or they believe he made it all up to get the deal. But I'm really concerned. They have all they need to convict this guy if Billy testifies."

"Do you have any type of defense at all, or just a general denial?"

"I think I'll probably have Angelo testify. I'm not sure at this point. I'm just going to wait and see what happens before I come to a conclusion on whether to take the chance. The guy has such a short fuse, I'm just afraid on cross, he may go ballistic. He has the shortest temper of anyone I've ever met, and I'm just afraid he could lose it all under any type of intense cross by Marvin. He's pretty damn good at cross, and Angelo is a bomb just waiting to explode, which is not a pretty combination when it comes to this type of confrontation. Especially, when, unfortunately, you're really rooting for the bomb to explode."

"Do you have anything else to offer the jury, or is that it?"

"Well, I do have his woman, Gail Harper, but I don't know if I'm going to use her or not. Again, I'm just going to need to see how everything goes before it gets to the point I need to call her."

"What's she going to testify to? Anything of relevance or just fluff?"

"Actually, she does have something to say, although, to be honest, I'm really not sure if it's the truth. She says on the night of the murder, she and Angelo were together. She says they were on their way to Knoxville, and he couldn't have been involved in the murder because he was with her. Like I say, I have no idea how her testimony will come across with the jury, but she seemed believable to me. I'll wait to figure out whether to have her testify after I hear the state's witnesses. I'm a little reluctant to call her. I really don't want her to perjure herself, and I have a bad feeling that may be exactly what she could be doing. I like her, but she's in a bad situation with this guy. Not sure how that happened, but I guess at this point, that's her problem and not mine."

"Now, this is the Gail Harper that lives in Brentwood, right?"

Rosa sat back and took a deep breath before she said, "Yes, that's the one. Do you know her?"

"Just to make sure we're talking about the same woman, the one I'm referring to is blond, about five-ten, great figure, good-looking, great dresser, and has a low, kind-of-sexy voice, right? Is that the woman you're talking about?"

"How'd you meet her?"

"She seems to have an interest in the arts. I was tailing a guy who went to this art show downtown, and I happened to run into a friend I hadn't seen in a while. She was with her and introduced us. She seems pleasant enough. She's pretty easy to look at too."

Rosa rolled her eyes. "You know, I've seen that look before, Stoney. You need to stay away from her. You know who she lives with! He would just as soon shoot you as look at you. And that brings us to a subject you and I really need to discuss—your choice in women. I know some of the women you've been seen with lately, and, Stoney, you're really making some bad decisions as concerns your love life. I really think you should start being a little more selective."

Stoney leaned back in his chair, the one that looked like it had been put together during the Holy Wars, smiled from ear to ear, and said, "And this bit of advice comes from the woman that just did David Goodson? Are you kidding me? You're giving *me* advice about my love life? Give me a break!"

"Stoney, I'm just telling you to be careful. You need to stay away from Gail Harper. I mean that. Stay away from her."

"Oh, I will. I did have a chance to visit with her again the other day, but just for coffee. She's really a pretty good person despite the company she keeps—you and I excluded, of course. Believe me, nothing will come of this. She's just a nice person to have a cup of coffee, that's all, just a cup of coffee and a little conversation. Nothing more."

Their conversation lasted only a few more minutes, and Rosa walked back into her office to prepare for another day of jury selection. But long into the night, her conversation with Stoney remained on her mind. He was a good friend and a good business partner, but he was making a huge mistake barking up the tree of Gail Harper. She had seen that look before. She knew what he was thinking, and if she was right, he needed to be extra careful. Stoney was playing a perilous game, unlike any he had ever played before, and his ultimate opponent was a man who would stop at absolutely nothing to win.

CHAPTER 4

Rosa *finally got out of bed a little before six, having lain there* tossing and turning for almost two hours. She had processed her way through direct examination of all her witnesses and potential cross of the state's witnesses time after time, just unable to stop reviewing the extensive possibilities and different directions the trial might take. She finally concluded it would be easier processing it with a cup of coffee in one hand and a pen in the other. At least, in that manner, she could make notes concerning any thoughts that might be relevant and which she might need to remember.

After jotting down a few ideas, she had a quick breakfast, then left for the office. She needed to pick up her files, determine if June had any issues, then drive to the courthouse in Nashville. Traffic, as usual, would be intense this time of day, but there was nothing she could do about it.

June normally arrived near seven thirty, and as Rosa parked her car, she could see her already seated, working her way through a stack of paperwork.

"Morning, June. I'm in a hurry, but is there anything going on here today we need to discuss? I'll be in court in Nashville all day."

"Morning. No, no, we're fine here. I'll just leave messages on your desk. Go ahead and go."

Rosa walked down the hallway, noticing Stoney's light was already on. She was somewhat surprised as he normally never arrived until at least nine.

She walked a few steps through his office door as she said, "A little early for you, isn't it?"

He looked up, smiled, and leaned back in his chair as he said, "Yup. But I'm under the gun in that Kroger dissolution. That trial's coming up soon, and I need to get out and hit the streets—try to dig something up for her. Today is the second day of jury selection, right?"

"Yes. I need to hit the road. He'll probably be waiting for me when I get there. Another fun day with my favorite client."

"I know he was out of town until late last night, so on top of his normal belligerent self, you'll probably have to contend with a lack of sleep, which will most likely make him even more difficult to deal with, if that's possible."

She took just a second to think and rethink whether or not she should ask the question, but she finally said, "How'd you know he was out of town, Stoney?"

"Oh, I had a cup of coffee with Gail last night about ten. She mentioned he was gone. She didn't tell me where, but she did tell me he wouldn't be back until early morning."

Rosa rolled her eyes, and as she did, he said, "I know, I know I shouldn't be with her. But it was just coffee. We weren't together long. It's no big deal, Rosa."

"I'm warning you, don't mess with this guy. If he ever concludes you're seeing his woman, you'll be lucky to come out alive. Stoney, you need to listen to me. For once, just listen to me."

"Okay, I understand, I get it. I'll be careful. Now, Mom, get out of here before you're late. I'll probably be here when you get back. Good luck today."

She hesitated for a moment trying to determine if there might be a better way to impress upon him the urgency of the situation, but finally just breathed a deep sigh, waved good-bye, and walked in to pick up her files.

Angelo and his "friends" were waiting in the conference room for her when she arrived.

"I thought you said meet here at eight thirty. It's eight forty. What the hell? Where you been? If we were to meet here at eight forty, I would have been here at eight forty. I don't like waiting for nobody. Why you late?"

"Traffic, Angelo, traffic. Now, do you understand what's going on? This has gone so smoothly, we may be able to finish voir dire today. If we do, we'll finish the selection process tomorrow and get the opening statements out of the way. Do you have any questions or thoughts before I go see the judge?"

"Matter of fact, I do. When is Billy supposed to testify? Do you know what day he's supposed to be here? And I wonder where he's being held. My friends tell me he's not incarcerated. Do you know if they're holding him somewhere else?"

"What friends?"

"Just answer the question, Rosa. Do you know where he's being held?"

"No, I have no idea where he's at. His testimony will probably start day after tomorrow. It just depends on how quickly everything else proceeds. Anything else?"

"No. But if you hear where they're holding him, you let me know. By the way, *be on time from now on*. I don't like waitin' for nobody." He dismissed her with a wave of his hand and turned to talk to Gail.

Rosa walked out, hoping the son of a bitch got hit by a truck on his way to his car after the proceedings today. She wondered who she might employ to do just that.

She walked in the judge's chambers where Judge Beason was already seated behind his desk, talking with Marvin, along with chief prosecutor John Winstrom.

"Morning, everyone." Rosa walked to the front of the judge's desk and took the last remaining empty chair.

After exchanging insignificant, unmeaningful, early morning chatter, the judge said, "Ready to proceed? I assume we just continue with jury selection today, is that correct?"

Both Marvin and Rosa nodded, indicating they were ready.

The judge looked at John and said, "Are you sitting in today?"

"No, no, judge, I was just checking on my number one assistant, making sure he didn't need anything before starting the proceedings today." He stood to leave. "I'm just headed out the door."

Rosa stood as he did and said, "I'll walk out with you, John. I need to discuss a couple of matters with you. Do we have a little time before we start, judge?"

"Of course. We probably won't start for another thirty minutes or so, Rosa. A couple of the prospective jurors called and said they would be a little late. Just let me know when you're ready to proceed."

John and Rosa walked out in the hallway together. At six-three, he was at least 6 inches taller than she. He had now been the district attorney for Davidson County for two and a half years, having defeated Leon Kelmer for the position. His term would only last another eighteen months, and he would then need to decide whether to run for the office or let someone else run, and accept a lessor position in the office at that time.

"John, how's the family? Kids okay? How's the divorce going?"

He smiled and said, "Everything is proceeding in as normal a manner as can be I guess. The kids are good, and Jacki, well, she's just Jacki. She already has another man in her life, which, of course, was also the problem while we were together, so I'd say she's fine. I'm hoping to get everything wrapped up in the next few weeks. We've agreed to everything, it's just a matter of the two of us signing the paperwork and getting a judge's signature. How's everything for you? Is your new office location working out?"

"Yes, yes, it's working out very well. Thanks for asking." She had never noticed how fit he looked. No one could wear a suit as well as he did and not be fit. The suit looked like it cost a thousand bucks and was handmade just for him. He was an impressive-looking man to say the least. "I wanted to visit a moment about that Novak matter. I met with him the other day. He's to be arraigned next week. Do you happen to know who's assigned to the case?"

"Off the top of my head, no, I don't, but let me get back to you." He hesitated a moment before he continued, "By the way, you look great this morning, Rosa. How's Stoney? How are you two doing? I don't think I've seen him in months."

"He's doing well. *We* aren't doing so well. We're still friends, but not involved anymore. It was mutual, and we still office together. All in all, moving to Mount Juliet was a career-defining move for both of us. It's been a good change."

"Sorry about you and Stoney. He's a good man, but to be honest, I could never really picture the two of you together. Maybe once my dissolution is final, we can get together and have a drink sometime. Believe me, nothing serious, but I would just like to get to know you better."

"Yes, that would be nice. By the way, it's really none of my business, but why aren't you trying this case? I figured a case of this magnitude would warrant the best your office could offer, and that would be you. Why is Marvin trying it?"

He smiled and said, "Marvin *is* probably the best the office has to offer. Besides that, I really want to get my personal issues out of the way before I jump into anything of this magnitude, especially against someone as competent as you. Everything is going fine, but personally, I just need to get all the loose ends tied down before I move back into litigation. Marvin is very competent as you know. I have all the faith in the world in him."

"You're right, he's certainly a competent prosecutor, but I did wonder why you didn't handle this case yourself. I can understand personal issues creating a problem though."

"Right now I'm concentrating more on being an administrator rather than a litigator. I'm just trying to make sure the right prosecutor is involved with the right case, and helping whenever I can. Give me a few weeks, and I'll be litigating right along with them." He again smiled that infectious ear-to-ear smile and said, "You better go. I'm sure your client is waiting patiently for your return."

"Oh, I'm sure he is. Just between you and I, I'm just hoping I get out of this alive. He's a difficult man to deal with, to say the least."

"I've heard that. I better get back to the office." He extended his hand and grabbed hers when she reciprocated. "Let's get together once this trial is over and have a drink somewhere."

"That sounds like a good idea. Give me a call, and we'll meet."

He nodded and turned to walk down the hallway. She watched as he walked away. As she started walking behind him toward the conference room, the only two words that entered her mind at that moment were *nice ass!*

CHAPTER 5

*H*e leaned back in his chair as he shut his eyes and yawned. Last night had been a long night for Angelo Bonaventura. This morning, after so little sleep, he fought a strong desire to just say "fuck all this shit" and go home to bed. Last night, he drove to Birmingham to talk to Mark Gladstone about paying back the money he borrowed from Angelo. The trip had been a success. Mark had been avoiding Angelo for months, but his unannounced arrival had taken care of the problem.

They had to wait, Angelo along with Rocco, until Mark had seen a few people and put together the money he needed to pay, but the wait had been worth it. He had been paid in full. After the money was securely in Angelo's pocket, he told Rocco to break Mark's arm just to make sure he remembered what happened to people that didn't do what they said they would do.

As they walked out of the building, Angelo, did, however, tell Mark it was a pleasure doing business with him, and they would gladly do so in the future. The loan was paid off, and that was really all that mattered. Angelo highly doubted he would see Mark again, but he would not turn down a conference with him to discuss another business opportunity, if Mark requested the meeting.

The trip had been successful, but it lasted well into the wee hours of the morning, Angelo not arriving home until 3:00 a.m.

Today he paid for his late hours. At sixty-four, keeping these kinds of hours was considerably harder than it was at twenty. He had tried handing off some of the more difficult work, such as last night's job—debt collection—to the younger guys; but for some reason, they didn't seem to enjoy the same level of success as Angelo did. They either came back empty-handed and let the guy go another week or killed the guy and got nothing. Unfortunately, there were just situations in which it was simply best for him to do what needed to be done, but many times, it resulted in late hours, last night of which was a prime example.

"Hey, Rocco, we did okay last night, didn't we?" Angelo talked through another yawn, which he tried to suppress, but couldn't.

"We did, boss. You know, I think Mark thought as soon as he come up with that money, you know, he was off scot-free. Don't you think that was what he thought, boss?"

"Absolutely. But he had to be punished a little. You did good. Snapped his arm on the first blow. I don't mind doing business with him, but if we have to go to Birmingham to collect again, it's going to be his neck this time."

Rocco laughed. "I can handle that, boss. The necks pretty easy. Probably easier than an arm. Don't you think? Probably easier than an arm?"

"Okay, guys, if you don't mind, I really don't need to hear this. Thanks for the graphic details, but if you don't mind, I would really rather not hear all this."

"Oh, don't be so prissy, Gail. You know what I do. You know what we do. You've heard it before, you'll hear it again. You sure never complain about spending the money our line of work provides you."

She gave him one of those looks, but sat back in her chair and said nothing more.

Angelo wondered if it was time he dumped her. He had been with her for almost ten years now. She loved the money, and that factor, in and of itself, would probably keep her in line. The problem was she knew too much for him to ever just send her away. He was afraid he would have to "dispose" of her if their relationship ended.

Lately, he had become somewhat concerned she might be seeing someone else. This was not the first time. He could tell when she was spending time with someone else. It was easy. Subtle changes in her demeanor, in her conversations with him, always told the tale. She quit conversing with him as often as she normally did. She didn't tell him how her time was spent in quite as much detail. She wasn't quite as quick to take care of his sexual needs. Lack of attention to detail always told him she was seeing someone.

It had already happened twice, and both times he had confronted her. Both times she admitted it, and both times it had ended quickly, without involvement on his behalf as concerned the one she was seeing. Her actions in the past few days seemed to indicate this was happening one more time, and he had to admit it was getting old. She had been with him longer than any of the others, but it would not be difficult to replace her. It would not be any more difficult to terminate Gail than it had been to terminate his son-in-law.

"You go out somewhere last night, Gail? Security camera looked like you went out and didn't get back until right before I did. Where'd you go?"

She hesitated a moment before saying, "Just went down to that all-night coffee place and had a few cups of coffee. I couldn't sleep anyway. I was home when you got home. At least give me credit for that." She smiled and turned away.

She was seeing someone. There was no doubt in his mind. But that issue would need to be placed on the back burner. It would need to wait until this trial was over.

"Rocco, you hear anything from Billy? Has he contacted you at all in the last day or two?"

"No, boss, not a word. I have no idea where he might be. If I hear from him, I'll let you know, but I ain't heard a word. I got people out looking for him. We'll find him."

"Better be pretty damn soon. I couldn't believe someone put up his bail. Now he seems to have vanished. Just find him. Don't care how, just find him."

"Oh I will, boss, I will. You can bank on that."

As he looked at Rocco, he continued to wonder why he had never been charged with killing Chuck. He had been there too—why didn't Billy tell them? Both Rocco and Billy had been friends for many years. He figured Billy knew it was him, and not Rocco, they were after, so he just never said anything about Rocco being there.

Angelo shut his eyes and thought back on the number of times in his professional career he needed to find someone, to try to determine where they were located, right now, and do whatever needed to be done. He was getting too old for this kind of work, but he had tried quitting once before. He almost went insane. He had no control—over anything. He needed to feel he was in complete control of all elements of his life, and when he had tried to retire, he lost control over seemingly everything. In addition, the adrenaline rush was gone—that incredible rush he got when he did it right, like last night, when he collected, broke the guy's arm, and went home with his money.

Maybe in a few years, he would try again, but not now. Even as tired as he was at this very moment, and even in spite of this fucking trial, he would carry on his life's work for a few more years. Maybe being a little more selective with his employees would help. People like Billy and his son-in-law had made his whole line of work just that much more difficult. He had handled Chuck, and he would handle Billy. He just needed to find him.

Rosa walked in the conference room door, shut it behind her, and took a chair.

"You ready to go? Not too much for you to do today, but listen. Again, if you have issues with anyone I question for the jury panel, be sure and tell me."

"I understand. We been through this before."

"Rosa, I have a question. What happens if, God forbid, Angelo is convicted? Will he have time to put his affairs in order before he goes to prison? We've never discussed that before. What happens if they find him guilty?"

"Gail, why the hell would you ask such a question?" Angelo asked, his voice increasing in intensity as he ended the sentence.

"I just think we need to discuss all the options before they happen. I didn't mean anything by it, I just—"

Angelo slammed his fist down on the top of the conference room table, stood up, leaned halfway across the table, and yelled, "That's not gonna happen. What do you think *you're* gonna do anyway, take it all over yourself? Is *that* what you have in mind? Not gonna happen. Not in my lifetime, not in yours."

Rosa stood up and said, "Sit down, Angelo. It was an innocent question and a good one, now calm down."

He turned, looked at Rosa, and said, "Don't you ever tell me to calm down again—ever." He straightened his tie, straightened out his suit coat, and, while still glaring at Rosa, sat back down in his chair. He then calmly said, "They ain't gonna find me guilty of anything, and that's a fact. We're not going to discuss that possibility again. "

Rosa continued to remain standing while everyone took a deep breath. Finally, she looked around the room and said, "It's time to go, Angelo. You ready? You need a little more time to compose yourself, or are you ready?"

Angelo smiled. "I'm as ready as I'll ever be." He looked at Gail. "Honey, you ready to go?"

"Yes, I guess so," Gail responded.

They all stood and, with Rosa leading the way, walked across the hall into a courtroom full of prospective jurors.

Angelo had never considered the possibility he would be found guilty. If that option ever presented itself as a viable possibility, he would determine his plan of action at that time.

For now, he had a plan in effect, which should take care of all the issues involving this trial. Time was running short, but he expected to implement his idea shortly, and if it worked, which he fully expected, this charge would disappear as quickly as the bodies of all those he had murdered. He just needed a little more time.

CHAPTER 6

*A*s day 3 began, the jury had been selected and would be ready to hear evidence as early as this afternoon. The schedule for this morning's activities needed to be reviewed and discussed with Angelo and his "friends." As she entered the conference room, Rosa hoped she would be able to spend only as much time alone with them as need be. *Anywhere* without them was better than being with them in this room.

As she took a chair, she said, "Angelo, let me go through the procedure for this morning with you. Once we get started, the assistant district attorney will read the complaint in open court, the attorneys will give opening statements, and the state will begin with their testimony. Their witnesses will probably take the next three or four days, and then we'll have the opportunity to put on our case. Do you understand the process—is there anything we need to discuss about that procedure?"

"No, I get it. I've been down this road once or twice before, Rosa," he said, in his sarcastic, demeaning delivery he used too often. "I don't forget anything, *ever*. I understand the process. When is Billy to testify?"

"I don't know whether he will be first up or last, but I assume he'll be one or the other. Probably last. I'll let you know when I know. Now remember, the judge is busy concerning other issues tomorrow, so we won't have court. We'll reconvene with the state's witnesses day after tomorrow."

Angelo stood, looked at Rocco, and said, "I gotta go take a leak. You wanna walk along with me?"

"Sure, boss."

They both walked out, leaving Rosa alone with Gail and Katy. Once the door had closed, Rosa looked at Katy and said, "Are you wanting to testify? You and I have discussed that possibility but only briefly, and you've never been very definite about it one way or the other. You're certainly welcome to get up on the stand and testify if you wish."

Katy stole a quick glance at Gail, looked down for a moment, and said, "For which side?"

Her answer caught Rosa completely off-guard. She finally asked the question she felt she probably didn't want her to answer. "Do you have a feeling your father did this?"

"I don't have a feeling, I know he did. I can't testify on his behalf and won't. Obviously, if I testify against him, he'll have me killed. You already know about his temper. That's the way he is every day of every week of every month of the year. He's impossible to work with, to reason with, but he wants me right here with him all the time. He must be in complete control of everything in his life. Once he feels he's lost that element of control, he does whatever he needs to do to regain it, including murdering anyone that gets in his way. That's the way he's been since I was old enough to remember. In answer to your question, no, I can't testify, and I won't."

Rosa turned to Gail and said, "Gail, you're testifying you and Angelo were together that night. After what Katy just said, I probably shouldn't ask this question, but is that the truth? Were you together or not?"

Gail turned away to briefly look out the window and, when she turned to look at Rosa, said only, "Yes, we were together, just as I told you."

Rosa turned to Katy, who would only look at the floor, and immediately knew her whole defense was based upon a pack of lies. If she would have had the benefit of discussing the issues with Katy before the trial began, she could have withdrawn from further representation, but it was too late now. She would need to play the cards she was dealt, and hope for the best.

Angelo and Rocco walked back in as Rosa walked out. She needed to meet with Marvin and the judge to discuss in detail the day's activities. She didn't feel she could handle another minute in the conference room with the company she was keeping.

Marvin was already in chambers with the judge, and as Rosa took a seat, she said, "Marvin, what's the story with Billy Martin? I understand from our conversation the other day, he's out of jail? What's going on?"

"Yes, he's out. As you already know, we made a deal with him, and part of the deal was that he would be placed in protective custody with his wife until it was time for him to testify. It was really important to him that he be able to spend some time with her prior to pleading, so he's with a couple of officers now, but he'll be here to testify when it's time."

"Apparently the fact he had a girlfriend that squealed on him didn't matter to his wife?" Rosa said with a grin.

"Apparently not. They're now together, and that's all I know."

"Doesn't really matter to me. I just found it strange you let him out, but I assume the state would do anything to get him to testify the way you want."

"Now, Rosa, you'll have your chance to cross-examine *him*, so leave *me* alone. The jury will determine whether or not he's telling the truth or was overly influenced by the deal we made. But I think they'll find the guy pretty convincing. I'll probably call him as our last witness."

"So am I to understand this morning we'll have opening statements and start with evidence after the lunch break?" Judge Beason said. "If that's the case and the opening statements don't take the rest of the morning, let's make sure my jury instructions look okay to the two of you with the time we have left. Then right after the break, Marvin, you can present your first witness. Is that acceptable to both of you?"

Both attorneys indicated that was an appropriate plan for the rest of the day.

Rosa walked back to the conference room, and as she walked in, Angelo said, "Did you find out what the fuck is going on with Billy? Is he to testify or not? And why is he out of jail?"

Rosa said, "Yes, he's going to testify. Apparently, as part of his plea deal, he was allowed to spend some time with his wife prior to testifying and entering his plea. I have no idea where he is, only that he is under guard with a couple of officers, and he's with his wife. He's to be the last witness to testify. Let's go. The judge is just getting ready to start the morning session."

The four of them followed Rosa into the courtroom where opening statements consumed over two hours. It was shortly after eleven once the statements were completed, and the court sent the jury out for an early noon break so the attorneys, along with the judge, could work on jury instructions.

Court resumed promptly at one, and the state called their first witness. The medical examiner for Davidson County testified as to cause of death, testimony that was uncontested by Rosa. She never bothered asking him anything on cross knowing it would do absolutely nothing for their case. She was okay with simply accepting the examiner's statement the victim was killed by multiple gunshot wounds to the back of the head.

Motive was a major issue. There just didn't appear to be a reason Angelo would want his son-in-law dead. So the state did what they could do to produce at least a scintilla of evidence concerning a purported motive, by having coworkers of Chuck testify as to different statements made by him indicating the relationship between him and Angelo was not a good one. Each time one testified, Rosa would object as to all the testimony offered based on statements made by Chuck. It appeared to be clearly hearsay, but the judge overruled every objection, letting each witness testify without restriction.

Once they were all finished, Marvin said, "Your Honor, the state and the defendant's attorney have entered into a stipulation concerning the make and model of one of the defendant's vehicles, and I would like to introduce the paperwork establishing the ownership of that vehicle into the record."

"Any objection, Ms. Norway?"

"None, Your Honor."

Angelo leaned over and whispered, "What the hell are you doing? Why did you agree to that?"

"Do you honestly think they will be unable to get that into evidence? They were going to get it in anyway. You have to pick your battles, Angelo. We weren't going to win this one, and it's a small issue anyway. By the way, let me handle this. You hired me to try this case, now let me do my job."

"Oh, I will, Rosa. You just better know what the hell you're doing, that's all. You better know."

The paperwork indicated Angelo was the registered owner of a black Mercedes.

The next witness was then called to the stand, and after the obligatory questions concerning his personal information was satisfied, Marvin said, "Now, Mr. Gordon, where were you at around ten p.m. the night of September 29, 2014?"

"I was just walking out of an all-night pharmacy. I had some sinus issues and needed something to help me get through the night."

"Can you tell me where the pharmacy is located in relation to Webber's Furniture Store?"

"Yes, it's the first store to the south."

"Did anything catch your eye about that time, as you walked to your car? Anything out of the ordinary?"

"Yes, I saw a vehicle moving at a high rate of speed through the parking lot of the furniture store. I noticed it because the lot was empty, and there were no other vehicles in the area. It was moving away from the building, and then just disappeared into traffic once it reached the street."

"Can you describe the vehicle you saw for the jury?"

"Yes. It was a dark Mercedes, late model, four-door."

"Handing you what has already been marked as exhibit 16, would you please read the description of that vehicle, and tell me if it appears to be the same make and color of the vehicle you saw leaving the parking lot?"

He studied the exhibit briefly and then said, "Yes, that's an exact description of the one I saw leaving the lot."

"Thank you, Mr. Gordon. Nothing further, judge."

"Ms. Norway, cross?"

"Mr. Gordon, were you able to see any of the occupants inside the vehicle?"

"No."

"Could you tell how many people were inside?"

"No."

"Could you tell what they were doing?"

"No."

"You had no idea who was in the vehicle, who it belonged to, or why it was there, did you?"

"Nope."

"Nothing further, Your Honor."

"The state has no redirect, Your Honor."

Angelo leaned over and whispered, "Well done, Rosa, well done."

Rosa never even acknowledged his comments. She knew why Mr. Gordon was called. He was called, at least some extent, to verify the testimony of Billy Martin and to help solidify the statements Martin was about to make. The witness had served his purpose well. The state's case was just starting to come together. If the jury believed the state's witnesses, when the jury's verdict was read, knowing what she already knew about the defendant's temper, she would want to be as far away from him as she could. In fact, the back row of the courtroom might be just right.

CHAPTER 7

"*Are you happy with your house insurance?*"

Rosa slowly looked up over her cup of hot, steaming coffee, at Nicki Johnson, who was clearly deep in thought as she posed the question and was waiting for a response.

"I bought it through you, and I've never needed to use it. Based on those two factors, yes, I'm very happy with my house insurance. Why do you ask?"

"Just wanted to make sure. Do you have any burial insurance? I mean, funeral costs are out of sight anymore. Who's going to bury you, and pay for it? I can get you insurance to cover that. The premiums are really low. Do you want me to look into it for you?"

Other than a weekend, today was the only day Rosa would have free during the week for the next three or four weeks. She had a number of items she needed to handle, but she had decided to take at least part of the day to reconnect with an old friend, Nicki Johnson. She had first filed some pleadings with the clerk of court in Davidson County, and then met Nicki at a Starbucks near the Vanderbilt campus in Nashville.

She had been best friends with Nicki all through high school, but they went separate directions when it came time for college. Once Nicki moved back to Nashville, they had occasionally spent time together, but it had only been in the last six months that they had cultivated their friendship and become close. However, one of the negatives about the relationship was that Nicki sold insurance, and did it all the time—day and night.

"Move on, Nicki. I don't wanna talk about dying and being buried. I'll probably be cremated anyway."

"Oh good, this insurance covers you there too. Let me get you some—"

"No, no, no! I don't want any insurance of that nature at my age. Now, can we move on?"

"Can I just ask you one more question? Do you have any life insurance? If you do, is it term or whole life… or…"

"One more insurance question, and I'm out of here. Are you done?"

"Okay, okay, I'm sorry. I need to tone it down. I'm sorry. Let's move on. What's going on? Why are you here today and not in court? I thought you had a big case going on somewhere. What happened? Whoa, did you see that guy that just walked in? He's so *hot*!"

Amy was small in stature, but most of the time, no one noticed her height. Her eyes were what people noticed. She was a striking young woman with huge brown eyes that caught your attention immediately. She was a friend Rosa knew she could trust. There was never any doubt that everything she told her would remain in confidence. The only other issue with Nicki was a small problem she had remaining focused. She had an attention deficit issue, and was definitely experiencing its symptoms today.

"Nicki, look at me."

"Man, that sucker is really built. Do you see him, the guy I'm looking at? Turn around, turn around right now and look. Okay, why are you here? Did you explain that yet? Why are you here, and not in court?"

Sometimes, when there were a number of distractions, as there certainly were today, it took all the self-restraint Rosa had not to just reach over and slap her—tell her to focus. Today would clearly be one of those days.

"Court's in recess until tomorrow. Tough case, tough client, but just part of doing business I guess."

"You want another donut. I need another donut. Who do you represent? Who's your client?"

As Rosa started to answer, Nicki got up and walked to the counter ordering more donuts. Rosa just sat back and waited. She had endured this behavior many times before, and if she hadn't been such a good friend, she would have given up long ago. She waited patiently for her return.

"Who's your client?" she said as she took her chair, and started to consume a chocolate-covered donut with some type of sprinkles on top.

"Angelo Bonaventura."

"Not *the* Angelo Bonaventura? Is *he* who you represent? Is that the case involving the murder of his son-in-law? Wow. What's he like? He sounds like an animal. Is he an animal because he sure sounds like one? Want a donut?"

"No. They're all yours. He's a tough man to represent. The case is going to be difficult to win. But it's just part of what I do. I'm glad we had the break today though. It gives me a little time to take a breath and get a few things done that I needed to do."

"So how long's this trial going to take?" Before Rosa could respond, she said, "You need a refill?" She grabbed Rosa's cup, then walked over to dump the old and fill the cup with freshly brewed, hot coffee.

As she set the cups down on the table, Rosa said, "Probably another couple of weeks."

"So, is this guy guilty? Did he kill his son-in-law?"

"I don't know. I have a feeling he did, but I'm just not sure."

"How do you represent people you think might be guilty? Is it tough?"

"Sure it's tough, but they're innocent until the evidence establishes guilt beyond a reasonable doubt. End of story. Now, let's move on. What've you been up to? I think it's been a couple of weeks since we've seen each other. How's that Andy guy you were dating? You've been with him a couple of months, haven't you?"

"Sure have. In fact, we slept together for the first time just last week. Oh God, Rosa I have to tell you about it."

Rosa watched as Nicki grabbed the last remaining donut and started to consume it, continuing to remain silent, obviously moved by the particular flavor of the pastry.

"Well, I'm waiting. Go on. Tell me what?"

"Oh, oh, about him. Okay, so we went to his place, and he turned the lights out, we got undressed and got into bed, and I felt down there, you know, between his legs, and there was almost nothing there… you know… nothing there. It was like a fourth of normal. And his staying power was consistent with the size of his thingy. He was done, had his teeth brushed, and was asleep before I could even say 'oh baby, baby, that feels so good.' What a joke. I got up and left. He never even knew I was gone. You should hear him snore. Holy shit."

By then, Rosa was laughing so hard she was starting to draw attention from the others in the room. "Have you seen him since?"

"He called me and wanted to know what the hell had happened. I just told him I forgot to feed the dog. He never questioned me, and I haven't taken his calls since. Not a good fit, so to speak, not a good fit at all. You want anything else to eat? By the way, how's your love life? I always think mine's bad, until I reflect back on yours. Been involved with any judges lately?"

Rosa looked down as she considered her brief, but disastrous, relationship with now-deceased Judge Hampton. "No. But I think of him almost every day. What a shame. What a shame he's gone, and at such a young age. I loved him and probably always will."

Nicki immediately noticed the pain on Rosa's face. "I shouldn't have brought that up. Sorry. What about Stoney? You two still friends?"

Rosa looked up. "Sure. We're the best of friends. We just couldn't handle that boyfriend-girlfriend stuff. I was always afraid we wouldn't make it. Our relationship grew out of one trial, and the resulting mess afterward. He and I were thrown into that situation by chance, and once it was resolved, it was like the common thread between us had been broken, and we just had nothing to bind us together anymore. He's a great guy, and we really work well together, but the romance is gone."

"So, you dating anyone?"

"Nope. Haven't been, and not in a hurry to start. I'm the world's worst at picking a man, and I'm done pushing it. If it happens, it happens."

"You've had some tough luck with men, that's for sure."

Rosa looked down at her cup of coffee, at least what was left of it, and said, "I think I'm just better off single. I just can't seem to get this couples game figured out."

"Don't worry about it. Better to have no one than to be like me, and have to deal with a guy that has a two-inch dick. By the way, who do you have your car insurance through? I can get you a really good deal on car insurance right now."

CHAPTER 8

*T*he next morning, as she drove to Nashville on Interstate 40, surrounded by four eighteen-wheelers, she couldn't help but smile as she reflected back on the prior day's conversation with Nicki. She was quirky, but she was a good friend and a very successful saleswoman. She never quit selling. Didn't matter where she was or who she was with, she always had "just the deal" for you. To her credit, normally she was right on the money—the deal she had for you was precisely the insurance package that fit your needs. She listened until she figured out what you actually did need, and then she would pounce, and pounce and pounce. She was relentless, but her results were extremely successful. Her description of Andy brought a smile to Rosa's face each and every time she thought of it.

Everyone was waiting for her once she walked through the conference room door.

"Rosa, Rosa, so nice to have you join us. Did you enjoy your day off? How was that friend of yours? Nicki, her name is Nicki, isn't it? Hopefully, in addition to having coffee with your friend, you spent a considerable amount of time preparing for my trial today."

"She's fine, she's—how'd you know where I was yesterday? You following me now, Angelo?"

"No, no, not at all. Just had a friend that saw you at that little coffee place on West End Avenue, that's all."

"Don't follow me, Angelo—don't you ever follow me. I don't need any additional preparation for your trial. I'm as ready as I'll ever be. Now, as concerns today's procedure, they're calling an additional employee of the store, and then I believe they'll call Billy. I need to meet in chambers with the judge and Marvin to make sure of the remaining witnesses, but it's my understanding that's where we're at. We'll probably need to present our case starting later next week."

"That sounds great, Rosa. You're just doing a bang-up job here, you really are."

"You seem in a particularly good mood for someone in the middle of a murder trial. Anything you wanna share, or are you just overly happy you were able to tail me yesterday?"

"Now, now, don't be so antagonistic, Rosa. You know I'm always in a good mood, always upbeat. By the way, I wasn't tailing you. I have way too much going on in my business to take the time, or have one of my employees take the time, to follow my lawyer around. It's just a good day, Rosa, just a good day."

She said nothing, stood, and left the room, watching as Marv entered the judge's chambers at the other end of the hallway. Angelo worried her more every day. This case couldn't end soon enough. She never figured he would follow her. But then again, maybe he didn't, how the hell would she know?

"Morning, everyone," Rosa said as she entered chambers.

Both Judge Beason and Marvin simultaneously bid her a "good morning" as she took her seat alongside Marvin.

"So, Marv, where do we go today? Who do I get to cross-examine first? Do you anticipate Billy Martin testifying today or tomorrow?"

"I have a store clerk to put on the stand today, and Billy will probably be tomorrow morning if that's acceptable to the court. We might have some free time this afternoon, but I thought maybe we could again review the court's instructions to the jury and make sure we are all good with their current form. Are you okay with that, judge?"

Judge Beason looked at Rosa. "Are you okay with that timetable? Probably means you will need to produce your first witness on Monday morning. Will that work for you?"

"That's fine with me, judge. We'll be ready on Monday morning."

"Why don't the two of you give me about fifteen minutes? I'll meet you in the courtroom. Marv, be ready to present your employee, and we'll get started."

Both attorneys stood and left chambers. Marvin walked into the courtroom as Rosa walked towards the conference room to gather up her entourage and march them into the courtroom.

Once everyone was seated, Marvin called Tom Hanson to the stand.

After the foundational requirements were met, Marvin said, "Now, Mr. Hanson, did you, at one time, work at Webber's Furniture Store here in Nashville?"

"Yes, I did."

The witness was clearly nervous. He made no eye contact with the defendant whatsoever.

"Mr. Hanson, you appear somewhat nervous today. You aren't here voluntarily, are you?"

"No."

"We needed to subpoena you to make sure you would appear today, didn't we?"

"Yes."

"Why?"

He looked down for a moment before glancing quickly at Angelo. "I didn't want to testify against my former boss."

"Afraid of him?'

Rosa stood and said, "Your Honor, I'm going to object to this particular line of questioning as being irrelevant and immaterial. He's here. Whether he did or didn't want to testify means nothing."

"Yes, Ms. Norway, I agree. Objection is sustained. Move along, Mr. Jackson."

"Certainly. Now, Mr. Hanson, were you an employee of the store on September 29, 2014?"

"Yes."

"So you were an employee during the time Chuck Harris was murdered?"

"Yes."

"Did you go to work the day following his murder?"

"Yes. I, of course, couldn't get anywhere near the crime scene, but I was allowed access to the rest of the store after the officers had looked around."

"Did you have a chance to check on other cash registers within the building"?

"Yes. One or two of them had been opened, but there were three or four that hadn't been touched."

"What about the safe near the far wall? Was it left open? Were the contents touched as far as you could tell?"

"I made the mistake of leaving it open that night. Have no idea why I left it open. That happened only one other time."

"Did it appear to have been rifled through or the contents handled by someone that wasn't supposed to have opened it?"

"No. It was exactly as I left it."

"So, there were other locations containing money within the building that were left unaffected by these so-called burglars, is that correct?"

"Yes."

"Was there cash at all these locations?"

"Yes. I would say well over five thousand dollars. All of it was still there the morning after the robbery."

"Did it appear to you these were either very inept robbers, or the motive really wasn't robbery at all?"

"Objection."

"Yes, yes, objection sustained. Calling for a conclusion this witness is not qualified to answer. Sustained."

"Nothing further, Your Honor."

"Cross-examine, Ms. Norway?"

"Yes, Your Honor. Mr. Hanson, how long did you work for Mr. Bonaventura?"

"About two years."

"And why were you terminated?"

"Because I left that safe open."

"But there were other problems with your employment record there too, weren't there? We don't need to go through them, but there were other problems, weren't there?"

He hesitated a moment before he said, "Yes, there were some problems."

"You have no idea how many people were involved in the robbery, do you?"

"No."

"You have no idea whether something interrupted their progress through the store, or they just ran out of time, or whether they had any one of a number of other reasons for stopping what they were doing that night, do you?"

"No. I wasn't there, I just don't know."

The hallway door into the courtroom opened, and the clerk of court walked in. She moved past all the participants as everyone watched; she walked up the few steps leading to the judge's chair, leaned over, and whispered something in his ear.

She then walked back through the door and into the hallway. The judge appeared speechless. Rosa glanced at Marvin, shrugged her shoulders, and looked back at the judge for clarification. Finally he said, "Ladies and gentlemen, something has come up. We'll be in recess for fifteen minutes. Remember my admonition to you about discussing the case with no one. We'll be in recess."

As everyone stood, Rosa looked over at Angelo and said, "Let's walk back to the conference room while we're in recess. I have no idea what's going on."

Together they walked out the courtroom door. Once they reached the conference room, all took seats around the conference table.

As they started to discuss the employee's testimony, the clerk of court knocked on the door, and then opened it just wide enough to give Rosa a verbal message.

"The judge wants to see you."

Rosa nodded and walked down the hallway to chambers.

Marvin was seated in front of the judge's desk, with his head down. No one said a word when she walked in or while she took her seat.

Finally, Rosa said, "Judge, what's going on? What's happened?"

"Rosa, someone apparently determined where Billy Martin was being held. We were just informed both cops assigned to protect them are dead, and Billy and his wife are missing. They're assuming both of them are also dead, but at this point, no one knows for sure."

Rosa let out an audible gasp and said, "Oh my god, that's horrible. When did this happen?"

"About an hour ago. They were staying at the Montourage Motel in west Nashville. There was a shootout, and both officers were killed."

Marvin looked up and said, "Judge, I'm not sure we have enough to convict without his testimony. He would have tied it all together.

Obviously, we need to continue everything until we know whether they're alive or dead, and whether he can testify."

"Certainly, yes, that's what we'll do. Let's continue everything until the first of next week. Surely by then, we'll know something. Even then, if we don't have some definitive word concerning their situation, we could begin putting testimony on for the defense. It would be out of order, but we could do that to keep everything moving along. In any event, I'll continue everything for today. I'll just tell the jurors to return Monday morning."

Both attorneys stood, said nothing, and walked into the hallway. Rosa had no idea what to say to Marvin, figuring he already had an opinion as to who had taken them.

She walked in the conference room door. Angelo looked up at her and, with an ear-to-ear grin, said, "Don't tell me, don't tell me, Rosa. Let's see, I'll bet Billy Martin has disappeared. Is that what you were about to say? Oh, please, Rosa, tell me it ain't so, just tell me it ain't so."

CHAPTER 9

*R*osa *looked around her office at pile after pile of active and inactive files.* She had planned on being in court all day, but after the news of the missing witness, she found herself in her office with nothing on her schedule. She knew the prudent course of action would be to dive headfirst into each and every pile, sorting through each individual file one by one. The inactive files needed to be given to June for her to file in the dead file drawers. The remaining active files could then be reviewed to determine which files needed immediate action, and which could wait a day or two. That was exactly what she should be doing, and she should be doing it right now. So why was she still sitting, motionless in her chair, taking no action whatsoever?

As she sat in dead silence trying to determine whether she should just take the day off and rest her weary mind or plunge headlong into the stacks of piles, she heard the office phone ring.

"Rosa, Marvin Johnson is on line one. You wanna visit with him?"

Rosa hesitated for only a moment before she said, "Yes, I better."

"Marvin, have you heard anything yet?"

"No, I've heard nothing. They're searching everywhere, as you can imagine, but have found nothing. Of course, I, along with everyone else involved in law enforcement, know who's behind all this, but as usual, no one has any proof or evidence that Angelo orchestrated it."

"Marvin, I'm sorry it's worked out this way. Obviously, from my standpoint as an attorney representing Mr. Bonaventura, I would have a happy client if this just all went away, but, as a friend and colleague of yours, I can't help but feel sorry for you. You've worked hard on the case, and unfortunately, it appears to be falling apart. What are you going to do if they can't be found, or worse, if they're found dead?"

"I'll probably have to dismiss. We're all reviewing other options, just in case Billy can't testify, but those options, as you can well imagine, are pretty slim. Our whole case centered around him. I clearly made a tactical error. I should have *started* with his testimony. That would have alleviated all this drama."

"Hindsight is always so accurate, isn't it? No, I think, looking at it from your standpoint, you did the right thing. You were going to leave the jury remembering that last witness, Billy, the only eyewitness, and clearly the most important witness in the case. You did the right thing, Marvin. The issue that now complicates everything was unpredictable, and certainly no fault of yours or the district attorney's office."

"Thanks, Rosa. I'll keep you informed, but I just called to tell you if he can't testify for whatever reason, I will most likely dismiss. I'll stay in touch."

Rosa terminated the call. As she did, she noticed the light in Stoney's office came on. She waited for him to organize the rest of his day, and then she walked across the hall.

"Rosa, what're you doing here? I figured you'd be long gone. Isn't that trial still in progress? Is it over?"

She took a chair and said, "We ran into a small problem."

"Oh, really. What's that?"

She studied him for a moment and said, "You already know, don't you? You already know their key witness is missing. I've seen that look a thousand times, Stoney, that 'tell me about it, but I already know' look. Let's see now, we only found out this morning. How could you possibly have found out so quickly, unless, unless you got a little inside information? You're still seeing her, aren't you? You've talked to her this morning, and she told you."

Rosa had moved forward in her chair and was now pointing her finger at him. Her voice had become elevated, and she was clearly upset. "I told you to stay away from her, Stoney. I told you—"

Stoney started to smile, calmly sat back in his chair, and interrupted her in midsentence. "Now, just calm down, Rosa. Quit pointing at me with that menacing index finger. Yes, I did talk to her this morning, and she told me what was going on. Angelo was out again, and she called."

Not wanting to quit the battle, Rosa said, "What the hell are you thinking, Stoney? I don't understand."

Stoney said nothing.

"Do you really know about this guy? He kills people if they don't do what he wants them to do, and never thinks twice about it. I've heard stories about him you wouldn't believe." She stopped, took a deep breath, and sat back in her chair. "I give up. Last time I'm saying anything to you about this. You're a big boy. You've been warned."

"C'mon, Rosa, lighten up. I know what I'm doing. Angelo knows nothing about us. I have become involved with her, I can tell you that. I have no idea where this is all headed. We're just taking it day by day. Don't worry about me. I'll be fine. You have a lot more to worry about than I do. If you don't get him off, unless they take him into immediate custody, you may need a bodyguard." He smiled that infectious smile, leaned back in his chair, and said, "By the way, I've been known to do that kind of work."

Rosa's retort was on her lips, when her cell rang.

"Hi, John. Wait just a moment please." She got up from her chair and said to Stoney, "I need to take this in the other room. You and I *will* resume this conversation later."

As she walked out his door, Stoney said, "Whenever you're ready. You know where I work."

She closed her office door as she said to the Davidson County district attorney, "How're you?"

"Well, you can probably imagine how I am after this morning's events. Not well!"

"Yes, that was a shock for all of us. Has anyone heard anything yet?"

"No, and to be honest, I'm really pessimistic about ever finding either of them alive. This has turned into a nightmare. But to be honest, it isn't why I called."

"Really? What's the problem?"

"It isn't really a problem, but after our conversation the other day, later that afternoon, all of my paperwork was signed for our dissolution. The judge is looking everything over on Tuesday of next week, and I wonder if you might have time to get together—maybe just have a drink together after the judge signs the paperwork. Whatta ya think?"

She hesitated. "Tell you what. Let's wait and see what happens concerning the trial. I really think I need to finish this up before I see you socially. Even though it's not you that's trying the case, it is your assistant, which does create a possible ethical issue. But even beyond that, if anyone from Angelo's extended family saw us, I would never hear the end of it. I love the idea, but the timing is off. Can you wait until we see where the trial is going before we get together?"

"Sure. Why don't you give me a call when you're comfortable with meeting me? You now have my cell number. You call me when you're ready."

Rosa terminated the call shortly thereafter, but as she sat at her desk, she smiled as she considered the idea of seeing him romantically. He was good-looking and smart and… June's piercing voice unfortunately cut through her physical evaluation of John.

"Rosa, Angelo's on line one. You wanna talk to him or call him back?"

She punched line one and picked up the phone. "Hi, Angelo. What can I do for you?"

"Just checking in. Have you heard whether they found Billy yet?"

"No, I haven't. They probably will though, Angelo. I'll let you know as soon as I hear anything."

"Okay, you do that. By the way, I'm thinking they probably won't, at least not alive. If they don't find them, let me know what they wanna do about the case. If I hear nothing from you, I'll just see you at the courthouse on Monday."

"That's fine. Thanks."

She terminated the call as quickly as possible. She did not want to discuss their disappearance any more than need be.

She had only just hung up, and June walked through her office door. "Rosa, Gail Harper is on line two. Do you wanna talk to her?"

"Gail Harper? Did she say what she wanted?"

"No, only that she needed to visit with you."

Rosa looked at the blinking light shining immediately above the button that would connect her to Angelo's lover. This didn't feel right. Hesitantly, she pushed the button and said, "This is Rosa. How can I help you?"

"Rosa, this is Gail." Her voice normally soft and breathy was now even softer, more difficult to hear. "I think I need your help."

"What's the problem?"

"Is this conversation confidential? Does it remain only between you and I?"

"Certainly, Gail, yes, certainly."

"I need to get out of this relationship with Angelo, and in a hurry. Can you help me?"

The tone in her voice clearly indicated concern, with just a small dose of fear added in. "Gail, that's not something I can discuss with you. Not now. I represent Angelo, and until the trial is over, I can't really discuss anything that might be adverse to his interests. There are a number of other attorneys I could recommend if you—"

"No, no, I want you! I want you to represent me. Once his criminal case is over, can we talk?"

"Yes, certainly we can at least talk about it. Can you wait that long?"

"I have a feeling the criminal case may end soon. I need to get off. I'll talk to you after the trial ends. Thanks for your time."

The call ended abruptly. Rosa sat quietly, thinking through their conversation before she hung up the phone.

She finally hung up, looked around the room, stood up, and walked out to June's desk. "You know what? I've had all I can take today. I'm out of here. Take messages. I'll return them when I can."

She waved good-bye and walked out the front door. Enough, enough! It was only one ten, but she needed a drink. Her day talking business was over. She would have a couple of drinks at home and go hike, or take up knitting, or play solitaire—anything to get away from all the turmoil. She needed a break.

Today, Saturday and Sunday, would continue on without that fucking David, that bastard Angelo, that idiot Stoney, and June and Gail! Fuck those files! Fuck the phone too! When Monday comes, she would face whatever she needed to face, but no more today—*not today.*

CHAPTER 10

*S*toney looked at his watch—5:05—almost time to go. He had no desire to leave the warmth and comfort of their hotel room. They had been here almost four hours, and during that time, there had been little talk, but lots of sex.

The room was small, the bed large. Their clothing was scattered about the room. It lie where it had come to rest—his pants in a corner, her bra over the lamp shade where she tossed it, one shoe near the bed, three shoes in a small pile halfway between the door and the bed, huddled together as if in conference. Nothing had been moved since each item hit the floor.

They had been able to check in at one, and since then, he had lost count of the number of orgasms Gail had enjoyed, but it was many. Stoney had been able to perform twice in four hours, which was considerably short of his record set when he was twenty-one. He just wasn't the man he used to be, but then who cared. He had been able to satisfy her on a number of occasions, and at his age, that was more important to him than his own performance.

This was their first time—the first time they had had the opportunity to spend time alone—away from coffee shops, mutual friends, and crowds. Gail had informed Stoney that Angelo would be gone from morning to night on Saturday, and Stoney jumped on the opportunity. He had made a reservation at an old, but well-maintained hotel in Murfreesboro, roughly thirty miles from downtown Nashville, and told her he would meet her there at one o'clock. She never resisted. She couldn't leave during the evening and be gone all night during one of the many nights Angelo was gone. She told Stoney he was keeping an eye on her, and being gone all night would not work. But by meeting during the day, she could explain she had gone shopping. Being gone all night was not now, nor would it ever be, an option.

He was lying on his side, his head propped up with an arm, looking down at one of the most beautiful women he had ever seen. She lay on her back with the sheet pulled up only to her waist. Her eyes were closed, but he noticed a single tear make its way slowly down the side of her cheek.

He wiped it away as he whispered, "Hey, hey, what's wrong? Whatta you thinkin' about? I should tell you I have a little problem with women who go through the best I have to offer, then cry. That, to me, is an inconsistent response. What's going on?"

She opened her eyes and started to smile. "It's not you… and it has nothing to do with us. I've just got myself into a situation I can't get out of. I don't know what to do anymore."

"You mean with him?"

She turned away. As she did, she said softly, "Yes."

He had no idea how to respond. He knew little about her relationship with Angelo. On those occasions when they had been together—when they had met for coffee—if he tried to break through that wall that she used to shield her life from him, she changed the subject. He finally just decided to enjoy his time with her, create their own world, and stay out of her life with Angelo. There was little else he could do unless she was willing to discuss it, which she wasn't, at least until now.

"What would you do if you could break free?"

"It's what I wouldn't do that's important. I would never ever get into this type of situation again. I was so young, so immature, when I met him. He offered me the moon. I grabbed hold. What a fool. What a fool I was. Now I pay the price. For one immature, stupid decision, I just pay and pay and…"

Her voice trailed off as she turned away.

He used his free hand, gently taking hold of her chin, turning it toward him. "There's always, always, a way out. You just need to figure it out—take it one step at a time."

"I called Rosa. I thought maybe she could go through some options with me, but she wanted to wait until his trial had concluded. I understand that. But it sure doesn't help me right now. I don't even know where to start. He has men everywhere. He has security cameras. He would just as soon shoot me as look at me. I just don't know what to do."

Again, she turned away as she started to cry.

"Has he ever hurt you?"

"He's never beat me, if that's what you're asking. The only time I've had any type of physical injury was during sex. He's rough, and as you can imagine, it's all about him. Today was the first time I've really enjoyed sex in a long time. I can thank *you* for that."

"I understand. You know, if and when you're ready, I can get you out of there—protect you, if you wish."

"For how long? And against his whole world? He has people everywhere. I think the only thing that will save me is if he dies. I really don't think he would even let me go, if it was *his* idea. He would kill me first. I know too much. I have too much information about his operation. He's an animal, plain and simple."

Stoney hesitated, considering his next question, before he asked, "Am I your first, or have there been others?"

"No, you're the only one. Until now, I've been afraid to even think about being with someone else. You're special, Stoney. You really are. I needed this. I needed you. I was about to go insane."

"What about this trial? If he's found guilty, won't you be okay? I mean if he goes to prison, you should be free from him."

"I've thought about that, but I'm just afraid there's no way in hell he'll ever be convicted. He has me lying about where he was when it happened—I'm his alibi. And in addition, if they can't find Billy, the state has nothing. From what I hear, they most likely will either never find him, or they'll find him and his wife dead. There's no way they'll convict. Either way, they'll dismiss it, and I'm right back where I started. What a fun future to imagine. I either live with this bastard until he dies, or until he's had enough of me and kills me."

Stoney looked at her for a moment. "Just remember, you didn't have me, didn't have this, six months ago. You've made some progress. Look how far you've come!"

She started to smile. "You're right. I do have you."

"Who knows, Gail, anything could happen. We need to remain positive about this. Let's just carry on the way we are for now. Hopefully something will happen that gets you out of there. You know I'll be waiting for you if it does."

"I know. Other than you, the only one I can ever express any of my feelings to is Joni. She does all the housework and actually oversees the staff. She's been there about five years, and hates him as much as I do. I think she's probably running from something. I really don't know for sure, and it's none of my business, but I have that feeling. She would be out of there in the blink of an eye if she could, but we're all afraid of him. He's simply a horrible man." She turned away, closed her eyes, and whispered, "I have no idea what to do."

Again, he took her chin, turning her face in his direction. He leaned down and softly kissed her.

"There's always a solution. Always. Sometimes it just takes a little longer to reveal itself, but there's always a solution."

"We need to go. He told me he'd be gone all day, but I know I better be there when he gets home."

"Okay. I don't wanna do anything to anger him at this point in time. Hopefully we can do this again soon. It's really a great way to spend a Saturday—to hell with my golf game."

She reached down between his legs and gently rubbed. "Speaking of a game with balls, how're yours? You got any 'game' left, Mr. Stone?"

He smiled. "I could probably sink one more shot. Now get rid of that sheet so I have room to maneuver."

He moved on top of her. Shortly thereafter, he discovered he had way more "game" than even he knew. He simply concluded that playing on the right course made a hell of a difference.

CHAPTER 11

As she continued to finish cleaning Mr. Bonaventura's bedroom, she listened for the return of both Angelo and Gail. Joni Carsten had worked for Angelo over five years and knew him well. He liked everything in its proper order, and proper order meant Gail being in the house whenever he returned. In this household, when all was not as it should be, all hell broke loose, and right now, all was not as it should be.

It seemed all she ever did anymore was look over her shoulder. She was either concerned something wasn't quite right in the Bonaventura house, which meant incurring the wrath of the owner, or she was making sure her past wasn't running just slightly faster than she was, and had finally caught up.

The house was nearly clean. Her day had been spent cleaning up and establishing a work schedule for the other domestic employees. She didn't normally work on Saturday, but they had held a large party last night in the home. The resulting mess needed to be cleaned up. They called her at 6:00 a.m. telling her she needed to come to work. Even though it was her day off, and she had planned on spending it with her two daughters, she knew what was best. She was cleaning the house by seven.

Angelo left midmorning. Gail left near noon. Joni asked her where she was going, but received no response. Over the last few

years, they had become close. Gail was not difficult to read. She figured something was amiss, but it wasn't her business to press the
issue. As she walked out the door, Gail told her she would be back
later in the day, after she finished shopping.

As Joni cleaned up the bathroom, she wondered if it would just
be easier if she turned herself in. The warrant out of Alabama was
now over five years old. It involved felonies, and crimes of which
she was certainly not proud. But they happened at a time when she
was with a man she subsequently learned was abusing her daughters;
when she found out what he was doing, she shot him, leaving him
for dead. She later learned her aim wasn't as good as she thought.
She hadn't quite killed him, and he told a completely different tale
to the authorities. The end result involved charges filed and an arrest
warrant issued.

Joni left the state, moved to Nashville, and never looked back.
But Angelo, after she had applied for and been given the job, found
out about the warrants. Once employed, she was fine as long as she
stayed in line. Her daughters were fine as long as she did her job and
did it the way he wanted it done. He had made it clear, when Joni
tried to quit in prior years, she just needed to stay put, to clean the
house, and supervise the help. He would tell her she had no reason to
quit—he liked how she handled the house for him—she just needed
to stay put. Joni hated him. She hated everything he stood for. But
she had no choice.

Joni was just finishing the last of four bedrooms when she heard
a car door shut. She quickly walked down the hallway toward the
back door of the enormous home and arrived just in time to greet
Gail.

"Is he home yet, or has he been here while I've been gone?"

"No. I was worried you wouldn't make it in time." She put her
arms around Gail and held her.

"So was I. What I wanted to accomplish took longer than I thought it would."

They both walked through the kitchen and into the main living area. They remained silent, knowing because of security cameras nothing could be said of a confidential nature. There were security cameras in every room of the house except his office. Nothing occurred on the grounds, consisting of over three acres, or in any room other than the office without it being recorded. Each recording may not have been viewed the next morning, but no member of the staff said anything that might be considered unfavorable as concerned Angelo or his work, just in case that particular recording *was* reviewed the next day. No one could take the chance. Everyone knew the nature of Angelo's work, and everyone on the staff knew better than to speak out against him in any form or fashion.

His office was the exception. He wanted nothing recorded that was said or happened in that room. Joni just assumed there were meetings held, and statements made, that no one other than the participants were to know about—ever.

"It's a beautiful night," Joni said. "Y'all wanna sit out on the patio while we wait for Angelo to return?"

"Sure. Let's grab a cup of coffee."

The outside area had security cameras, but audio was not recorded.

Once outside, Joni said, "Where the hell y'all go? You've been gone almost all day. I'm sure glad you got back before he returned." Joni, from past experience, knew Angelo would know when Gail left and when she returned because of the cameras. Gail always made sure she returned at an "appropriate" time, and as a result, coming and going wasn't so much an issue as being home when he arrived. That was something he *demanded* and a rule she observed.

"Had a lot to do, Joni."

"Okay, I'm gonna be just pretty damn blunt here, Ms. Gail, but you seeing someone else? I have the feeling you're seein' someone. Am I wrong?"

Gail took a sip of coffee, thought for a moment, and said, "You know as well as I, it's best you don't know the answer to that question. It's just much better if you don't know. As far as you're concerned, I just shopped my ass off all day." She smiled, set her coffee down, and looked up at a sky filled with stars. She turned to Joni and said, "How did everything go here?"

"Oh, fine. I got everything done. Just afixin' to go home. Both the kids are alone—have been all day. Need to ask y'all something. Do you think there's any way you can get me out of here without incurring his wrath? I'd really like to move on, but you know how hard it is to get loose of this place."

Gail considered her response and finally said, "Why don't you just wait 'til the trial's over? Maybe it'll all work itself out. You know I want out as much as you do. Hopefully this whole episode involving Billy will turn out for the best for both of us."

"Whatever. Y'all know not one damn thing's goin' to come of—"

Before she could finish her sentence, Angelo and three of his associates drove around the back of the house, pulling to a stop nearby. They all got out and walked toward the patio and back entrance to the home.

"Good evening, ladies." Angel leaned down and kissed Gail as he said, "What happened here today? Anything of which I should be aware?"

Gail said, "I'm not sure. I was shopping all day. Joni, anything he should know about?"

"No, no, sir. Just another day. Got the house mostly cleaned up. I was just afixin' to leave."

"Gail, you were shopping all day? I'll wanna see what all you purchased. Maybe a little show later this evening would be good."

Quickly Gail said, "Most of it had to be altered. I'll model it for you after I pick it all up next week."

Joni stood up immediately and said, "Mr. Bonaventura, I need to get home to my daughters. Everything's done here needs being done. I'll see y'all on Monday."

Angelo continued looking at Gail for a moment longer and finally turned to Joni as he said, "Fine, fine, I'll see you then. You can pick up your check for the last couple of weeks then too. I'll have it ready."

As she walked to her car, she heard Angelo say, "So, Gail, what else did you do today?"

She drove down the long drive to the street, and as she did, she couldn't help but feel guilty. She should have stayed. She should have remained to help Ms. Gail. It was obvious he didn't believe she had been shopping all day, and she had brought nothing home to show for it. But it was impossible for her to be there all the time when issues of this nature arose. Besides, she was sure Ms. Gail knew plenty about how to defend herself. This was certainly not the first time he had confronted her, nor would it be the last.

She needed to figure out her own dilemma. Joni had been offered a number of other jobs in Nashville. Good jobs, with good families. But each and every time she mentioned something about leaving, he had subtly informed her that would not be in her best interest, *or* in her *daughters'* best interest.

If she were to leave, she would need to pack up everything she owned. Move out in the middle of the night. She would need to run again. Even if she did run, she had no assurance he wouldn't find her. There was no doubt in her mind, if she left without his approval, he would find her. And when he did, it wouldn't just be her who would pay the price, her daughters would also incur his punishment.

For now, she would watch and listen, hoping the results of the murder trial would send him up the river, and she would be free, hoping that they would put him away for what he did to his son-in-law—that possibly Chuck's murder, would somehow, in the end, result in a benefit to both herself and her daughters. If that didn't work, Joni simply had no idea how she would finally free herself from the grip of this man she knew would do whatever he needed to do in order to get whatever he wanted.

CHAPTER 12

*I*t took effort, but she forced herself to stay away from the office all
weekend. She normally worked on Saturday, and sometimes,
Sunday mornings, but not this weekend. Rosa knew it would be
counterproductive. She needed to take a two-day break, watch a little
TV, read a book, and consume a full bottle of wine, by herself, and
that was exactly what she did. The first time she observed the front
of her office after her exit on Friday, was on Monday morning, when
she entered the front door.

She walked past June and said, "Morning, June. How was your
weekend?"

June never looked up. She was typing while talking on the telephone. Didn't matter. She was there doing her job, as she was paid to
do. *That* was what mattered.

She noticed Stoney was already in his office, again somewhat
earlier than normal.

"Morning, Mr. Stone. How was your weekend?"

"Great. How 'bout you?"

"Did nothing, which was exactly as planned. I needed to get
away from everything for a day or two. Never even came to the office.
Did you go anywhere or do anything exciting?"

He smiled as he said, "No, not really."

"Hmmm. I know that look. I also know your weekends are rarely spent alone. Who were you with?"

His hesitation told her all she needed to know. Rosa thought for only a moment before she said, "The only person I know that you might be reluctant to tell me you were with is Gail Harper. You with her this weekend?"

He sat forward in his chair and said, "No, no, not at all. I…"

She turned around, clearly disgusted with the direction the conversation was taking, and said, "Worst liar ever! You are, Stoney, you're the worst liar ever!"

"C'mon now, wait a minute."

She walked in her office, picked up the Bonaventura files, and walked toward the door.

Stoney followed her. She heard him say as she walked out, "Wait a minute, will ya? Let me explain."

She was wasting no more time talking to him about the evils of his relationship with Gail Harper. She realized now she would need to convince his dick, not his brain. Unfortunately when it reached that point with Stoney, dick always prevailed. *Been there, done that,* she thought. Not doing it again.

She arrived at the courthouse prior to eight forty-five, walking directly to the conference room. Angelo was there along with his entourage. After the usual pleasantries were completed, Angelo said, "What happens today? How long do we wait for them to find Billy? What happens if they don't find him? Are we done here?"

"I don't know the answer to any of those questions, Angelo. I need to visit with the judge. He'll tell me whether he wants us to continue the proceedings or just wait. Let me go visit with both he and Marvin. I'll let you know the judge's thoughts when I return."

"I assume if they can't find him, they'll dismiss the case. Is that what'll happen, because that's what should happen."

Rosa stood and said, "I'll be right back."

She figured the best way to get the answers he needed was straight from the horse's mouth. She had no answers, but the judge did. It was time to find out where this show was headed.

"Morning, judge."

"Morning, Rosa. Marv and I were just discussing what direction we should take from here. They still haven't found the witness or his wife, and obviously they are important, perhaps crucial, to the state's case. I'm willing to grant them some additional time, but I do *not* want the case to sit on hold while they continue to look. This is a very unusual situation."

He sat back in his chair as Rosa sat down. "Here's what I propose. Why don't we allow the state to rest, subject to the testimony of one more witness, and have the defense start putting on their evidence. I simply do not want these jurors to go home, and become somewhat disconnected, while we wait. This way we could keep it moving along, and by the end of the week, or by the time Rosa is finished, if the witness hasn't been found, Marv, you can either rest with what you've submitted, or it can be dismissed. Your thoughts?"

"Obviously, on behalf of Mr. Bonaventura, I can't agree with that process. We'll need to make a record in that respect. But sitting here in chambers, between the three of us, that sounds like a logical approach to me."

"Marvin?"

"That's really the only option the state has. We would certainly concur with that procedure, judge. It's not normal, but this is an unusual situation."

"Let's go in and explain it to the jury. Rosa, you can then call your first witness."

Both attorneys stood and left chambers, Rosa walking toward the conference room, Marvin into the courtroom. Once Rosa reached the conference room, she said, "They still haven't found Billy. But the judge wants to move on. He doesn't want to let everything remain

dormant while they continue to look. So we're going to start presenting our evidence, and when we've finished, the state will either stand
on what they've already offered, and we will submit it to the jury as
is, or they will be allowed to call Billy, if he's been found. Everyone
ready?"

Angelo stood up. "What the fuck kind of circus is this? Isn't the
state supposed to present the witnesses they have, rest, and then we
put our evidence on? Have you agreed to this procedure?"

"No. I'm going to make my objection on the record once we
start this morning. But we have no choice, Angelo. If that's the way
the judge wants to proceed, that's the way it's going to be. Now let's
go."

Angelo was clearly becoming more agitated as the conversation
continued. "What the fuck is going on here?"

Rosa put up her hand in midsentence and said, "Now look. I
don't like this any more than you do. But this is an unusual situation.
I'm going to make our objection. I'm going to preserve my objection
on the record, but there's no more I can do. Now let's go." No one
moved. "Get up, let's go, *now!*"

Everyone stood. Rosa led the way across the hall and into the
courtroom. The jury was seated in the jury box. The judge had
already taken his seat behind the bench.

"Ladies and gentlemen, I need to inform you of a slight proce-
dural change we're going to make. The state still has one witness to
call, but because of a small problem, he's unable to testify until a later
date. Because of that, and because I wanna keep everything moving
forward, I'm going to allow the defense to start putting on evidence.
This will continue until they either conclude presenting evidence or
the witness for the state testifies. I understand this is slightly unusual,
but I do *not* want you folks to sit around and wait until he finally
testifies. I wanna keep this moving along. If either attorney has an
issue with the procedure, feel free to make your record now."

Clearly, the jury was in agreement with the process. A number of the jurors nodded affirmatively, agreeing with the change in procedure so everything could continue to move forward.

"The state doesn't have an issue with the procedure you recommend, judge."

"Ms. Norway?"

Before she could stand, Angelo stood up and said, "I don't know about her, but this is a bunch of bullshit. I don't agree with—"

"Mr. Bonaventura, sit down, *now*. You're out of order. If you say one more word, I'll have you removed. Now *sit*."

Angelo, who had now turned a complete shade of red, clearly agitated beyond words, stared at the judge, but did reluctantly take a chair.

"Now, Ms. Norway, keep your client under control. He does that again, I'll let him watch the proceedings from another room. Do *you* have an objection to this procedure?"

"Yes, I do, Your Honor. This is exceptionally unusual, and, of course, because it's so completely contrary to the rules of criminal procedure, we feel it necessary to voice an objection. We feel the state should present what they have, and if they don't feel it's enough, they should dismiss. It's time for them to present what they have or rest. It's either A or B. there is no C. there is no other procedure provided for in the rules or anywhere else. This is highly unusual and—"

The clerk of court entered the courtroom and walked immediately to the bench. She whispered in the judge's ear. The judge immediately said, "We're in recess. I wanna see the attorneys in chambers immediately."

Angelo whispered to Rosa, "What the hell's happening?"

She whispered, "I don't know any more than you do. Take everyone back to the conference room. I'll see what's going on and meet you there in a few minutes."

Rosa walked into the judge's chambers. Judge Beason was seated, leaning back in his chair, clearly in distress. Marvin was pacing nervously back and forth deep in thought.

Rosa said, "What's going on?"

The judge looked at her and said, "They just found the witness and his wife. They're both dead—murdered. They were shot. The witness, Billy Martin, had his tongue cut out. They just found them in a dumpster in the Antioch area."

Rosa gasped as she sat down. "Oh my god, how horrible. Is there any indication who might have been involved?"

Marvin looked at her and said, "Whatta *you* think? No! But you know as well as I who did this. There's no evidence to prove anything at this point in time, but you know as well as I who's behind this."

Rosa said, "Where do we go from here, judge?"

"Marvin, this is your call. Whatta you wanna do?"

"Let me talk to John. Give me until this afternoon. I'll let you know then."

The judge said, "Fine. Rosa, why don't you send your people home? I'll call you this afternoon when the state determines what they wanna do. I'll tell the jurors to return tomorrow morning, unless they hear otherwise from the clerk of court."

Rosa stood and left the room. As she walked down the hallway, there was no doubt in her mind who was behind the murders. She figured the state would now dismiss. Everything she had concluded in prior days about Angelo had just been confirmed. He was, without doubt, the most ruthless animal she had ever encountered. Unfortunately she had the dubious honor of calling him her client. What an *honor!* What an honor to have spent all that time in law school learning a trade that "allowed" her to deal with this type of animal—*what a fucking honor!*

CHAPTER 13

*O*nce she reached the conference room and explained the situa-tion, she heard all the differing views from everyone there, none of which mattered to her. All she could think about was Billy and his wife—two young lives cut short. Billy may have been facing hard time, but once he was released, at least he would have had a future, something to look forward to with his wife and kids.

She wiped the tears away as she drove back to the office.

When she walked in her office door, June looked up and said, "What are you doing here? I thought you said you'd be involved with court all day."

"Ended a little early."

She walked down the hall to her office. She set the files on her desk and turned to see if Stoney was in his office. His light was on, but that didn't necessarily mean he was physically present. She walked across the hallway and stood in the doorway, silent. He was there, but he had apparently just returned from somewhere, as he still wore a light jacket.

She started to cry. He took his jacket off as he moved toward her. Neither said a word as he put his arms around her and pulled her close. She never resisted, putting her arms around him, pulling him tightly to her body, and continuing to cry. They both remained silent, until he finally said, "Obviously, things didn't go so well. Wanna talk about it?"

"They found the missing witness and his wife dead this morning. They were both murdered. The state has no idea what they're going to do with the case. There's no doubt in anyone's mind who did it. Angelo did it, but of course, they have no proof of any kind linking him to their murders."

Stoney backed up, and grabbed the tissue box, moving with her as she took a chair. He handed her the box as he sat down. "You have no doubt he did it?"

"None at all. He's a horrible man—and guess what? He's also my fucking client."

Just then, she heard the door open. She could hear muffled conversation and then the steps of June as she walked down the hallway toward their offices.

"Rosa, Angelo's here. He wants to see you. I told him you were tied up, but he won't take no for an answer."

Rosa looked at Stoney. He offered nothing. She dabbed away the remaining tears and followed June to the reception area.

"Hi, Angelo. What can I do for you?"

He was accompanied by Rocco and his daughter. For some strange reason, Gail apparently had not thought it prudent to visit Stoney's office.

"Didn't you tell me they would let you know this afternoon— that they would call and let you know what they were gonna do with the case?"

"Yes. I had planned on giving you a call as soon as I found out."

"I just figured, since my calendar was clear anyway, we would just wait here until you heard. That's all right with you, isn't it? We won't bother no one. We'll just sit quietly until you hear. Got any coffee?"

Rosa looked at June while determining the best course of action. Finally, she said, "June, get them what they want. Angelo, I have work to do. As soon as I get the call, I'll let you know."

She walked back to Stoney's office, stopping in front of his desk, and whispered, "Your most recent sex partner's boyfriend is sitting out front. He's parked there until I hear what the state is doing with the case. For some strange reason, Gail decided not to come with them. I would advise you just to remain comfortable back here until I can get rid of them, unless you wanna meet him. You want me to introduce the two of you?"

He looked up at her with a halfhearted grin and whispered, "Just let me know when they're gone, will you?"

She walked into her office hoping the call came sooner rather than later.

An hour later, as she was preparing for her next trial scheduled to start on Monday, she heard the phone ring, again. Each time it rang, she expected it to be the call that would determine the fate of Angelo's trial, but it hadn't come yet—maybe this would be the one.

She heard June walking down the hall and concluded this was the call she was in fact waiting for. Instead, June whispered, "Gail Harper is on line one. Do you wanna talk, or do you want me to have her call back?"

"Did you mention her name out loud while you were talking to her?"

"No."

"I'll take the call. Just hang up out there, and don't mention her name. Close the door as you leave."

June said nothing, following instructions and closing the door as she left Rosa's office.

"Hi, Gail. How can I help you?"

"I hope you aren't with Angelo right now. Is he with you? I don't want him knowing I called."

"No. He's out in the reception area. Gail, if you're calling about the same thing you called about last week, I just can't go into that with you yet. This case is *not* over, and right now, I'm not sure when it will be. Why don't you let me call you when I'm able. I have your number, and once this is all over, I'll give you a call. At that point, we can set you up with an appointment to discuss your issues. Is that okay with you?"

"Yes, yes, that's fine, but the sooner the better."

"I understand. I'll call you as soon as I can."

It hadn't been half an hour when the office phone rang again, and June, this time using the intercom, said, "Rosa, John Winstrom is on line one. I assume you'll wanna visit with him."

"Yes, I do. Thanks."

"Hi, John. What's your conclusion concerning Bonaventura?"

"Good afternoon. We're just going to dismiss. I really don't think we have a choice. Our main witness is now dead. I understand from Marvin that Angelo's woman was going to testify they were together the night Chuck Harris was murdered. We have absolutely nothing to offset that. I don't think at this point we have a choice. I'll go ahead and dismiss it this afternoon. It's not what I want, but I just don't think I have a choice. I'm setting up a news conference this afternoon to explain why it's being dismissed, so the public understands and just doesn't blame our office for bailing out for no apparent reason."

"Okay, I understand. John, I'm sorry. I obviously have a vested interest in the outcome, but I really didn't want it to end this way."

"I know, Rosa. None of us did. But you know as well as I, in this business, sometimes you just play the hand you're dealt, and we simply don't have a choice. By the way, since this case will shortly be just a bad memory, you wanna have a cup of coffee with me in the near future?"

She thought for just a moment before responding, "Absolutely. Why don't you give me a call later this week? We can set something up then."

"I will. You be sure and give Angelo my best when you give him the news."

"Oh, I will."

She got up from her chair and started the long walk to the reception area.

"Angelo, I have some good news. They're dismissing the case. You're a free man. They'll exonerate your bond later today, and you should be done with this. Congratulations."

Angelo started to smile. He then stood, walked over to Rosa, and embraced her.

Rocco stood and yelled, "Yes, yes," walking over to pat Angelo on the back while Angelo held Rosa in a tight bear hug.

Angelo leaned back. As he did, he said, "Rosa, you're the best. I will never ever look for another attorney. You did this. You got me through this. You got me out of this. How can I ever thank you enough."

Rosa backed away. "You'll get my bill. That's good enough for me."

"I'll pay it the day I get it. Rosa, I simply cannot thank you enough for what you've done. You babied me through this whole process. You've seen me at my worst and found a way to get me through all this without me losing my sanity. I'll never forget what you did. You're a genius."

"No, no, Angelo. I think you did plenty yourself, at least as concerns the dismissal. Just glad it turned out for you the way it did."

They left the office a few moments later. Through it all, his daughter said nothing. She knew. They *all* knew what her father had done. If Angelo Bonaventura ever walked in her office door again, it would be too soon.

As she walked back to her office, she vowed never to represent him again, *concerning anything*. As she sat down at her desk, she prayed she would never ever have to eat those very words.

CHAPTER 14

*I*t had been over three weeks since the dismissal of charges against Bonaventura. Rosa had cleaned up a number of small problems that had surfaced during the trial, but which she just couldn't stop at the time and fix. In addition, she continued to prepare for a burglary trial in Wilson County that was to begin in three days. She was prepared, but she knew it would be a tough case to win.

She was seated in a small coffee shop only a matter of blocks from her office. The weather was nice, so she had walked, and now she waited for John. He had called her a couple of times trying to set up a time to meet with her. The first attempt resulted in failure. She had a trial scheduled, and the timing just wasn't right. But the second time he called, she had the time, and the desire, to meet with him. They agreed to meet in Mount Juliet, at a coffee shop just a short distance from her office.

Since the trial, Angelo had called her on numerous occasions, wanting her advice concerning a plethora of issues, all the way from questions concerning income tax to advice on where to buy organic food. It was apparent he would be a lifetime client unless she made it clear she no longer wanted his business. It was going to take some type of action on her part to stop him.

She had reconsidered her position concerning further representation once the horror of his trial ended. She did not, as a matter of fact, know who was responsible for the murders of Billy and his wife. She *assumed* he was, but she really didn't know. Once he paid her fees, it too softened all the negative issues of the trial. The money was good, and as long as the issues remained simple, she would continue to advise him. Once again, she felt like she might be doing a dance with the devil, but she felt she could play the game for as long as she wanted and quit when she wished.

However, while analyzing her position, she concluded it might be analogous to all her woman acquaintances who had had a baby and said "never again, never again." Of course, a year later, they found themselves saying, "You know, that was fun. Let's do it again, let's have another baby." Time away from the pain always seems to make a hell of a difference.

He was late. She had already finished her first cup of coffee when he walked through the door. Rosa had located a small table for two near the back wall where their conversation would remain private. He waved, and motioned to her, wondering if she wanted a fresh cup, to which she nodded affirmatively.

He was dressed in a suit, and certainly worthy of the looks of many of the young women already seated in the café. If physical appearance were the defining issue, he was certainly a keeper, she thought as he made his way to the table.

"Morning, Rosa. Sorry I'm late. I got wrapped up in a couple of issues before I left the office, and couldn't get out of there. I hope I haven't kept you waiting long."

"Hi, John. It makes no difference. It was just a relief to get out of the office for a few minutes. That trial with Bonaventura put me behind the eight ball, and I've been trying to catch up all week. It feels good to catch my breath for a minute."

As he took a chair across the table from her, he said, "By the way, you look great. Looks like life away from the big city agrees with you."

"It's worked out well. Business is more than I can handle. Speaking of business, was there any public fallout from the dismissal of Bonaventura's case?"

"No. There really wasn't much anyone could say once the issue of the death of our prime witness was disclosed. Most people understood there was nothing we could do—our hands were tied. What about Angelo? He had to be overjoyed."

"He was. I, of course, have no idea who might have been behind the murders. I have my suspicions, but no proof. What about you? Anything turned up that might point to him as the killer?"

"Not one shred of evidence of any kind. We have nothing. Let's stop talking shop. Let's talk about you. How's your life here in Mount Juliet, Rosa? Do you still enjoy living here?"

"Yes. The pace is much slower, yet it's easy to drive into Nashville anytime I wish, and pick up the pace without a problem. Of course, I'm developing friends here as I did in Nashville. But my situation did change substantially in one respect when I moved here. I had a relationship with Stoney then, I don't now. That did complicate issues when I first moved here, but it's all worked itself out."

"You and Stoney still good friends?"

"The best. But the romance has run its course." She hesitated for a moment, looking away before she continued that thought. "My love life is crap, but I do love where I live. Can't have it all I guess. I'm happy right now, and that's worth a lot."

"I understand how you feel. We just finished our divorce, and of course, my love life, like yours, is also 'crap.' But like you, I'm much happier. It's interesting looking back now. All those years I put up with her running around on me, always wondering, always guessing what she was doing, but afraid to ask, not wanting to know, but needing to know. I'm just glad it's over. So I take it by your comments you're not seeing anyone?"

"No. Not looking either, but no, I'm not seeing anyone."

He hesitated while considering her response. "I get a few mixed signals from you, Rosa. I want you to know I didn't drive to Mount Juliet today for the coffee. They really have pretty damn good coffee in Nashville. I drove out here to see you, to spend a small amount of time over a cup of coffee, *with you*. And the point of it all is that I want to spend *more* time with you. I don't want you to misunderstand why I'm here. You'll learn I always lay my cards on the table and let the chips fall where they may. That's always been who I am. That's what I'm doing right now. I wanna spend time with you, Rosa. I hope that's okay with you. I know I fumbled my way through that pretty badly, but do you understand what I'm trying to say? I'm a hell of a lot better at finding the appropriate words in the courtroom than I am in this type of situation."

He looked down, obviously distraught over his inability to say exactly what he felt. She reached over, placing her hand over his. He looked up as she said, "I understand, John. Yes, I get it. I would love to get to know you better and to spend a little time with you doing just that. You need to know beforehand that my success rate in the romance game is pretty bleak. But with that in mind, I'm always willing to give it another shot."

He looked up and smiled, placing his other hand over hers. "Thanks for 'getting it.' I'm sorry I'm not very smooth. I'm just out of my element here. So, does that mean we could go out for dinner, perhaps next weekend?"

"Let me check my calendar." Without ever removing her eyes from his, she said, "You know, I just happen to be free. What time and where?"

Before coffee ended, they set up a time and place to meet in Nashville the following Saturday night. They continued their conversation well into the morning, discussing business and pleasure, evaluating prosecutors and defendants, both finally leaving the café near noon. Rosa had so many fires to put out that she had her mind on her work before she ever left the café.

She walked in the office as June left for lunch. Stoney was still in his office, and as she sat down to review additional issues involving her upcoming trial, he came to her office door leaning against her door frame, waiting patiently until she acknowledged him.

She finally put her pen down and looked up. "Morning, Stoney. Obviously you need a little attention, so let me stop what I was doing and give you some. What's going on? You been busy?"

"Ouch, that did hurt a little. Yes, I'm busy as hell, and all because of you. You keep sending me all this business. I've no time for a social life of any kind."

"That's good. I'm probably saving your life. Work will hopefully keep you and Gail away from each other. You still seeing her?"

"How was your coffee date?"

His comment removed the smile from her face immediately. "How'd you know about that? Who told you about that?"

"June said you and John had a coffee date. How'd it go?"

"I need to tell her to keep her mouth shut about my personal life. It went fine. And it wasn't a date. We just had coffee, plain and simple. He's a pretty nice guy though, I will admit that."

"You make any future plans with him?"

"None of your business. That's just none of your concern. Now, are you still seeing her?"

He smiled that smile she knew so well whenever he teased her. "If you ain't telling me about your love life, I ain't telling you 'bout mine. Now, y'all have a nice day."

With that, he turned around and walked down the hall toward the reception area.

"Stoney, get your ass back here," she yelled. "*Stoney.*"

She heard the front door shut and heard him lock it as he left, to remain that way until June returned from lunch.

The most frustrating man that ever walked the face of this earth—*ever*. But without doubt, one of the most loveable characters she had ever met. She went back to work acknowledging he was an extremely important element of her life, but also one of the most irritating individuals she had ever met—all wrapped up in one very loveable package. Now, where was she...?

CHAPTER 15

*I*t had been a week since her coffee date with John. Rosa was camped at a small table in a coffee shop near downtown Nashville. She had been waiting almost an hour for Nicki to make her appearance, and wasn't going to wait much longer.

Waiting for her was not necessarily out of the ordinary, but waiting this long was unusual.

Just as she decided to toss what was left of her lukewarm coffee and walk out, Nicki sauntered through the front door. As she walked to Rosa's table, she said, "Been here long?"

"Just since the time we were *supposed* to meet. Let's see, that was an hour ago. Where the hell you been?"

"Just a moment." She turned around and walked up to the counter. Rosa continued to wait while she ordered and was then handed her cup of coffee.

She turned to walk back to the table, starting her conversation about halfway there. "I was working with this guy on some insurance. Just couldn't get away. I think I about got him hooked. I'll know more tomorrow night. You hungry?"

"You couldn't call? You couldn't let me know you would be a frickin' hour late?"

"Didn't want to interrupt the flow of the sale. He wants me to meet him at his apartment tomorrow night and finalize the deal. You hungry?"

Rosa said, "Do you think that's a good idea? I mean, meeting some guy you barely know at his apartment. That doesn't sound very smart to me."

"Oh, I've known him for a while now. I'm wantin' him to buy some life insurance." She started to grin. "I know he's interested, but I'll probably have to sleep with him to finish the deal."

Rosa nervously cleared her throat. "Now wait a minute. Are you nuts? Are you really going to sleep with him just to sell a policy? Is that your normal process? Is that really necessary? Do you have no more ability to sell than that—that you have to sleep with them to sell? Whatta you do if it's a woman?"

"Not sure. Hasn't come up yet. But I'd probably sleep with her too. Just the name of the game for me, Rosa. Get the sale at any cost. Now, let's talk about you. Whatta you been doin'? Where've you been? You need any burial insurance? You know, important shit like that."

"Well, for starters, I assume you already heard how the trial ended. It's certainly been well covered."

"Yes, I did. Whatta you think happened to the witness? You're client kill him?"

"I don't know. I assume he did. But I have nothing in the way of evidence to show that's what happened. Everyone thinks he was responsible, but no one can prove it. I continue to work with him, and probably will until it's established he did it."

"So is he off scot-free?"

"Yes. Everything's been dismissed. I'm thinking it's probably over. Law enforcement can find no one that will come forward and say what happened. They're all afraid of him, probably for good reason. So what about the insurance business? You been busy?"

"Always. Now, let's talk about your love life? Last I knew, you were going out with that John what's-his-name, that prosecutor. Did that happen? I've waited until we were together to discuss that with you. I know you were going to have dinner together, but did that finally happen?"

Rosa started to smile and briefly put her thoughts together before starting the enjoyable process of discussing their first dinner date. "Yes, it did. We decided to get together last Tuesday. There's a small restaurant in Lebanon called Mo Cara that I've been to a number of times. It's quiet and the food's good, so I asked him to meet me there. It's also away from the eyes of Nashville, which was what I wanted."

Nicki was clearly immersed in the conversation, and the break in the flow of information from Rosa obviously irritated her. "So, go on, go on, what happened?"

"Well, we met, we had supper, and we both went home—to our *own* homes. Luckily, I don't have to worry about selling insurance to make a living, and didn't have to go to bed with him to make a sale."

"Smart-ass. What happened? You have a good time? What's he like?"

"Yes, I had a good time. He seems solid as a rock. He just finished terminating a bad marriage. His relief in ending that relationship was apparent. But yes, we had a good time. We talked about everything under the sun. We were probably there a couple of hours."

"So, what's next?"

"Well, there's that Vanderbilt Hospital benefit in Nashville next weekend. We're going together. He asked me, I was free, and so I said I'd be glad to be his date. It should be fun. Really, nothing going on yet, Nicki. We've both been down this road before. We're both taking it very slowly. But I do like him. He's so easy to be with. We had a good time together."

"Doesn't he have children? I was thinking you told me he had kids."

"Yes. He has a couple of boys, ages five and seven. John and his wife have joint custody. The kids will end up being with both of them about half the time. He's really proud of them. From what I understand, they're excellent students—just all-round good kids. But my only information is from him too, so who knows."

"Can you handle being a stepmom?" Nicki said with a wry smile.

"I'm just not going there with you. I have no idea where this is all headed. I know I enjoy being with him. That's as far as the relationship has gone."

"Just for discussion, what would happen if you two got married? How would that work with you being a defense attorney, and he a prosecutor? Is that a conflict?"

"Obviously, not in and of itself, but we would need to be careful. I probably wouldn't practice as much in Davidson County. When I did, I would probably refrain from trying anything against him. I would maybe just try matters that involve the assistant district attorneys. But even then, if something did come up, I'm assuming if the client waived the conflict, it would probably be acceptable. Let's move on. We're talking about a situation that doesn't exist and probably won't."

"Just keep me informed, will you? Don't make me pull everything out of you. Let me know what's going on." When Rosa failed to respond, Nicki said, "You seem distant this morning. You okay?"

Rosa turned away for a moment, clearly deep in thought.

"Hey, you okay? What's going on? You don't seem yourself today."

Rosa looked at Nicki and said, "Sorry, I'm sorry. It's probably nothing, but Stoney hasn't been in for a couple of days. I'm a little concerned about him."

Nicki rolled her eyes and said, "Why, are you his keeper? You've told me in the past there have been six or seven days in a row he wouldn't be in, and then he'd walk through the door and give you a line of bullshit about being on a drunk for a week with some broad from Knoxville or somewhere. You didn't seem worried then, what's changed?"

"Did I tell you he seemed to be having some type of relationship with Gail Harper, Angelo's live-in? I don't remember if I told you that or not."

Nicki sat back in her chair, hesitating a moment before saying, "That sounds like a bad idea—a real bad idea. And no, you never told me that. You need to tell me these things, Rosa. I have to pull everything out of you anymore. Did you talk to him about it?"

"Yes. He laughed at me. You know him. Most everything in life, except his work, is one big joke. To him, there's nothing that can't be resolved or worked out, normally over a drink and a good meal. I told him you don't work things out with Angelo. He's an animal. It's his way or no way. Stoney just laughed it off. I'm worried about him. I still care for him. He's one of the best friends I ever had, and of course, we're basically in business together." She looked away for a moment, and as she turned back to continue the conversation, she smiled and said, "Forget it. It's probably nothing. Just worries me a little. Probably wouldn't worry me at all if he wasn't screwing around with Gail. Forget it."

"How long's it been?"

"He hasn't been in the office for three days. I can't seem to reach him by phone. He always leaves his cell on. I've left a couple of messages for him, but I've heard nothing. I'm only going to wait a couple more days before I contact the police department. This just doesn't feel right."

"Maybe the two of them ran off. Maybe they're having a wild sexual experience in Las Vegas. Remember, what happens in Vegas stays in Vegas."

Rosa laughed, in a halfhearted way, but she was concerned. He wouldn't just walk out on her without saying something. She would wait a couple of days, and if she hadn't heard anything, she would report him missing. He was an important part of her life. Even though he had been gone just a few days, without him, she felt an uncomfortable change in her own day-to-day existence. Perhaps when she returned to the office today, he would be there. She would like nothing more than to be able to verbally assault him about not pulling this stunt again. Hopefully, he would be there...

CHAPTER 16

Sleep was an unattainable goal. She had been awake for hours. She watched TV, she finished some office work she brought home, she paced, but nothing worked. Rosa simply could not figure out where her friend and business partner might be. She called his friends and business associates throughout the day into early evening. His disappearance was now serious. Early in the week, it was simply an uncomfortable situation. Now it was serious. He had never been gone this long from the office without telling someone where he was or what he was doing.

She called Gail's number, also without success. Were they together? Surely not! Especially for this long!

It was now 5:00 a.m. She had had enough of lying in this bed. Rosa figured maybe she had slept for a couple of hours, but no longer. It was time to get moving, to think about something else—about work, about anything other than where he might be. It wasn't just that he was gone. That wasn't the only issue at play. It was that he was gone while he was in a relationship with Angelo's woman. That was what concerned her most.

Rosa got up, dressed, and was at the office by seven. She first checked his office. Nothing had been moved, nothing had been touched since she left the night before. She checked the office answering machine—nothing.

If no one had heard from him by noon, she would contact law enforcement. *If* he returned, and was upset because she contacted them, maybe he would learn a good lesson. He needed to remain in contact with friends and with business associates who cared for him. Maybe the situation would embarrass him to the extent he wouldn't put her through this again.

She had three trials coming up in rapid succession within the next couple of weeks. Two of them were in Wilson County, one in Davidson County. The one in Davidson was to be tried by John. She had mixed feelings about trying a case against him. She was excited about the day-to-day contact while trying the case, but concerned about beating him. This would certainly be a new experience, and one she wasn't entirely certain she would enjoy.

June had only been at work a short time when she said, "Rosa, Chief Spring is on line one. Do you wanna talk to him or call him back?"

Jack Spring had been chief of police for almost three years. He was good at his job. He and Rosa had become good friends over the last year. Jack was all business at work, but when it was time to leave the job and "get down," he could do that with the best of them.

"Morning, Jack. How goes the battle? Any of those drunks you picked up off the streets last night need a good defense attorney?"

His silence at the other end quickly told her this was not a personal call. This call was strictly business.

"Morning, Rosa. Unfortunately, this call is a little more serious than that, and one I really didn't wanna make. I wanted someone else to make this one, but figured I was probably the most appropriate one to make it."

Rosa sat back in her chair as her heart skipped a beat. "What's wrong? What's going on?"

"Rosa, Stoney was found dead this morning."

She said nothing. She took a deep breath and really just wanted to hang up the phone, pretend she never heard what he had just said. "I don't understand. Found dead where? What happened? Are you sure it's him?"

"It's him. He was murdered, Rosa. Do you want me to go through the details with you on the phone, or would you rather drive down here?"

"I'll be right down."

She walked by June, explaining she would be back shortly. She would say nothing to her until she knew all the facts. The drive to the station, located a few miles from her office, was something later she wouldn't remember making. Everything was a blur. It was as if her vehicle knew the way on its own. Her mind was on everything but traffic signals and stop signs.

Upon arriving, she was taken to the chief's office where he embraced her as he said, "I'm so sorry, Rosa. You have no idea how much I hated to make that call."

He walked behind his desk and sat down, while Rosa took a seat on one of two ugly, well-used chairs sitting in front of his desk. She noticed as she sat there was what appeared to be a couple of photographs turned upside down, lying in front of him.

"Are those of the crime scene?" Rosa asked.

"Yes."

Her voice trembled as she said, "May I see them?"

He hesitated before responding, "You know, Rosa, I think it might be best if I just told you what happened. These are really graphic, and I would rather—"

"May I see them?"

He stared at her for only a moment, before reaching out and slowly pushing the photos across the desk.

She picked them up. There were only two. As she looked at them, she struggled to comprehend what they depicted.

It was Stoney. He was lying on his side. And there was someone with him. Gail—it was Gail. They were face-to-face, bound together by what appeared to be a rope. They were both nude. She looked away. What had this monster done? She looked at the pictures one last time before she shoved them back across the desk.

Rosa pulled a tissue from her purse as she started to cry. It was him. He was gone. The lack of sleep, his disappearance, and now his death was more than she could handle. She started to sob uncontrollably. Chief Spring stood and walked around his desk, putting his hand on her shoulder.

"I'm so sorry, Rosa. I know how close you two were, and of course, you were also in business together. I hated to be the one to tell you."

"Where were they found?"

He walked around his desk and sat down. "In a ditch just south and west of Mount Juliet in Davidson County. They had been there a day or two. It seems to us someone wanted them found. Otherwise, they could have just buried the bodies, and they probably would have never been located. The medical examiner feels she might have been shot somewhat before him, but while they were bound. So Stoney would have been alive, tied together with her dead body for at least some time prior to the time they shot him. No doubt, a horrific situation for both of them, but particularly bad for Stoney."

"Any indication who did it?"

"No, at least not yet. They're doing the autopsies as we speak. Hopefully something will come out of that. Do you have any idea who might have done this—and why those two are bound together? Do you have any thoughts on all this?"

She looked away as she thought for a moment. "No."

"No one was harboring a grudge against him that might do this?"

"Not that I know of. I need to go." She stood. "Thank you so much, Jack, for being so thoughtful—for taking the time to notify me personally."

He stood as she did, and he said, "Again, I'm sorry for your loss, Rosa. If you think of anything that might help, let us know. Davidson County will be handling the investigation, so you should probably contact them direct."

She said nothing, turned, and walked out the door to her car.

Once she arrived at the office, she gently informed June. While Rosa retained her composure, June fell completely to pieces. Rosa told her to make a small handwritten sign for the front door, then put a verbal response on the answering machine with both indicating they were closed because of a death, and then go home. Rosa decided to remain closed until after Stoney's funeral, which she assumed would be early next week.

June did as she was told, placing a small note on the office door and a short message on the answering machine. Rosa locked the door behind her as she left.

She then shut all the lights out in the reception area, walked back to her office, and fell apart. She sat at her desk and cried as she thought of all they had been through. She remembered all the issues involving the Jake McKay case she worked on with him in Nashville, during which they had both been shot and nearly killed. She remembered all the time in rehabilitation, which they went through together, making love, setting up the office together in a new town, all the good times they had enjoyed with each other.

She walked across the hall to his office. She turned on the light and looked around his room. There were so many reminders of their time together. Now this, this is the way it all ends–at the hands of a madman!

She knew who did it. But Rosa was smart enough and knew him well enough to know that *knowing* who did it and *proving* it would be two entirely separate issues. One thing was certain. Angelo would pay for this. He would never get away with the murder of Stoney, not as long as she could still take a deep breath.

She could not forget the image of the two of them tied together in that ditch. Rosa knew she had made a mistake in looking at the photos. She would never forget those images... bound together... forever bound...

CHAPTER 17

*F*ocusing *was indeed an issue. She just realized he had been in her office* discussing his marital problems for quite some time. A sneak peek at her watch indicated he had been discussing his "issues" for almost forty minutes. During that time, Rosa had made two comments, and he had used the other thirty-nine minutes and thirty seconds to tell her how big a bitch his wife had become since their marriage.

She tried to focus on her client's issues today, just as she had so many other clients that had asked for her advice and assistance since Stoney was murdered. The course of conversation always seemed to proceed in exactly the same order—she was interested, she made notes, she wasn't interested, she didn't care, end of appointment. One item, and one item only, occupied her mind: Stoney's murder.

His funeral had been large, even for Nashville. People from all over middle Tennessee had attended. Many knew him, and they all had one thing in common—an incredible degree of respect for a man who exuded integrity and honesty throughout his career.

Gail's body had been transported back to her hometown, the town in which her family lived. They had her funeral there, and that was where she would be buried. For some strange reason, Angelo would not even identify her body. He was making it difficult for law enforcement to set up a conference with him to discuss her murder.

It was apparent to Rosa, and to law enforcement, why he was acting in that manner, but until they had some type of proof, something to indicate he was actually involved, their hands were tied. She understood. She didn't like it, but she understood. To her, the case was cut and dried, but her evidence too was considerably short of proving what she actually believed happened.

"Rosa, Chief Spring is on line one. You wanna take the call or call him back?"

"I better take it. Tell him to hold a minute."

She quickly terminated her appointment, indicating to her new client she would prepare the necessary paperwork. He could stop in the first of next week, with his retainer, of course, and sign all the papers, which would commence the dissolution process. He was glad everything would be ready that soon and left her office with a smile from ear to ear. Rosa was just happy to get rid of him.

"Morning, chief. Anything new?"

"No, unfortunately, we have nothing more to go on than we did when we found their bodies. The autopsies gave us nothing. They were both shot at close range. Nothing on their bodies provided anything that would give anyone an indication of who might have done this. I just got off the phone with the Nashville Sheriff's office. They wanna visit with you when you have time."

"I'll stop in the next time I'm in Nashville."

"Okay, thanks. I wish I had more information for you, but we have nothing so far."

"Rosa, Marvin Jackson is on line two. Do you wanna take it or call him back?"

"I'll take it. I need to go, chief. Keep me informed if you don't mind."

"I will, Rosa. Thanks."

"Marvin, do you have anything new concerning Stoney's murder?"

J. B. MILLHOLLIN

"Nothing like getting right down to business. Good morning to you too."

"I'm sorry. Good morning. It's just that this is all so overwhelming. It's all I think about day and night. I can't believe this happened."

"I understand. We have nothing of an evidentiary nature to tie this to Angelo. I know you're in somewhat of a difficult position—in that you were Stoney's business partner, and you're Angelo's attorney—but any help you can offer us would really be appreciated, Rosa."

"You need to know I'll do all I can to help determine who did this. My hands are somewhat tied, but as time goes by, if there's any way I can help you, I will."

"I'll keep you in the loop. Thanks, Rosa."

Once she terminated the call, she sat in silence, thinking back over the past week. How quickly life had changed. Not only had she lost her best friend, but she had lost a business associate. She relied on him to assist her in ascertaining the facts and underlying issues in so many of her cases. Even in a financial sense, his death would impact her life. He paid half of all the expenses for the office, including June's salary.

Late last night, when sleep was impossible, she drove to the office, and in a room illuminated only by a small desk lamp, she started the process of going through all his paperwork. She was named executor in his will and was charged with the responsibility of overseeing all his financial issues along with cleaning up loose ends involving his business. As she went through file after file, including all his personal papers, she would need to stop and brush the tears away as the story of his life unfolded, event by event. She stayed at it for over two hours and then knew it was time to try to sleep, if only for a short time. Today she paid the price. She was tired, depressed, and confused.

"Rosa, you have a visitor. John Winstrom is here. Do you want me to send him back, or do you wanna come out here to see him?"

She hesitated before she answered. She had not seen nor talked with him since their dinner date, and she just wasn't sure now was the right time. Finally, she said, "Send him in." Rosa stood as he entered the room, and said, "I wasn't expecting you. What's going on?"

The look on his face clearly expressed the purpose for the visit. He walked toward her slowly as he said, "Rosa, I'm so sorry. I know how close the two of you were."

She walked around the end of her desk, and as she started to cry, he took her in his arms and held her. She didn't resist and, in fact, embraced him. They stood quietly, until she said, "I'm getting mascara all over your suit. I'm sorry." She pulled away as he grabbed a tissue from her desk, handing it to her.

"Forget it. It'll come off. How're you? How's everything going? Is there anything I can do to help you?"

Rosa sat back down at her desk, continuing to dab at the tears. He also took a seat. She couldn't help but notice the wet mascara stain on the shoulder of his light-tan suit coat.

"No, no, there's nothing you can do, but thanks for asking. I was his executor. I'm just starting to figure out what needs to be done. What's happening at your end? Any idea who might be behind this?"

"You know as well as I who's behind all this, but once again, it's a matter of evidence. I've turned everything over to Marvin. He'll handle it from now on. I talked with him briefly this morning, and they're still processing the scene, but so far, nothing has turned up."

"I talked to him earlier today. I wondered at the time why you weren't handling it. Big profile case like this would seem to be right up your alley."

"I know, and I thought about it, but Marvin went after him the first time and really wanted to handle the investigation concerning this case. Besides, don't you still represent Angelo?"

"Well, yes, but I wouldn't represent him if he was charged with Stoney's murder."

"I didn't know how that might all work out for you, and I didn't want to get caught in some type of conflict. I just don't want that issue to pop up. These kinds of cases are difficult enough the way it is, without having those types of ancillary problems raise their ugly head. It just seemed the right thing to do."

"Rosa, your next appointment is here. I also have a call on hold, along with two calls you need to return as soon as possible."

"Okay, okay, June, thanks."

John stood. "I need to move along. I know you must be overwhelmed with work after all the personal issues you've had to deal with, but I wanted to see you. I wanted to tell you how concerned I was and ask you out for dinner within the next few days. I know my timing isn't the best, but I also know life moves on. I just didn't want to wait until I felt you were fully recovered from all this. I figured if I waited until I was sure, it might be into next year." He smiled and said, "What about Saturday night? Maybe Husk or Etch or some other restaurant of your choice? Just let me know. You don't need to tell me now."

She stood and walked around the edge of her desk, reaching out her hands to take his. "You have no idea how much this means to me—driving all the way out here to basically just say you care."

He pulled her close and held her. "You mean a lot to me," he whispered in her ear.

Later, as she waited to dial the number for one of those many calls she needed to return, her thoughts weren't on John, but continued to remain fixated on Stoney's murder. No one knew anything.

They had nothing. Just like the murder of Chuck. Not enough. Just like Billy's murder. Not enough.

She slammed her fist down on her desk. This man needed to be stopped! It was time for her to commit, to take a stand. She would do nothing, make no decision that might affect the possibility that at some point in time, she might be in a position to provide information or participate in an activity that would put this man behind bars once and for all.

Now was the time to listen, to observe, and to do nothing that would place her outside Angelo's circle of associates. If she needed to extend the boundaries of the canons of ethics somewhere along the way, so be it. *Enough was enough.* At that moment, she concluded she would stop at nothing to make sure this man, this animal, in whatever manner might be available, was brought to justice.

CHAPTER 18

leepless nights—assiduous days. The pattern seemed never-ending. Such was the schedule Rosa had endured since Stoney's murder. It had been almost a month since they had found their bodies, and still no evidence of any nature had been uncovered indicating who might have committed the crimes.

Nicki had called earlier that morning and informed her she had to see some clients in Mount Juliet. She wanted to meet Rosa at the coffee shop a few blocks from her office and planned on meeting around eleven. Rosa really had no desire to small talk her way through a conversation with another individual. She would meet her, not because she was looking forward to the conversation, but only because she was a good friend.

Nicki was seated with a cup of coffee and a couple of donuts when she walked in the door. The coffee shop was packed with people having a near-noon shot of coffee with a sandwich or pastry. Rosa walked to the counter, ordered a small coffee, and joined Nicki.

"You're late. You're never late. Any reason?"

"Not really. I just had trouble getting going this morning I guess. Have you seen your clients yet?"

"I have. They bought nothing. Wasted trip."

Rosa smiled. "Not really. You get to see me. Surely that's worth something."

"That's true. By the way, have you given any more thought to purchasing burial insurance? You saw what happened to Stoney. You just never—." She stopped in midsentence and reorganized. "Sorry. That was really callous. I'm sorry. I never should have said that."

"No problem. You're certainly right about one thing. You never know. And of course, there's all those other similar clichés you could also throw out like, 'One never knows what's right around the corner,' or what about 'Life's short, better enjoy it now' or 'You only live once,' and all those other bullshit phrases I've heard over and over in the last two weeks. I thought about the applicability of those phrases the first time someone mentioned one, but just tell me, how the hell does someone change their life to live a phrase? We all just live it the best we can based upon our own specific situation. You can't change your life just because you need to live *now*. Thanks for the advice, but sorry. I've heard all those clichés once too often in the past couple of weeks."

Rosa looked into her coffee cup, but said nothing. When Nicki failed to respond, she said, "Okay, okay, I'm the one that should be sorry. That was probably a little harsh."

"We need to talk about it, get it all out on the table. Let's talk about how you're handling it. This is really the first time we've had a chance to discuss it in depth since he died. How're you feeling about all this?"

Rosa wiped a tear away with her finger and never looked up. She said, "I'll never get over losing him. I know that now. We were close in so many ways—ways that I didn't even consider before he died. There are so many times I wish we could visit, just talk for a moment, about a problem I have in my own life, or just about anything. It's been really hard. No question the most difficult situation I've ever been through." She looked up, smiled as she continued to wipe away tears, and said, "I'll be fine, Nicki. Have to be. Need to *move on*, as they all say."

"The day I talked to you, I believe you mentioned you were the executor of his estate, is that right?"

"Yes. I'm responsible for handling all his possessions, and either disposing of them, cashing them in, or selling, whichever is appropriate. I've been in contact with his former wife, and she's been wonderful to deal with. Most of what money he had, he put in trust for his children. He made his former wife the trustee. She wanted many of his personal possessions for his children. She's made my job a whole lot easier." She hesitated, and then in a whisper, she said, "But going through his desk and all his personal items was so damn tough..."

"I can only imagine. What about Angelo? You told me you thought he might have done it. What's the story on him?"

"I've talked to him once. He knows he's being investigated. I told him to just sit tight and wait and see what happens. I knew it was too soon for me to talk to him. I didn't wanna burn a bridge yet and just tell him to go to hell. So he seems to be content to let everything lie as it is. At least he's quit calling me. For a while, I really thought, if June told me he was on the phone one more time, I was going to shove that phone down her throat."

"Let's move on to a different subject for a moment. Let's talk about something positive. What about John? Have you seen him or spent any time with him? What's the story with John?"

"I thought I told you I had supper with him. Maybe not. Everything has been such a blur lately. Yes, we had supper together. He came to Mount Juliet, picked me up, and we ate at Mo Cara in Lebanon. I had a great time with him." Rosa smiled for the first time since the conversation began. "We have a lot in common. He's really easy to talk to."

Nicki leaned forward in her chair and whispered, "Well, go on. What happened after supper?"

"Nothing happened, Nicki, absolutely nothing. Oh, he kissed me when he took me home, but it's way early in the relationship for anything else. Besides that, I need to move on from Stoney's death before I get involved with anyone."

"So whatta ya think? Is he a keeper, or is he disposable?"

"Let me put it this way. I like him. I always have. This change in our association has not changed any of that. But as I said, I need to get past Stoney's murder. I just need some time I guess." She looked down as she once again started to cry.

"Okay, since we apparently can't move away from the subject, let's talk about Stoney again. What are you thinking? What's going to need to happen for you to be able to move on?"

She looked up, wiped away the single tear still remaining on her cheek, and said, "Find out who the fuck did this. I'll never rest easy until it's solved. I think I know who did it, I really do, but until it's finished, until it's really concluded, I'll have trouble moving on with my life."

"What are you going to do? How are *you* going to solve this? Don't you think the police know what they're doing?"

"I know how this man works. I've seen him in action more than once. He's an animal. Nothing gets in his way. Right now, I'm in a position to keep my eyes open and my mouth shut, to perhaps help in solving Stoney's murder, and I won't rest easy until I've done all I know I can do or it's solved, one way or the other."

"Are you going to continue to represent this guy Angelo?"

"I am for now. I'll continue to until I know he didn't do it, or until I can somehow help in establishing he did. Whatever it takes. Whatever I need to do, I'll do to help solve Stoney's murder."

"Don't you have a few ethical issues you need to consider if you still represent him?"

"I'll handle them if they come up. I'm not even going to try to guess what might happen in that respect. I'll just take it day at a time until it's over."

Nicki sat back in her chair, deep in thought. Finally, she said, "Want some help?"

"Help for what?"

"Help in figuring this all out, help in determining if he did it, and if you determine he did, what to do with him then."

"From whom, you?" Rosa started to smile. "You gonna try to sell him burial insurance, maybe just add a question to the app asking him if he murdered Bill Stone? No, I'm fine. I'll handle this myself."

"I didn't mean me. I have a client by the name of Kat Rickter. Interesting person. I've known her for a couple of years. Through the course of our conversations, I've heard some interesting stories about situations she helped resolve, involving men that were out of control."

Rosa sat back in her chair, clearly interested. "Really? Is she employed by law enforcement, or does she work alone?"

"She works alone. You might wanna talk to her. She's an amazing woman. I think your type of situation is what she lives for. By the way, she's independently wealthy. She works on cases like yours because she wants to, not because she needs the income."

"Just one of those man haters, huh?"

"No, not at all. She doesn't hate all of them. But she won't take shit from *any* of them! Believe me she can handle herself, and your type of situation is what she thrives on. Can't hurt to contact her. I'll call you with her number."

As Rosa walked back to her office a few minutes later, she considered Nicki's comments. She had not formulated a plan, *any* plan concerning her approach to acquiring enough evidence to put Angelo away for Stoney's murder. There was no doubt in her mind he did it. Proving it would be difficult to say the least. But it wouldn't hurt to have a partner. It wouldn't hurt having someone help her put this son of a bitch away for the rest of his natural life. Partner or not, that was exactly what she was about to do. She would see this through to the end, as she knew Stoney would have done for her.

CHAPTER 19

"*This wine is amazing.*" *Rosa toasted her date as she swallowed a second taste.*

"It *is* good. I wasn't sure whether it would live up to its name, but it really is good."

John had driven to Mount Juliet and picked her up in time to make a 7:00 p.m. dinner reservation in Nashville. Upbeat was an up-and-coming restaurant in the Five Points area of Nashville. The restaurant was intimate and would not appear to feed more than fifty to sixty people at a time, but the reviews were good, and both John and Rosa were interested in giving it a try.

The conversation centered around work while they indulged on liver pate and fried green tomatoes. Between courses, he reached over, taking her hand, a motion she did not resist.

They each ordered another glass of wine with their main course, which consisted of North Carolina trout on a bed of cheese grits for John, and chicken with risotto for Rosa. As the discussion concerning business wound down, the inevitable discussion concerning Stoney began.

"How are you handling office life without Stoney?"

It had now been six weeks since he had been found dead together with Gail Harper. Life was starting to settle into a routine without him. Hard to do, but necessary. She knew settling into a new routine was inevitable, but it didn't make it any easier.

"It's difficult, John. Most of his business activities have been concluded, and his clients have made other arrangements, but it's become much more difficult for me. I used him in many of my domestic cases. Now I've needed to reach out to other people I've never dealt with to perform the services he handled for me. It'll all work out fine, but the transition, as concerns business, has been difficult."

"What about handling his personal affairs? How are you coming in that respect?"

"Good. I've handled most of his personal issues that needed to be tended to. Luckily, my relationship with his family, particularly his former wife, continues to remain good. I still need to deal with a few creditors, and then I think I'll be ready to wind everything down."

"You going to have someone take over his office space or leave it vacant?"

"I'll leave it as is for now and figure that out in the future. I'm just not sure what I'm going to do in that respect. Not to change the subject, but what about our friend Angelo? Any additional information concerning his involvement?"

"No. They've found absolutely nothing, although Marvin said he was working on an angle that might pan out. He said he would tell me more about it if it appeared to be something we could use. At one time, I know you were really, really bitter about the fact that you felt Angelo was somehow involved, and you were concerned he would never be brought to justice. You still feeling that way?"

Rosa had been concerned her personal feelings about Angelo might be the subject of conversation before the evening was over. She had decided that until she had formulated a plan, an idea that would help bring this man to justice, she would not reveal to anyone—*any-*

one—how she felt or what she had in mind. That *anyone* included the man sitting across the table from her.

"No, no, I'm going to leave all that in the hands of law enforcement. They are best suited to handle the investigation. I'm keeping my nose out of it. Obviously, I initially figured Angelo was involved, but hell I don't know. Could have been anyone. I've never been one to convict anyone of anything until there was at least some evidence to review, and in this case, there is nothing that points the finger at Angelo. At least nothing of which I'm aware."

"That's a wise approach. Glad to hear that's how you're looking at it. I'll be sure to keep you informed if we come up with anything. But for right now, for the moment, are you ready for some dessert, or are you ready to go home?"

"No dessert for me. Yes, I'm ready to leave."

While walking to his car, he put his arm around her waist. As they drove to Mount Juliet, she wondered about confiding in him how she really felt concerning bringing Angelo to justice. She figured she had taken the correct approach. There would be plenty of time to express her thoughts.

Upon arrival, she said, "Would you like a quick nightcap before you drive back to Nashville?'

"Absolutely."

They walked through the front door, and Rosa walked directly to the kitchen. He stood beside the island, located in the middle of the kitchen floor.

"Baileys work for you?"

"That's fine, yes, that's fine for me."

She leaned over and removed the bottle from the lower kitchen cabinet. As she stood, he walked around the island, stopping behind her and placing his arms around her waist. She turned to face him, and as she did, he kissed her. She put her arms around him as he said, "Does this place have a bedroom, or do you sleep on the couch?"

She smiled as she said, "Down the hall, first door on the left."

He kissed her, picked her up, and carried her to the hallway. As he reached the first door on the left, he walked in and let her down. He took off his shirt and removed her blouse. He then unsnapped her bra; she lowered her arms, allowing it to release its hold and, suddenly, no longer needed, drop harmlessly between their legs. He removed everything else he was wearing, then unbuttoned her pants, lowering both her pants and panties to the point gravity took over, and they, without further assistance, dropped softly to the floor.

With only the indirect light from the front room shining through the doorway, he once again picked her up, carrying her to the bed. He gently laid her down without bothering to turn down the bedspread or any of the sheets.

She tried to take it as slow as possible, but both were ready for the intimacy, the close contact. It wasn't but a few moments until he entered her. He was gentle from beginning to end.

Once her heart had returned to beating on a regular basis, she realized he had fallen asleep beside her. She got up, lifted up the comforter, and covered him.

Rosa walked out into the living room, without dressing, guided only by the indirect dim light of a small lamp she had left on in the kitchen. She sat down in one of the four overstuffed chairs in the room. In the darkness, she tried to sort through, in a reasonable fashion, what she was feeling.

Did she love him? Should this have happened this soon? Should she have allowed it to happen at all?

He was a good man, of that she was convinced. She cared for him. Maybe love was a little strong, but she did care for him. Was this the appropriate time in their relationship to become physical? Maybe, maybe not. But it happened, and it was clearly something they both enjoyed.

Where should they go from here? She literally had no idea. Recently, her life had changed radically in so many aspects. This would seem to be one of those spontaneous events, which occasionally happen throughout the course of a lifetime. Neither had anticipated tonight, but now that it had happened, she needed to go with it, just see how it all turned out. She wouldn't fight it. She wouldn't push it. She would simply go where it took her.

Rosa walked back into the bedroom. John was sleeping soundly. She pulled the comforter aside and lay down beside him. His back was toward her. Rosa moved in closely, putting her arm around his waist. With her immediate concerns settled for the evening, she figured now the only remaining issue was what she would fix for breakfast. Unfortunately, she concluded, after determining what she had in the fridge, that question might indeed be the most difficult of all those she had considered during the last few minutes.

CHAPTER 20

She sat quietly, in the sanctity of her office, contemplating the small piece of paper she was holding in her hand. It was early morning. June hadn't even arrived yet. Rosa knew it was time to commit. He had been dead over two months now, and it was time for her to jump off the fence and move one direction or another.

Law enforcement had uncovered nothing concerning Stoney's murder. She knew it would only be a matter of time before it became a cold case, and the attention of the department would turn to other, more pressing, problems.

Not long after his death, when she concluded she would let it lie, let law enforcement do their thing, she always came back to the same basic question. What would Stoney have done? Would he have let it lie if she had been the victim? The answer always remained the same. He would have died trying to determine who had committed the crime. That was just the way he was.

Ultimately, her conclusion was simple. She had to do everything she could to solve the crime. The only issue now was where to begin. This was not her specialty. She could try cases, and she could read people, but investigating crimes—where to begin, who to talk to, where to look—those were areas in which she was not well versed. That brought her back to the number hastily written by Nicki on the piece of paper she held. Should she dial it, or should she do some additional research? She already knew the basics concerning the woman, but knew nothing specific.

She punched in her number.

"Kat Rickter."

"Morning, Ms. Rickter. Rosa Norway, attorney in Mount Juliet."

"Saw your name come up on caller ID. How can I help you?'

Right to the point. One mark in her favor.

"Kat, I got your name from a mutual friend, Nicki Johnson. I wonder if you would have a few moments today to discuss a problem with which I need help."

"Guess I'm going to need to have to have a talk with Nicki. Don't really like her giving my number to anyone. What kind of problem?"

"Nicki is a longtime friend and was only trying to help. I need some investigating done if you have time. If you have a few minutes, I would like to discuss the details with you here in the office. I don't know if you noticed the media reports concerning the murder of my associate, Bill Stone, but that's what it involves."

"I don't do that kind of work."

"I understand. The man whom I believe responsible for this, I also believe, killed his girlfriend and has been involved in numerous activities of that nature for quite some time. He's also a client of mine, which complicates issues even more."

She hesitated. "Is the guy an abuser? Do you know if he's a longtime abuser?"

"I've seen him at work. Worst I've ever seen. The sex of the individual really makes no difference. He abuses them all—male and female."

Again, a hesitation. "No promises, but I guess we could at least visit. I'm busy most of the day, but I could get away about four. That work for you?"

"I'll make it work. See you then."

Without a word, Kat Rickter terminated the call.

Woman of few words. Another mark in her favor.

Rosa's apprehension involving her initial contact with Kat Rickter was over. She was seated before her, and the initial unimportant exchange of data between two unknowns had concluded.

It was clear Kat Rickter was not someone with whom you wanted to do battle, either mentally or physically. She was as physically fit as any woman she had ever met. In addition, she was stunningly beautiful. Every question asked, every answer given by Kat was brief, to the point. As she had already determined, Kat was clearly a woman of few words, but when she *did* talk, you listened.

After closing her office door, Rosa said, "Let me briefly explain the problem. Maybe you can determine if you even want to get involved before I go into the details."

"Works for me."

"My partner in this office was Bill Stone. He was a private investigator I knew very well. We worked together the past couple of years. He was murdered along with the woman he was seeing, who, by the way, was the murderer's live-in. She wanted out of the relationship, so I believe he just killed two birds with one stone, but I have no proof. Nothing has been uncovered concerning his murder. I need some help in ascertaining who did it."

"Why hasn't law enforcement uncovered anything yet?"

"The man I believe responsible seems to be untouchable. This is at least his third and fourth victim, and that's only since I've known him. He apparently makes no mistakes when he kills these people because they can't seem to catch him."

"Did you mention he's also a client?"

Rosa hesitated a moment before finally saying, "Yes. I assume you understand nothing can leave this room. This conversation, for obvious reasons, must remain only between you and I."

"Who is the guy?"

"Angelo Bonaventura."

"*The* Nashville Bonaventura?"

"Yes. You know him or heard of him?"

"Heard of him. Not a nice man. Did you say you think he murdered his girlfriend too?"

"Yes. At least, I believe he did. He previously also either murdered or had murdered his son-in-law along with a key prosecution witness in a case in which I represented him. None of these murders were ever solved. As I say, he seems untouchable. Of course, I have a conflict-of-interest problem also, so I must be extremely careful who I talk to about the problem, but this man needs to be stopped."

Kat leaned back in her chair as she became more comfortable with the situation. "Going to need to be a little careful with this conflict issue, aren't you?"

"Yes. I want him brought to justice. However, I don't wanna be disbarred, so the situation is extremely touchy for me. But I need help. I need someone to guide me through this and help put this man away. I didn't quit representing him because I thought somehow I might be able to aid in the process if I continued to handle his legal issues."

"Obviously, this means a lot to you. You're putting your life and your professional career on the line." She hesitated while her eyes continued to bore a hole through Rosa. Finally, she said, "I might be interested. Let me think about it a day or two."

"Before you go, since I've opened up to you about this whole situation, can you just briefly tell me a little about yourself?"

"Sure. First off, I'm independently wealthy. No one supports me but me. I'm unmarried. I was married to Mike Rickter, a cop with the Nashville police department, who was killed while on duty. Because I was married to him, I still have a number of contacts in the

Nashville department, men I can rely on and that I trust, so acquiring information about this Bonaventura won't be difficult."

"What do you do? What specifically is your line of work?"

"I help women get out of abusive relationships. I either council them or I actually intervene."

"How long have you done this?"

"My first case ended about a year and a half ago. It involved a man by the name of Roy Brakus. Most abusive man I ever knew. He and I had a couple of serious confrontations. That was when I knew there was a need for someone like me in this world. I've helped many, many women get out of bad situations, and I plan on continuing to do that as long as I'm able."

"That's certainly admirable. What about this Brakus? What happened to him?"

"Can't go into it, but I can assure you, since our final confrontation, he's never again been seen in this area and won't be. That's all I'm going to say."

"What about being paid for your efforts?"

"Money isn't an issue. Don't need any more than I already have, and these women, at least most of them, have no money anyway. Let me ask you, how do *you* intend on helping me?"

"If you conclude Angelo did this, I'll do whatever needs to be done. Clearly I would rather it remain only between the two of us, so I don't lose my law license, but we can let the circumstances dictate what I need to do. We can figure that out as we go along."

Kat stood to leave. Rosa walked around the desk, extending her hand. Kat shook it and said, "I wanna research this guy, both on the Net and through some limited discussion with law enforcement. Don't worry, your name will never come up. Once I've finished, I'll give you a call and let you know if I'm interested. We can go from there."

She opened the office door, and Rosa followed her to the reception area.

"How soon will I hear from you?"

"I'll get back to you within the week."

Rosa watched her walk to her car and drive away. As she walked back to her office, she appreciated the fact Kat and her were not at odds, about anything. She had a feeling being involved in any type of physical or verbal confrontation with Kat would result in a quick conclusion, of which Rosa had a very small chance of success.

CHAPTER 21

arvin Jackson took his job seriously—*in fact, probably too seriously.* He would obsess over losing cases. He would obsess over his inability to prosecute when he knew someone had committed a crime, but had insufficient evidence to charge him. But he was at his worst when, for any reason whatsoever, he had to dismiss a case in the middle of a prosecution, as he did with Angelo Bonaventura. That had now been months ago, and he still lay awake many nights wondering if there was something he could have done to secure a conviction.

The case totally fell apart once Billy Martin had been found dead. He knew the case centered on Billy's testimony from day one, but it didn't make it any easier to dismiss the case. He knew it was only a matter of time before he would get another chance to prosecute Bonaventura, but the dismissal only confirmed what he had known from the beginning—this guy would be tough to convict of anything. He seemed to cover up his sins in an effective and efficient manner each time he was involved.

Even now, trying to solve the murders of Stone and Harper had taken far more manpower than a normal murder investigation in Davidson County deserved. From the beginning, they had so little to go on. He had some basic information from witnesses who had heard Angelo ask Gail if she was seeing someone. He had witnesses who had seen Stone and Gail together, but he didn't have that one witness who might tie it all together, until now.

"Good morning, Marvin."

John Winstrom, district attorney for Davidson County, just walked in his office. He and John had worked together as prosecutors for over ten years. John was now technically the boss, but Marvin had been allowed to run his own show ever since John had been elected. Marvin had been assured repeatedly by John that he trusted his judgment and that the decisions Marvin made would be wholly supported by the district attorney under each and every circumstance.

"Morning, John. You have a few minutes?"

"Sure. I saw your note wanting to see me. That's why I'm here."

"As you know, the sheriff's office has been devoting a considerable amount of time to the murders of Stoney and Gail Harper. The other day, we got some information concerning an individual that's working for Bonaventura. One of his housekeepers, and one that's been there for quite a few years, is apparently under indictment in Alabama for an offense which occurred a number of years ago. I thought about having her brought in to determine what she might know about the murders and to also discuss those pending charges. Do you have a problem with that?"

"No, of course not. Are you thinking if she has some information, you might work a deal with her?"

"Yes. I have no idea what she might know, but providing testimony from someone on the inside like that might be all we need."

"You going to be able to protect her?"

"Yes, I think so. We'll need to do a better job than we did with Billy Martin, but I think we can handle it."

John thought for only a moment before he stood to leave the room and said, "Go for it. Good luck. Let me know what happens."

As he left the room, Marvin picked up his phone and quickly punched in the number for the detective working on the murders.

"Bring in Mrs. Carsten immediately. Also, pick up her two girls. Hold them at Protective Services until I'm sure how we're going to proceed."

An hour later, Joni Carsten walked in his office, along with an accompanying law enforcement officer.

Marvin stood and said, "Good Morning. Please have a seat, Mrs. Carsten."

Joni was dressed in a pair of old jeans and a sweatshirt. Clearly she had no time to put on makeup or even brush her hair when they picked her up.

"What's the meaning of all this? Why am I here? And if I have to be here, couldn't y'all have at least called me in advance so I had time to clean up before y'all brought me in here? As you can see, I'm a damn mess."

"Officer, please wait outside. Close the door behind you."

The officer complied immediately, leaving them alone.

"Please, Mrs. Carsten. Have a chair."

She looked at him for a brief moment and then grudgingly took a seat.

"Why am I here? What have I done?"

"Well, first of all, you have done nothing here, in Tennessee. We have no problem with your life here. But in a prior life, I believe you were actively involved in some illegal activity in the state of Alabama. Am I correct?"

She looked at him for only a moment before her shoulders slumped; she lowered her head and, in a voice barely audible, said, "Might have been. That what this is all about?"

"Partially." He smiled. "But don't give up yet. All is not lost. That's why you're here, with me, and not in jail. We need to talk about another aspect of your life, the part that may set you free from all your past sins."

She looked up and said, "What y'all talking about?"

"You work for Angelo Bonaventura?"

"Yes, why?"

He took a deep breath and said, "Ever hear him talk about what happened to Bill Stone and Gail Harper?"

"Why?"

"Because we may be able to work out a deal if you did. Now, did you ever hear him talking about those murders?"

"What kind of deal?"

"I need to know what you heard, if in fact, you heard anything."

She sat back in her chair, obviously considering her options, which Marvin knew were few. Finally, she said, "Yes. I did hear some things about the murders, but very little."

"What did you hear and when?"

"Before they was killed, I overheard him asking his men if he knew whether Gail and Stone were involved. They didn't seem to know. He would rant about what he would do if he found out they were involved. How he would kill both of them. Then, after they was murdered, I heard them all laughing about it. How they know they had both gone to a better place, most likely together since that's how they left this earth."

"Did you ever hear him say he killed them?"

"No."

"Do you have any other information indicating Angelo was somehow involved?"

"No."

"Okay, I believe what you have is what I need. I need your testimony against him. I think with what we have and with what you just told me, we may be able to secure a conviction. Are you willing to testify?"

She stood up and leaned on his desk. Her eyes were full of rage as she spit out her words, "Are y'all crazy? Hell no. He would slaughter me and both my children before he allowed that to happen. No way."

"Take it easy, take it easy, just sit down. First of all, I've picked up both your daughters at school. They're with Child Protective Services. I didn't want to take a chance someone might see you walk in here and do something stupid with the girls. They're safe. Secondly, we've found a safe place for all of you. It's a witness protection program out of town, and the location will be known only to myself and the officer taking you there. No one else would know."

She returned to her chair, but was still clearly agitated. "You protected Billy real well now, didn't y'all? It's impossible to get away from him. He'll find us."

"No, he won't. We made the mistake of underestimating Angelo the first time. That won't happen this time. We should have removed Billy from Nashville, and he would most likely still be here. You and your daughters will be safe, that I can guarantee."

She looked away and started to cry.

"Now, here's the rest of the story, Joni. I'll have your record wiped clean in Alabama. I've already visited with the authorities, and they have agreed, in return for your testimony, to dismiss all pending charges. In addition, I'll set you up with a new identity, with recommendations from a number of people that will help you find employment. You can start over. I also have a fund from which I can draw enough money to keep you in groceries until you find a job."

She thought for a moment, then turned to look at Marvin. "Sounds like I got no choice." She looked down. "Besides that, it sounds like maybe it's best for me and for my children. When do we leave?"

"Now. I'll send an officer to the house to box everything up, and we'll terminate your lease. I'll probably bring the grand jury in to hear your statements next week, and you'll need to be here for that."

"I don't know whether to thank y'all or curse ya."

He smiled. "It's all going to work out, Joni. Even if he isn't convicted, I guarantee he'll never find you."

He stood, walked over, and opened the door. "Come in, Sam." He shut the door as the officer walked in. "She's good to go. Pick up the kids. Take them to the location we discussed. The house is ready for her. You're going to need to go box up her possessions later today and get them to her."

He nodded affirmatively.

As she walked out the door, she turned and said, "Thank you."

Marvin smiled and said, "This is going to work out just fine. I'll see you soon."

As he sat down, he picked up the phone and said, "John, I've got some great news."

He still wasn't sure it was enough to convict, but it was all they had, and hopefully, it would be enough to secure the conviction he should have had the last time he tried Angelo. Perhaps, just perhaps, this was the last piece of the puzzle, and he now had enough evidence to put Bonaventura away for the rest of his natural life.

CHAPTER 22

*R*osa sat alone, in her office, staring blankly into space. She was so far behind in daily office work, she felt perhaps the quiet setting of the office—before the manic day-to-day activity began—would help her at least review the stack of new calls she hadn't returned and phone messages she hadn't read. But as she sat there, her thoughts again turned to Stoney, and to better times.

For some reason, she remembered the time she was so sick she couldn't leave the house. A case of the flu kept her inside, in bed, and away from the rest of society. But about midmorning, she heard a knock on the door. She had barely enough strength to rise out of bed and make her way to the door, where she opened it ever so slightly. It was Stoney, and he had a delivery.

She opened the door just enough to make conversation slightly easier, observing he had brought her ice cream. He knew she was sick, and he was doing with her as he would have done for one of his own children if they were sick—bringing her ice cream. But when he saw her nightwear, those pajamas with the elephants on them, he burst out with laughter. Even as sick as she was, she too had to laugh. He never let her live that down. Months later, he would ask if she still wore those elephant pajamas. Of course, when they were a couple, she never wore anything—he always kept her warm. Long after her romantic relationship with Stoney ended, he never let her forget how cute, but how funny, she looked with those elephants plastered all over her pajamas.

"Morning, Rosa."

June had arrived. Rosa knew from past experience the phone would now start ringing, appointments would start arriving, and the office would swing into its normal insanely active mode.

She knew it was now time to stop living in the past as concerned Stoney. It was time to shift gears and move on to the next step. It was time to stop moving in slow motion on a day-to-day basis and move into the present. Moving into the present meant, as concerned her friend Stoney, moving forward concerning activities that would determine who murdered him. Since his murder, she found herself hanging on to the past and simply leaving the present on hold. That would end today.

"Morning, June. When's my first appointment?"

"Angelo will be in about ten. But you really need to call Marvin Jackson. He's called three or four times, and the last time, he asked me to tell you to call him first thing this morning."

"Okay. I wonder what he wanted."

"No idea."

She waited until eight thirty before she punched in his number. "Marvin, Rosa. I see you called. Is there a problem?"

He laughed. "Not really. In fact, quite the contrary. I expect to have an indictment in hand before the morning is over, charging your client Bonaventura with the murders of Stoney and Gail. I just wanted you to know."

Rosa was at a complete loss for words. Finally she said, "You're kidding. What evidence did you come up with that gave you enough to present his case to the grand jury?'

"His housekeeper. She's agreed to testify for the state. She has testimony that should tie down the motive issues completely."

Rosa hesitated, expecting more. When he said nothing, she said, "Is that it?"

"Yes. Hopefully it will be enough. That along with all the other witnesses that will testify concerning his statements about the two of them, combined with all the people that saw both Stoney and Gail together, we feel will be sufficient. I know its light, but it's all I have."

"You're correct, it's light, but maybe it'll be enough."

"What's your position, Rosa? You gonna represent him?"

She hesitated before answering. "We've known each other a long time, Marvin. I know whatever I say to you will remain in confidence. I'm assuming the call isn't being recorded, correct?"

"Whatta you think? The county has no money for such an expensive gadget as a phone recorder, you know that. No, it's not tapped, and this conversation is as confidential as any you'll ever have with anyone."

"I'm going to represent him. But let me tell you this. It's not his side I'm on. I'll do all I can to present a proper defense, but I have little doubt he murdered them. I'll be more than happy to lose the case. Does that answer your question?"

He laughed. "So you're gonna help me convict him?"

"I'm not going to go quite that far, Marvin. But let's just say, in public, I'm your worst enemy, in private, I'm your biggest fan."

"But how are you gonna handle this with Stoney being the victim? I can't imagine how you can represent the man that most likely murdered him."

"I'll handle it, believe me. I have my reasons. Just let me justify what I have to do. You present enough to convict, and I'll take it from there."

"Okay. I'm not sure how this will all work out, but that's good news for sure. I'll let you know when the indictment has been handed down, and you can make arrangements to bring him in."

"The sooner, the better."

She terminated the call. It sounded to Rosa like the evidence might be insufficient to convict. She wished he had waited and tried collecting more evidence before he submitted everything to the grand jury. But he did what he clearly thought he had to do. It sounded as though there was plenty of evidence concerning motive, but virtually none concerning method or opportunity.

"Rosa, Angelo is here. He's early."

She wasn't sure she was mentally ready for him. She felt drained after every visit with him, but quickly concluded it was just best to get him out of the way so she could move on with her day.

"Send him in."

"Rosa, Rosa, how are you today?" He stuck out his hand as he walked through her door.

She stood, shook his hand, and directed him to a seat in front of her desk. "I'm doing fine, Angelo. What brings you here?"

"Well, a couple of issues. The original issue which necessitated my visit was just to see if you had heard anything about Gail's murder. I really miss her, every day, and I wanna make sure someone is held accountable."

"What's the second?"

"Oh, it's really nothing, but I just lost my housekeeper. She failed to show up a couple of days ago. I figured you helped me with everything else, maybe you could help me replace her. I realize it's a small issue, but I really need someone, and I just figured you might be in a position to know of someone that needed a job."

"No, no, Angelo, can't help you there. Sorry. But, I *have* heard some news about the murders."

"Great. What have you heard?"

"Marvin Jackson called me earlier, and he believes the grand jury may indict you today on both murders."

He jumped from his chair and screamed, "Me? What the fuck? I didn't murder either of them. Where the hell did that trumped-up charge come from? What evidence do they have? This is fucking bullshit."

Rosa never took a deep breath, never raised her voice. She was used to his rants by now.

"Sit down, and calm down." He never moved. "Sit down, Angelo, or leave. Up to you."

He looked at her for a brief second, and then, obviously realizing he needed more information from her before he left, took a seat.

"Thank you. It's my understanding the housekeeper you told me just quit has turned state's evidence. She's going to testify you discussed killing both Stoney and Gail on more than one occasion."

He sat back in his chair and started to smile. "Where's the rest of their evidence? Do they have anything else? Is that it?"

"I believe that's it. But I won't know any more until I actually see the minutes of testimony."

"Do you know where they're keeping her?"

"No."

He looked down for a moment and finally said, "You going to represent me, or is that too much to ask?"

"You want me to?"

"Hell yes. You're the best attorney I know. I know you well enough to know that no matter what the evidence shows, you'll represent me with all you got. That's enough for me. Of course, you also know I didn't do this."

She smiled. The die was cast. She would now do all she could to walk that thin line, to put up a defense that was just enough for him to believe she was adequately representing his interests, and at the same time, she would do all she could to bring to justice the man she knew murdered her friend.

CHAPTER 23

*S*he watched as the flames began to subside, leaving nothing but glowing embers and a resulting coolness in the air. Kat Rickter sat alone, with her thoughts, as she often did, not because she had to, but because she elected to.

Late afternoon, she had started a fire in the fire pit located between the barn and her home. With a bottle of wine and her iPad, she settled into a comfortable chair, started the fire, and watched the sun set. Now, some three hours later, she found herself in the same spot, slightly influenced by three full glasses of wine, but not so far along she couldn't remember. Her thoughts turned to Mike, remembering the man that set her out on this mission, this mission to protect women from men who would take advantage, and to protect them from themselves.

Roy Brakus had been the first of many men she had confronted. He was a murderer, a user of women, an abuser, a sociopath. He had murdered her husband and left no evidence of any nature for law enforcement. They couldn't prove he did it, but she knew who killed Mike, and she had set out to even the score or die trying.

She remembered the day of their final confrontation, right here on this very farm. He was about to rape her at gunpoint, in the barn, and then kill her. As a result of a timely diversion, she was able to obtain the upper hand. All issues involving the two of them were brought to a conclusion on this farm. Since then, she had helped many women escape abusive relationships. Kat felt relieved she had never needed to again go to an extreme to stop their abuse, as she had needed to with Brakus, but once she agreed to assist, she committed herself to do whatever was necessary to protect the women she helped.

Now, it was time to research this man Bonaventura. Time to figure out what made him tick and why he was so untouchable.

She got up from her chair, her balance somewhat affected by the bottle, looked down to make sure there was nothing left to burn in the fire pit, which might create an issue, and walked back to the house. Tomorrow she would begin her search for information concerning Mr. Bonaventura.

The next morning, after breakfast and exercise, she sat down at her computer and started her research. It didn't take long to find his name located within many different areas of the Internet.

She first determined he was the owner of a furniture store. Research concerning that issue also brought up the apparent robbery and murder of his son-in-law, Chuck Harris, a murder for which Bonaventura was ultimately charged.

She was able to follow the proceedings right up until the time the chief prosecution witness was murdered, and the case was dismissed. His murder too had remained unresolved. It was apparent Bonaventura had, by then, gotten away with at least two murders, and her investigation had barely begun.

Through the course of the next two hours, she uncovered story after story in which his name was linked to a crime or a series of crimes involving robbery, prostitution, abuse of women, and money laundering. She never found an article about a conviction involving any of those allegations. It was clear this was a man who was involved in illegal activities of every nature. To date, no one had come close to stopping him. It was also clear, he would stop at nothing to success-fully conclude whatever goal he was attempting to achieve.

There was little doubt, based on her research, he was the type of man that she abhorred. He was the type of person she had vowed to stop. Kat needed some additional local information, other than what she read on the Net, to help her come to an appropriate conclusion. She knew just who to contact in that respect.

Captain Gleason had been on the force for over twenty years. He was her husband's immediate supervisor. She had become close to both him and his wife when Mike died, and had remained close since Mike's death. She knew she could trust him with her life.

"Hi, Cap. Been a while. Kat Rickter. Got time to visit for a moment?"

"It *has* been a while, Kat. Sure. I always have time for you. What's going on?"

"I need some information about a resident of your fine city. I just figured if anyone could tell me about him, you could."

She heard his chair squeak. She envisioned him leaning back and could hear him chuckle as he said, "You after somebody, again?"

"You know me too well, Cap."

"I also know how much good you've done for people, Kat. Your service for the women in this area has not gone unnoticed. Who you after this time?"

"A guy by the name of Angelo Bonaventura. You ever heard of him?"

There was a noticeable silence, and she could again hear his chair squeak as he apparently moved forward to continue the conversation.

"Don't mess with him, Kat. I'm telling you right now, stay away from the guy. He's like nothing you've ever dealt with."

Kat laughed and said, "Really? Is he that bad? Tell me about him."

"Yes, he's really that bad. In addition to how dangerous a man he is, he employs guys that are just as bad, people that would do absolutely anything. He's been associated with many, many crimes in the city, but never been convicted of one. He's not only mean, but he's damn smart. You really need to move in another direction, Kat. This guy's too tough, even for us."

"What type of crime?"

"He's been associated with everything—drugs, abuse of women, and even murder. But none of the charges ever stick. Even now, they're in the process of charging him with a couple of murders that happened a while back. But, I've talked to the prosecutor's office, and it seems clear to me the evidence is inadequate. They have a chance at a conviction, but it's far from a slam dunk. That's how it is with him, every single time. They just can't get enough on him to put 'im away."

She hesitated before continuing. "Okay, Cap. Guess that's what I need to know. As always, thanks for your help."

"Does that help?"

"Sure does."

"You gonna stay away from him?"

"Don't know yet. Probably not."

"What do I need to say to convince you to stay away from the man?"

"Cap, you told me what you needed to about him. I'll take it from here. Obviously, he's a problem. That's what I thrive on—men that are a problem. I'll figure it out from here. Thanks for all your help. Give my love to Martha."

She terminated the call, while considering the information he had provided. She ultimately concluded it was time for a short trip.

A few hours later, she was situated a couple of blocks from the Bonaventura home. She had a camera with a telescopic lens. For the next hour, she took pictures of people coming and going. She would place faces with names after she arrived home.

As she drove Interstate 40 east, toward home, she considered her options. This man, from all she could ascertain, was as evil as anyone she had ever dealt with. She was working on no other project at the time, so the timing for her schedule was perfect. Angelo Bonaventura interested her. If there were no other factors that she uncovered through her research tonight, in spite of the captain's warning, she would take him on as her next project. Hopefully she would be able to do what apparently no one else had ever been able to do—put this animal where he belonged once and for all.

CHAPTER 24

*R*osa *sat in silence, waiting, anticipating her next appointment.* Kat Rickter had called and made an office appointment for next week. Once Rosa had noticed June had placed the appointment on the calendar, she told her to call her back and reschedule for this week if possible. The appointment was rescheduled for today. The issues she needed to discuss with Kat were far more important than other people's problems. This was Rosa's problem. This was personal.

She heard Kat enter the front door. June messaged her asking whether she should bring her back, and Rosa acknowledged affirmatively.

"Good morning." Kat had on a white sleeveless button-up blouse. Her arms were sculptured, and as tight as the arms of a boxer.

"Good morning, Rosa." She took a chair in front of Rosa's desk, waiting for her to start the conversation.

Rosa stood, then walked behind Kat to close her office door. As she did, she said, "Have you had a chance to consider the issues we discussed the other day? What are your thoughts?"

Rosa's heart was in her throat as Kat started to respond. Rosa needed her. She couldn't do this on her own.

"I have. I also had an opportunity to do some research into the past, and present, concerning Mr. Bonaventura. Either you are a really good attorney or the guy was born with a silver spoon in his mouth. He seems to be able to avoid apprehension and conviction concerning every mess he gets into."

Rosa smiled. "Well, I have to admit I'm a pretty good attorney, but not that good. He figures out his escape plan long before he does the crime. He's well organized in addition to being a murdering son of a bitch."

"I need to know how committed you are to stopping this man. How far you willing to go? You ready to lose your license to practice if we get caught?"

"Obviously, I hope it doesn't come to that. I've asked myself that very question a number of times, but all I have to do is consider what Stoney would have done if the tables had been turned. There's no doubt in my mind he would have risked everything to figure out what happened to me. So in response to your question, yes, I'm ready to risk it all to confirm Angelo did this and bring him to justice."

"I've had a chance to review his history and to make a few phone calls to people who know of him, and whom I trust explicitly. All the research, all my contacts confirm the same thing. He's impossible to stop. At least he has been so far. You plannin' to continue to represent him while working with me to apprehend him? Is that the gist of it?"

"Absolutely."

Kat looked down for a moment, apparently considering her options based on the answers given by Rosa. Finally, she looked up, smiled, and said, "Let's get him."

"Music to my ears. Now, since you grilled me concerning my position, let me ask you a couple of questions. First of all, the story you told me about that first man you discussed, the one that got you started in this 'protect the women' phase of your life. How was that concluded?"

"Let me ask you a question. Is everything we say confidential? I assume nothing goes beyond this room."

"That's correct. By the way, I have much more at risk than you at this point, so I can assure you, none of what we discuss will ever go beyond me."

"I'm not going into details with you. Let me say he got exactly what he deserved."

Rosa sat back, took a breath, and said, "Holy shit. Did you kill him?"

Kat smiled and said, "Not going there with you. I can tell you he'll never hurt anyone else. If my farm could carry on a conversation, believe me, you would hear quite the story, Rosa."

Rosa thought for a moment, smiled, and said, "That's good enough for me. First of all, I think it's important once we get started, we not be seen anywhere together."

"I agree, and I don't think there should be anything in writing between us. Everything we say and plan should be verbal. This should also be the last time we meet here. When we need to discuss issues, we could meet at my house, or somewhere else private. Once this starts, there should be absolutely no indication we are friends or are in any way associated."

"What are you thinking? Preliminarily, what are you thinking about as a plan?"

"I need to find a way to get close to him or to someone in his group. I hadn't considered the method yet. I wanted to see how this conversation went first, and then plan accordingly."

"So I'm assuming the overall plan here is that you, through your eventual contacts with this man and his group, acquire information that will help prosecute him. You then tell me what you've learned, and I either use it in the presentation of his case in court or I make sure the prosecution is aware of what you uncover. Is that about it?"

"That's what I'm thinking at this point. I think most of our planning will probably take place once we start. It's just too hard right now to formulate a plan based on so few facts. Right now, we just need to know we are working together to put this guy away, and then go from there."

"Did you know he's in the process of being indicted for both those murders?"

"I did hear something about that. Do they have enough?"

"No, not as far as I'm concerned. If I thought they did, we wouldn't be having this conversation. The one bit of evidence that fell into place, and resulted in submitting everything to the grand jury, was that his housekeeper turned state's evidence. She's in protective custody now, but I don't think Marvin Jackson, the assistant district attorney prosecuting the case, even thinks they have enough to convict. He's just hoping Angelo's reputation puts him behind bars. But I think you and I need to make sure. We need to make sure when the trial starts, Marvin has enough to convict. You should know, Marvin is a good man. I've known him a long time, and he's honest and upfront. He'll be easy for me to deal with, especially if he thinks he might somehow acquire enough additional evidence to secure a conviction."

"So what're your thoughts about starting this show?"

Rosa thought for a moment. She started to smile. "Do you do your own housework, or do you have a housekeeper?"

"I do my own, why?"

"Wanna start a new occupation? How does 'Kat Rickter, housekeeper' sound to you?"

"What are you talking about? Hell no, I don't wanna be a housekeeper."

"Angelo came to me the other day bemoaning the fact he no longer has a housekeeper and was looking for one. What better way would there be, but for you to get inside that house, and come up with what we need to convict this guy."

Kat started to smile. "I have someone that could set me up with a new identity with references—good references. Once inside, I can guarantee you I'll get whatever Marvin needs to convict." She thought for a moment. "I wonder if they have security cameras throughout the house. Can you find out if they do and where they're located?"

Rosa picked up her phone, autodialed Marvin's personal number, and put the phone on speaker.

"Morning, Marvin. I need a favor."

"Hi, Rosa. What's that?"

"Can you find out for me from Angelo's housekeeper if they have security cameras inside the Bonaventura house, and if they do, where they're located?"

"I guess I can, but what for? What's going on?"

"Marvin, don't even ask. Let me put it is this way: what I'm doing will only benefit you, not me. Can you find out and get back to me?"

"Yes. I'll talk to her today. I'll call you when I know."

Rosa terminated the call.

"Get your references together, lady. You're about to be reborn, with a new name, and a new occupation. You worried about all this?"

Kat rose to leave. "Absolutely not. I faced the worst that ever lived in Roy Brakus. This should be a piece of cake."

Rosa got up, walked over to Kat, then embraced her.

"Here's to our new alliance. May it turn out as successful as your venture involving Mr. Brakus turned out."

"I agree. Hopefully, if this all concludes as it should, the last words uttered at the trial involving this SOB will be 'guilty, as charged!'"

CHAPTER 25

A week later, Rosa continued to remain optimistic about their newly established partnership. She told no one. Absolutely no one would be allowed access to any information concerning their alliance. Too risky. If Angelo were to learn of the connection between the two while she was representing him, the ending could be deadly for both of them. No one must know, other than perhaps Nicki. Nicki started the ball rolling, so she at least had some idea what was going on, but the specifics would never be divulged. She would need to tell her to forget she had ever given Rosa her number. She would have the opportunity to do that soon, very soon. Nicki was just walking through her office door.

"Rosa, Nicki just walked in, and is standing here. Your next appointment isn't until ten. Do you wanna see her, or should I send her packin'?"

Rosa laughed. "Send her in."

As Nicki walked through her office door, she said, "Do you often send friends *packin*? Sure as hell better not do that with me, that's all I got to say about that."

"Don't worry, Nicki. I wouldn't do that with you. There are a few people that walk in off the street who wanna see me immediately that we do send *packin'*. I think June was just having a little fun with you. What are you doin' in Mount Juliet? You're a long way from your normal territory."

"You're right, it is. But I needed to see that client I told you about one more time. Can't quite get the deal finished off. It could mean a hell of a lot of business for me, but I just can't quite seal the deal."

"So how's he in bed? He good enough for you or not?"

"Ya, he's great, but… hold on. Did I tell you I was sleeping with him? I didn't remember I told you that. How'd you know?"

"You told me. It really wouldn't have mattered whether you had told me anyway. That seems to be the way you operate anymore. I just assumed that was going on with this guy, as it apparently has with other 'clients.'"

"This is the last one. It's getting me a few sales, but not enough to make it worthwhile. I do like this guy though. He's a little more to me than just a sale. I'm not sure where this is all headed, but whatever happens, I sure would like to close the sale, I know that. Let's quit talkin' about me. You got any coffee in this place? I'd like a cup if you don't mind."

"Sure." Rosa stood, walked into the back office, got her a cup of coffee, and returned to her office.

"So what's happened concerning Stoney?"

"Nothing."

She turned away for a moment, before she looked at Nicki, and said, "They have no idea what happened or who did it. That's no surprise to me. They'll never figure it out. It'll end up as a cold case. That's why I contacted Kat."

"Are you two going to be able to work together?"

"Yes, I think so. Thanks for providing me with her phone number. I called her, and we got together the other day. I think, maybe, we're going to be able to work together."

"Great. I've met with her a number of times. I'll tell you one thing about her. She's honest to a fault. If she tells you she's going to do something, she does it. Not just occasionally, but every time. If she says she'll meet you somewhere at a specific time, she does it. Doesn't matter what she says she'll do, at least with me, she's never failed to do it. She's tough, but she's great to deal with. You always know where you stand with her."

"I could tell she was right up-front with me concerning everything we discussed."

Nicki leaned forward in her chair, as if the room was full of people and there was a desperate need to whisper while communicating a secret. "So, what's the plan here? What's going down, what's happening, is there anything I can do?"

Rosa had to laugh as she rolled her eyes.

"There's nothing you can do. Oh, except one thing. I know how close you and I are, and I know you never say anything about our conversations to anyone, but I need to ask you to be double careful about that concerning Kat and I. You can't say anything to anyone concerning the two of us teaming up. No matter how this turns out, it's going to be dangerous from day one. If Angelo ever gets word the two of us are working together, both of us could be in terrible danger. So thanks for letting me know about Kat, thanks for introducing us, now forget all about it."

Nicki sat back in her chair, thoughts of her participation in the scheme now shattered, and said, "Okay. If that's the way you want it. I'll never say a word to anyone. In return, just keep me informed."

"I'll do that. Where do you go from here, back to the office?"

"Hold on—just a minute here. We haven't even discussed the reason I stopped. What about John? Have you spent any time with him at all? Am I going to be a bridesmaid or best woman or whatever they call them now? What's going on in your love life? Anything? Anything at all?"

With the pressure concerning the issue of Angelo and Kat, off the table, Rosa sat back and smiled. "As a matter of fact, I've seen him a number of times since we last talked."

Nicki waited. Rosa offered nothing more.

Finally, Nicki said, "Go on, go on. What happened? I tell you everything about my love life, now give it up."

"Okay, okay." She took a deep breath. "Well, we've had dinner together five or six times, in Mount Juliet, Lebanon, and Nashville. We've really spent a lot of time with each other, especially in the last couple of weeks."

"So whatta you think?"

"I think he's easy to get along with, and I think I love being with him. We have many things in common, so there's always a conversation going on about something or another, and I just enjoy being with him. I don't know how far it'll go from here. I'm not thinking about that right now. I'm just enjoying the moment and enjoying our time together getting to know each other."

Nicki smiled broadly and said, "You in love with him?"

Rosa hesitated, obviously considering her answer not only as a response to Nicki's question, but in response to the same question she had recently asked herself.

"I care for him—a lot. I'm not sure if *love* is appropriate yet, but I really do care for him. I look forward to seeing him, being with him, and spending time with him. I enjoy all those things, so if that's your definition of *love*, then I guess that's where I'm at—in love."

"So..."

"So what?"

"Come on now. Have you slept with him yet?"

"I can't go there with you, Nicki. I know you have no problem with discussing your sex life with me, but I do with you. Let's just move on."

Nicki sat back in her chair considering Rosa's response.

"Okay, let's see, if you hadn't slept with him, you wouldn't have had anything to hide, so you would have simply said no. Your answer is a clear indication to me you did and you just aren't going to tell me about it. Now just tell me if my conclusion based on your answer is accurate."

Rosa only smiled and replied, "I'm not going there with you, Nicki. Now, change the subject."

Nicki was far from giving up. "So we've concluded you love him and that you've slept with him. Interesting. You love him enough to marry him?"

"We're done here. I have no idea what the future holds. We're both taking this slowly, one step at a time. All I can tell you is that we're compatible, and I really do care for him. That's it. You get no more out of me concerning that issue."

"What about his former wife and those kids? Any issues there?"

"No. I met the children once. They seem really nice, really well-grounded. I've never met her. He tells me she's a good mother, a great cook, an adequate housekeeper, but she was a pathetic wife. Three out of four just wasn't enough, and that was why he divorced her. There was nothing left in the marriage. They settled everything amicably, and each went their own way."

Rosa led Nicki to the door not long after Nicki had concluded Rosa would provide no additional information concerning her relationship with John, at least for today. But long after Nicki left, the questions she asked Rosa continued to command her attention.

They were, however, only part of her thoughts. She couldn't help but pause and consider how much had changed since Stoney's murder. Almost simultaneously, she lost her best friend, her business partner, and a strong male influence in her life. At the same time, in walks John, the first man she had spent any time with, to any extent, since her romantic relationship with Stoney had ended almost a year ago.

Rosa had always analytically considered every issue of importance in her life. She evaluated the problem and, drawing from available options, determined an appropriate solution, just as she was doing with Stoney's murder. That did not appear to be a feasible method of resolving the question concerning her relationship with John, and how it might ultimately conclude. At this point, there appeared to be no defined, acceptable option, or multiple options, available, only a series of inscrutable, nebulous questions, which failed to produce a well-defined answer of any nature.

For example, was she in love? No doubt! Did she enjoy every moment she spent with him? No doubt! *But* would she consider spending the rest of her life with him? That was a tough question. The probable answer: most likely*!*

On second thought, perhaps those questions and their resulting answers weren't quite as nebulous as she first thought. All in all, she was glad she had this little conversation with herself. Now it was time to close shop, drive home, open a bottle of wine, and hopefully, sometime this evening, talk to this man she just concluded she loved, and would someday marry, if asked.

CHAPTER 26

"Hey, Rocco, send her in." *Angelo Bonaventura was seated* behind a large wooden desk located in the middle of his office. He had paperwork scattered all over its surface, which he had reviewed prior to yelling out his order to "send her in."

Angelo's office was his sanctuary. It was his escape, where he went when all else failed, when life was sliding downhill, and he needed to think, to figure out what the hell to do next. His office was always quiet. There were no windows, there were no cameras. Whatever happened in that room stayed in that room. Many times he had found it necessary to clean up a bloodstain on his office floor the next morning. Many times his voice had echoed throughout the room, with door closed, as he berated or reprimanded one of his trenchermen concerning actions they had or hadn't taken the day before. When all else failed, there remained *his office.*

This morning, it would be used as an employment venue. He would interview a couple of women in a continuing effort to replace Joni.

Angelo knew it would be difficult to replace her. She was good at what she did, and she worked for little pay. He had those issues in Alabama to hold over her head. That motivating factor remained extremely effective, until now. She stayed with him, did her job, kept her mouth shut, and worked for virtually nothing.

"Good morning, Ms. Crabstone. Do you go by Jenny or Jennifer?"

She was tall and slender, about twenty-five, poorly dressed.

"Either. Either is fine."

"Please be seated. I've read your resume. You don't have much job experience, do you?"

"No. Not yet, sir. But I really think I could do y'all a good job."

"You realize you would be supervising a couple of other part-time workers too? Have you ever been in a supervising capacity before?"

"No, sir, but I'm sure I can handle it. I just really need a job."

"What about those pending charges against you in Louisiana for manslaughter? You get those all resolved, did you?"

She said nothing.

"You surely knew I'd find out about those, didn't you? You shot your boss, correct? Killed him. At least that's the information I got. Is that resolved or not?"

She looked away for a moment, then finally said, "No, but they will be shortly. I'm afixin' to take care of all that real soon now."

"Did you really shoot your boss? Is that really what happened?"

She sat up and, with a look of defiance, said, "Sure did, Mr. Bonaventura. Son of a bitch deserved it. He came on to me. He deserved to get shot."

"Rocco! Hey, Rocco."

His right-hand man bounded into the room. "What's up, boss? What's the problem?"

He hesitated for a moment, then smiled while still staring at the applicant, and said, "Escort the lady out of here. Did you honestly think I was going to hire someone who, first of all, was under indictment and, secondly, was under indictment for *shooting her boss*? Give me a fuckin' break. Now get out."

She never said a word. The look of defiance quickly left her face. She rose, following Rocco out the door.

Once Rocco had had enough time to walk her through the front door, he returned to Angelo's office. "Boss, Janice wants to visit with you."

Janice Kerr was one of his two remaining housekeepers. She worked on a part-time basis and had received all her instructions from Joni.

"What the hell does she want?"

"Something about the toilets."

"What the fuck? Send her in."

Janice timidly entered his office, a location she had never entered before today. "Boss, I need some advice from you. Do you have time? Boss, do you know what Joni used to clean the stools with? I can't find what she used. I don't know what to buy or where to buy it. Can you tell me?"

He sat quietly while contemplating an appropriate response. He leaned forward in his chair, and very softly, he explained, "I have no fucking idea what she used to clean up shit, I really don't. Now get your ass out of here, and go figure it out yourself, you idiot. Don't come back here again with a question of that nature, or I'll see to it you never work another day in your life. Now get out!"

She slowly backed out of his office without another word.

Such was a normal day since Joni had left. He fielded question after question concerning what cleaning products to use, where to take clothes to have them dry-cleaned, or what to do about an inoperative dishwasher. He needed to replace her, but the applicants all looked the same—incompetent. He needed to replace her to retain his own sanity.

"Rocco, Rocco, get in here."

"Sure, boss, what's up?"

"Don't bother me with any more questions about this house. You answer them questions, and get it right. Don't give them some cock-and-bull answer about some crap we use to wash the dishes that ain't right! You get it right. You understand me?"

Rocco suddenly looked like a deer caught in headlights. "But hell, boss, I don't have a clue. I can give them an answer, but I don't know if I'll always be right. Can't you have someone else do it? I don't *wanna* be responsible."

"No. You do it. Quit you're whining, you prick. Get it right, and I'm not asking, *I'm telling*. Now go find Danny and Andrew, we need to talk."

Fifteen minutes later, Rocco returned with both Danny Moss and Andrew Gross. After closing the door and taking a seat, Rocco said, "Boss, is that problem concerning giving some guidance to the help still open for discussion? I mean, can I voice my concerns concerning your particular resolution to that particular problem?"

"You bring it up again, I'll break your fuckin' neck. Does that answer your question?"

"That sure does. Yes, sir, the discussion is over. I'll take care of that problem."

"Are there any more applications I haven't reviewed?"

"No, boss. You seen 'em all."

Angelo sat back in his chair as he looked over his three primary henchmen. They waited patiently for the discussion to begin. Finally he said, "You all know Joni's gone. I never told you, but she's apparently going to testify against me. I hear they're about to indict me for the murders of Stone and Gail. I have no idea what they have on me yet. I really can't think they have much if all they have is Joni. Has anyone ever talked to any of you about those murders?"

"No, boss," Rocco responded. The other two shook their heads, indicating a negative response.

"Okay. First off, we need to find Joni. That will probably be hard to do this time. They most likely learned their lesson after being so lax about it with Billy. You guys did a good job finding him and handling the problem appropriately. But now, we need to find her. I don't think they have enough to convict me of anything anyway, but knocking her off won't hurt. So you guys start the process. Contact all your contacts and figure out where she is. Do you understand?"

Rocco responded with a yes, and the other two nodded affirmatively.

"Now, as concerns the second issue—knocking off Stone and Gail. Again, you guys are telling me no one has approached you asking questions about their murders, correct?"

They all nodded their heads affirmatively.

"Well, this one is going to be a little different than the other investigations we've been through. This Bill Stone was a former cop, he was well liked. And, of course, the other victim was a woman. I expect the investigation to continue right up until the trial, if they do indict me. You guys can't say nothin', absolutely nothin'. We were all involved, each one of us. They get one of us, they get us all."

"Boss, we've been with you, all three of us, a long time, and we ain't never said nothin' to nobody 'bout nothin'. That's not going to start now. Don't worry 'bout us guys. We ain't never saying nothin'."

Angelo smiled. "That's great. Because you all know what happens if you do. If you do, you're dead, or your family's dead. I'll get you one way or the other. Now, you two guys get out. Stick around, Rocco."

Once they left the room, Angelo said, "Rocco, do we have any more people that have expressed even the slightest interest in the cleaning job?"

"No, boss. You've reviewed all the written applications we've received. You've looked at all the online applications too. You've rejected them all."

Angelo thought for a moment. "Place another ad in the paper and online. Increase the size of the ad in the paper. List some type of benefits this time. Maybe that will bring in some new applications."

"What kind of benefits, boss? Us guys don't get no benefits. Will we get benefits too?"

"Sure will. You do it right, I won't fuckin' kill you. That's your benefit! Now get your ass out of here, and find me someone to clean this house."

Rocco said nothing more, slinking out the door, and closing it as he did.

Angelo was concerned about the pending indictment involving the murders of both Bill Stone and Gail, but concerned only to the extent of it being a simple inconvenience. He knew the system well enough to know they didn't have enough to convict. It would take time, and a little money, but in the end, he would win this one. It only amounted to a simple inconvenience.

But having a stool that was shitting dirty, now that was a major issue, and an issue he sure as hell wasn't going to live with much longer!

CHAPTER 27

*P*rior to sitting down, she walked to the kitchen window and looked out over the landscape. Before her stood the small barn, an area between the home and the barn where someone had built a fire pit, and finally the pasture beyond the barn, which was green and lush, a product of an abundance of middle Tennessee midsummer rain.

"Kat, your home and grounds are beautiful. I bet you love living here."

"Wouldn't give it up for the world."

"Is this where the war concerning Brakus was waged?"

"Yes."

"Any regrets?"

"Plenty."

"Really? That surprises me. I figured you for someone who once the decision was made, there was no looking back. That really surprises me."

"Prior to our confrontation here, I shot the fucker—blew him into the Cumberland. I really thought he was dead. But his girlfriend at the time saved him. For that good deed, he apparently murdered her, and disposed of her body. She was never found. Later, he killed my husband. That wouldn't have happened if I had initially succeeded. So yes, I do have a regret or two, but not about how it all concluded. It ended like it should have."

Rosa walked to the kitchen table, taking a seat across from an already seated Kat. Rosa drove to Kat's home after dark, making sure she hadn't been followed by one of Angelo's men along the way. Upon arrival, she drove her vehicle in the barn, out of sight.

Kat had prepared a large pot of coffee, and tonight, they would strategize—discuss different ideas as concerned uncovering additional evidence involving the murders of Stoney and Gail.

"I really think we need to talk to Marvin first," Rosa opined.

"You mean the prosecutor? Why? Why does he need to know anything?"

"It's really not a matter of him knowing anything as much as it is in learning what his evidence is, how weak or strong it is, and what additional evidence he might need to ensure a conviction."

"Do you know the location or phone number of this woman I'm replacing as Angelo's housekeeper?" Kat asked. "I need to ask her a few questions."

"No. But I have no doubt Marvin will. I'll ask him when I get him on the phone. Is that the only question you have for him?"

"Yes. My questions are primarily for that housekeeper."

Rosa tried reaching Marvin at home. It was shortly after 9:00 p.m. He still hadn't arrived home from the office, where her next phone call found him.

"Marvin, Rosa. Got a minute?"

"Actually, I was just walking out the door. Long day. What's up? Whatta ya need?"

"I need some information concerning Bonaventura. First of all, give me your candid opinion concerning your chance of securing a conviction. Do you have enough?"

He hesitated for a moment before he said, "Probably marginal. Especially with you representing him. My best evidence is the housekeeper, and even with her, I just don't know if that will be enough. But, I do have enough to present a prima facie case, and at least get beyond a motion to dismiss at the conclusion of my evidence, I do know that. I guess it may come down to what you present on behalf of the defense."

"That's what I figured. I assumed your case was weak. I'm working on something that might help you, but I need you to visit briefly with a woman I'm currently with. I don't want to be part of this conversation. Hold on."

She handed the phone to Kat. "Hi, Marvin. First of all, there's really no need for names. You don't need to know to whom you are talking. I need the phone number for the housekeeper. That's all I need. Just the phone number."

Marvin never responded.

"Listen, I'm on your side, believe me. If you trust Rosa, if her word is good, then trust me. If you want this guy like I think you do, just trust me. Now give me the fucking number."

She could hear him shuffling papers. Finally, he said, "Here it is."

As soon as Kat wrote it down, she handed the phone back to Rosa.

"Thanks, Marvin. You won't be sorry. By the way, has he been indicted yet?"

"No. the grand jury reconvenes tomorrow morning. I'll have them sign the bill of indictment then. I'll give you a call when it's been filed. Rosa, I hope you know what you're doing. Sounds like to me you're getting in pretty deep. By the way, how many people know about this?"

"Just the three of us. It must remain that way, Marvin. Don't even tell John. There's no reason for putting anyone else in harm's way other than us. The more they know, the greater the risk someone else will find out."

"I understand. Let me know if anything develops."

The call ended, at which time, Kat said, "I'll call this Joni now while you're here. I won't tell her you're involved nor mention your name unless I need to, but I want you to stay until I get what I need from her."

Kat punched in the number Marvin gave her. The call went to voicemail. Kat figured she might not answer once Joni saw where the call originated, and noticed it was from an unknown caller.

"Joni. I know you don't know me, but I need some information from you. I feel I might be able to help convict Angelo Bonaventura, but I need some help from you. Please return my call as soon as possible. Thanks."

She terminated the call and said, "Wonder how long this might take? You can go ahead and leave if you wish."

Before Rosa could answer, the phone rang.

"Kat Rickter."

"Hi, this is Joni Carsten." She hesitated. "Rickter, Rickter, your name is really familiar." Again, she hesitated. "Wait a minute. Are you the wife of that officer that was killed by some guy a few years ago? Your name is unusual. As I recall, it was your husband that died. He was murdered by some guy whose name I can't recall. Is that correct, is that you?"

"Yes, yes, it is, Joni. I'm going to try and help convict Bonaventura, but first you must promise me this conversation will go no further. If I can help with the information you can give me, it will benefit everyone, including you, by putting this guy away once and for all. Do you understand? Is that acceptable to you?"

"Yes, yes, of course." She hesitated. "But first of all, let me tell you how much I admire the way you handled your husband's death… with such class and dignity. I'm so sorry you had to go through that. Now, with that said, whatta y'all need to know?"

"Thank you. First of all, what exactly did you do for him while you were employed?"

"Just generally cleaned the house. I was also a supervisor of two others that worked on a part-time basis. Nothing out of the ordinary. I just cleaned the house."

"How many men does he have employed and are around the house on a regular basis?"

"Three, other than him. There are others, many others, but they come and go. He only has all of them there when he needs additional help. Day-to-day, there are only three there other than him."

"What about security cameras? Does he use them?"

"Everywhere."

"Outside and in?"

"Yes."

"Any other type of security other than that?"

"Just the men and the cameras."

"Anything unusual about him? Any traits or characteristics about him I should know?"

"What are y'all goin' to do? What kind of contact with him you gonna have?"

"I'm going to apply for your job. I'm going inside and see what I can do from there."

There was a decided pause while Kat's statement sunk in. "You're crazy. Believe me, Mrs. Rickter, you're crazy to do that. I honestly don't know how I ever came out of that house alive." She hesitated, then finally said, "But, I guess if that's the plan, may God go with you. Now, as specifically concerns your question, praise Angelo. Just kiss his Italian ass every chance you get. He loves that."

"Did he ever come on to you? Is that something I need to watch?"

"Are you kidding? I was the lowly help. He's above screwin' the help, believe me. No. No need to worry about that."

"Okay, I think that's about all I need for now. Sounds like a difficult—"

"Wait, I misspoke. I don't know if this matters, but there are no security cameras in his office. He doesn't have one there. One of the guys, during a conversation he had with me one time, told me Angelo wants nothing that's said or done in his office to be recorded—ever. That one area is the only area without multiple camera coverage. I don't know if that helps, but I did want to correct what I told y'all."

"Thanks, Joni. If I need anything else, I'll give you a call. By the way, again, absolutely no one can know about my involvement. Hopefully, I can, in some way, help get this guy convicted so you don't have to worry about him anymore."

"I understand. As far as I'm concerned, this conversation never took place. Good luck, Kat, good luck."

Kat terminated the call.

She turned to Rosa and said, "Everything should be ready within the next couple of days. I'll file the application then."

"You have no idea how much I admire what you're doing."

Kat smiled. "I just hope to hell it works."

They spent the next two hours talking about whatever came to mind. Politics, politicians, work, play, lovers, and husbands—nothing was sacred.

On her way home, Rosa felt she had just found a good friend. Everything about Kat was first-class. She just hoped the friendship wasn't short-term. If Kat found a job in Angelo's house, she was definitely walking into a lion's den. Unfortunately, getting in might be way easier than getting out—at least alive.

Chapter 28

*A*ngelo Bonaventura *sat in front of Rosa's desk, staring at her,* waiting for an answer.

"I assume they filed because they feel they have enough to convict. I assume that was why they presented it to the grand jury. I know of no other reason. It certainly wasn't just to irritate you."

"You know as well as I they don't have enough. This is an inconvenience, Rosa, a simple inconvenience. Even if Joni makes it to trial, and testifies, she has nothin' on me, because I didn't do nothin'. From what I can determine, she is literally all they have. I just don't get it. I can't believe a grand jury even indicted."

"Rosa, Marvin is on line one. You want it?"

Rosa picked up immediately.

"Good morning, Marvin. Did the grand jury indict yesterday?"

"Yes. He's been charged with murder two concerning both Stoney and Gail. I'll file both the indictments this morning. I just couldn't get them to indict on murder one. I tried, but I suppose I was lucky getting murder two considering how thin the evidence was. When do you wanna bring him in?"

She held her hand over the landline mouthpiece, looked at Angelo, and whispered, "You've been indicted—murder two. He's filing both the indictments this morning. When do you want to appear? I have time this afternoon. You wanna meet me at the court-house, say, around two?"

Angelo rolled his eyes. "Sure, why the fuck not? My time's worth *nothing*. I have nothing else to do, but clean stools and appear so I can answer to those bogus trumped-up charges. Yes, I'll meet you at two."

"We'll appear at two. I assume you're going to let the magistrate set bond according to the schedule? Any chance of releasing him on his own recognizance?"

"Whatta you think? Hell no! I'm going to recommend a mil-lion. If he wants to stay out of jail, tell him to bring a cashier's check."

"I understand. Thanks for calling, Marvin. See you at the courthouse."

"You on a first-name basis with all them prosecutors? I suppose all of you in the system are pretty close. Are you? You and that head guy, John what's-his-name, you pretty close to him too? That does make me a little uncomfortable, you know."

Rosa's heart skipped a beat.

"Did it sound like Marvin and I were close when we were sitting across from each other in the courtroom? Did it sound like we were good friends? You're frickin' paranoid, but you're also entitled to new council anytime you want it, Angelo, anytime you want it."

He smiled. "That's the spirit. That's what I love about you. You got the balls of a bull moose. No, no, no, I don't want anyone but you. I'm just a little frustrated with this particular proceeding. It's just so trumped up. In addition, I told you I lost my housekeeper, and that's turned into a nightmare. I've interviewed a number of women, but can't find the right one. In the meantime, you can imag-ine how tough it is to get some of my employees, some of the guys, to wash dishes. They fight me on it all the time. I would just really like to get someone hired and move on. *Now*, there's this criminal crap on top of it all. I'm a little frustrated as you can tell. Hopefully it will all work out sooner rather than later. I have a couple of applications waiting at home for me to review as we speak. Hopefully you can get this criminal thing thrown out so all is good."

"I can handle your legal issues, but I'm afraid I'm not much help with the dishes. I normally use paperplates around my house. I haven't cleaned a stool in ten years. I would offer you a little advice on the housekeeper issue though. Be patient. The way you tell it, you were pretty lucky with the last one you had, other than now she has turned state's evidence and is trying to convict you of murder. But as concerned her housekeeping abilities, apparently she was adequate. Just be patient. I'm sure the right one will come along."

Rosa knew Kat was still putting together her application and setting up a new identity. Without appearing to be interested in who-ever he hired, she wanted to try to encourage him to wait until Kat told her the application was in Angelo's hands.

"Good advice, Rosa. Thanks. Now what about this charge? Where do we go from here? Have you ever determined the where-abouts of Joni?"

"No, and I'm sure they'll never tell me. Most of the law enforce-ment community thinks you murdered Billy and his wife. If they had one shred of evidence, you would have been indicted on that one too. They're not going to tell me where she is. Really, as concerns her testimony, what difference does it make to you anyway? You didn't do anything, right? We can look at the minutes of testimony today. We'll determine exactly what she's going to say at the trial, and pre-pare accordingly. But her location isn't important, is it?"

"No, no, of course not. She can't offer testimony about those two murders because you're correct. First of all, I didn't do it. Second, she's never around when I'm visiting with the boys anyway. I'm always in my office. She's never invited in, so if she says she overheard some-thing about those murders, she's lying. They have nothing."

"Why don't you just meet me at the courthouse this afternoon around two? We can get a copy of the indictment, you can make your appearance in front of the magistrate and then bond out. Bring a cashier's check for a million."

"A million? You shitting me? Are you kidding?"

"You want out, or do you want to wait for your trial date in jail?"

Angelo gave her a quick condescending smile and said, "Sure, whatever accommodates the system. I'll have it, and I'll see you there at two."

They met a little after two, in front of the magistrate's courtroom. Rosa already had the clerk's office make a copy of the indictment. She had it in hand as Angelo presented himself before the magistrate for the purpose of bond. Once it was set, Angelo walked in the clerk's office and gave them a cashier's check. They both then found an open conference room, which they would use to review the allegations contained in the indictment.

After each had had the opportunity to review not only the charges, but the testimony of each of the state's witnesses, Angelo said, "It's just like I told you, Rosa. They don't have shit. They have people that say I was upset about Gail's relationship with Stone. Joni said she overheard me say I would kill them—blah, blah, blah! But they have nothing to establish I *did* anything. It's all circumstantial. They have nothing."

"I agree they don't have much. Do you want me to fast track the trial and forget about any type of pretrial discovery?"

"How much difference in time would it make?"

"If we fast track it, we can probably try it within the next sixty days. Otherwise, if I take everyone's depo, go through the normal discovery process, we might be ready by winter. You're probably talking an additional six months."

"No, no, no, I wanna get this over with. We know what everyone is going to say anyway. Let's forget that discovery business. Just get it set for trial as soon as you can."

"You know the routine, Angelo. They probably don't have enough to convict, but I will most likely want you to testify, to tell them you did nothing wrong. I'll want them to see a charming, sweetheart of a man. Unfortunately, you're reputation precedes you. It's not the best. I want to offset that to some extent by having your smiling face up there on the stand. You ready to do that?"

"Sure. I'm pretty good at persuading people anyway. I can handle that. Not a problem."

"Angelo, is there anything I should know about these two killings? I need to know everything you know. I need to know all the facts if I'm going to defend you. Is there *anything* you should be telling me about this situation?"

Angelo leaned back in his chair and said, "I know absolutely nothing about those two murders. I miss Gail every day, as I'm sure you do Mr. Stone. *On my mother's grave, I know nothing about either of those murders.*"

They left the courthouse shortly thereafter. Rosa now sat in the quiet sanctity of her office late that afternoon, after June had gone home, and the lights had been turned off.

So far, all had gone as planned. She had been somewhat concerned he might have already hired someone as his housekeeper. That would have necessitated a change in the plan. She was glad to hear he hadn't. Kat called later in the day and told her the application was ready and would be submitted online this evening.

Rosa thought about his remarks concerning "his mother's grave." She never really felt he would stoop so low as to make a statement he *knew* was false, backing it up with a reference to his mother. Unfortunately, if the truth were known, he probably killed his mother too, or at least had a part in her death.

She had tried to set the stage, at least to some degree, this afternoon when she told Angelo he may need to testify. If everything
continued to work according to plan, his testimony would indeed
come into play. His personality—so self-assured, confident about his
ability to persuade, to convince people, so sure of his ability to sway
people to his way of thinking—might indeed be the very trait that
brought him to his knees. There were so many factors that needed
to fall into line, but so far, everything was working well. Hopefully
as they continue to set the trap, all the other elements would also
proceed as planned.

CHAPTER 29

*S*he had been seated at her desk for over three hours, and it was only 7:00 a.m. She had watched the sun rise above the horizon. She awoke around 3:30 a.m. and hadn't been able to fall back to sleep, so she got up, made a pot of coffee, and continued her research concerning Angelo Bonaventura.

Kat's paperwork was spread all over her office. The process had been consistent all morning. She would uncover another small note about Angelo's antics, print it off, and place it in a pile earmarked for the particular characteristic he had displayed in the article. As she stood to place the latest article on the appropriate pile, she hoped she had no early morning visitor, especially someone she really needed to see. Kat slept with nothing on, and had not bothered to dress before she sat down to do her additional research. It would be difficult to travel from her office to the upstairs bedroom without being seen. Didn't matter to her, but it could certainly bother a Seventh-Day Advent brother looking through her kitchen-door window, waiting for someone to let him in.

One key factor in setting everything up was to make certain there was no visible connection between herself and law enforcement. She did not want someone from the prosecutor's office or someone from law enforcement testifying they were working "with" her. That issue could possibly create a problem involving entrapment, which could potentially negate all the hard work she was doing to apprehend him. Even if discovered, it most likely would *not* be an issue, but she just wanted to make sure it never even came up. So far, that had worked well. She had not had any contact with anyone in the case except Joni; and their mutual goal, the removal of Angelo from the general population, would seal Joni's lips forever. Of that, she was certain.

After another hour of research, Kat got dressed, had an abbreviated breakfast consisting of yogurt and fruit, then placed a call to Joni Carsten.

"Good morning, Mrs. Rickter."

"Good morning to you, Joni, and call me Kat. Do you have a sec?"

"I do for you, absolutely."

"I just wanted to reconfirm the fact that Angelo has no security cameras whatsoever in his office. Is that a fact? Are you certain that's the case?"

"Yes. I'm certain. I know that for a fact."

"Is there a particular time he's always gone? Do he and his boys all ever leave there at the same time?"

Joni thought for a short minute. "As a matter of fact, they all meet at a restaurant south of Nashville, in the Antioch area, once a week. They have a meeting. All his employees eat together to discuss problems or issues of any kind. It's normally Wednesday."

"Does that happen every week?"

"Yes."

"Did you remain in the house while they were gone, and continue to clean?"

"Yes."

"How long are they normally gone?"

"About two hours, give or take."

"Thanks, Joni. Again, you must never say a word about our conversations, both for your sake and mine."

"Did you get the job?"

"Not yet, but I will, I will."

Kat terminated the call a short time later. As she again reviewed all the issues involving Angelo Bonaventura, she was somewhat amazed. He had been associated with every criminal offense in the book, but he had never ever been convicted. Either the witness disappeared, or died, the case was dismissed, or Rosa got him off because of a lack of evidence.

She sat back in her chair, cup of coffee in hand, and watched as the sun quickly moved upward over the top of the barn. She wondered if she should reconsider her role, her involvement, concerning this monster. She had been warned by Chief Gleeson. The detailed description of this man by his own attorney, Rosa, would have been enough to stop most people from becoming involved.

Perhaps this time she was getting in a little too deep.

As she continued to consider that possibility, she remembered her vow, after Mike died, to do whatever she could to stop men like Brakus from ruining the lives of women. Angelo put his pants on just like the rest of his type. Nothing made him any different. She wasn't going to back away just because the task might be slightly more difficult. Her success would be just that much sweeter.

She picked up her phone and called John Rivers. He had been with the Nashville Police Department for years, involved in computer crimes of every type. John was an expert with the computer, with the Internet, and with everything that involved the Internet. He had quit the force a few years ago and was now self-employed in the private sector.

"John, Kat Rickter. How're you comin' with my new identity?"

"Hi, Kat. Good. I'm finished. It's all online. Your new name is now Catharine Ramey. I added a considerable amount of positive information online concerning your housecleaning abilities and set up two references for someone to call to confirm your abilities.

They're both wives of former officers and are expecting the call from Angelo. Of course, all that information will disappear as soon as you're hired. I'll send you an e-mail as to where it's all posted. Of course, the primary Web site we're using is Craigslist. You joined a number of other women looking for housekeeping jobs, but your credentials put you in a much better position than any of them."

"Great. I'll review it all later today. By the way, you know this is never to be discussed with anyone else, ever. Didn't figure I would need to emphasize that with you, but I felt I should."

"I understand. Not a problem. Good luck. Let me know when you want it all removed."

"I will. Send me a bill."

She terminated the call, then went straight to Google, typing in her new name. Catharine Ramey came right up—no picture, just a complete bio with both women's names for her references.

She punched in Rosa's personal number.

"Hi, Rosa, Kat Rickter."

"How's everything going, Kat?"

"Good. I'm a new woman, a woman named Catharine Ramey." She laughed. "Don't feel much different, but according to my new Internet bio, I'm an absolute cleaning bitch. I clean up everything from animal shit to kitchen counters. It's been posted on Craigslist and a number of other Internet sites, so we'll see what happens."

Rosa laughed. "By the way, I might need someone for my own house if—"

"Don't even go there. This is it. If Angelo doesn't bite, that crap is all coming down so quick it'll make your head spin. Whatta you hear from him?"

"As a matter of fact, he was here yesterday. He's been indicted. We went to the courthouse, and he's already bonded out. But he was really bemoaning the fact he still hadn't hired a housekeeper. I told him to be patient. He should jump all over your app. I'll let you know if I hear any more from him."

"Thanks. I'll do the same."

She had a number of errands to run in and about Nashville and wasn't able to return home until late afternoon. Upon checking her e-mails, she had six responses from women all over the Nashville/ Mount Juliet area wanting to set up an interview.

The last one came only minutes ago. It was the one she was waiting for. It was from Angelo. He wanted to set up an interview, at her convenience, but as soon as possible. He had taken the bait. All she needed to do now was reel him in. She used a burner phone she had previously purchased and placed a call to the number noted, setting up an interview the next day, late in the afternoon.

She was already nervous. She had never gone to this extent to stop someone. She knew the stakes were high. She knew her life was on the line. If he found out who she really was, she was most likely as good as dead. But the stakes were equally as high for him. If she prevailed, if she did her job and did it right, the son of a bitch would never hurt another living soul. That was, in and of itself, enough to drive her, to eagerly look forward to her first encounter with him tomorrow afternoon. There would be no middle ground, no standoff in this encounter. There would be one winner and one loser. She just hoped after the smoke all cleared, she was declaring victory, and he was cursing the day he ever interviewed her.

CHAPTER 30

"*Good morning, Ms. Ramey. Can I get you a cup of coffee?*"

"No, I'm fine. I'm a little nervous, so I would probably spill it all over anyway. Wouldn't that be a good way to start an interview?"

He stood, laughed, and motioned for her to sit. After sitting down, he said, "As you know, my name is Angelo Bonaventura. Most people, except my enemies, call me Angelo. Whatta you go by? What, for instance, do your friends call you?"

"Normally just Catharine. That's what I prefer to be called."

After her abbreviated conference with Joni, and her statement that Angelo had never tried to take advantage of her during the years she worked for him, Kat had decided to bundle up. If he wasn't that type of employer, then letting her girls flop around and displaying all she had to offer was probably not a good approach. Instead, she put on a long-sleeve white blouse, which buttoned up to the neck, and a dark pair of slacks. She would approach her initial meeting with Angelo on a very conservative basis in every respect.

"I have had a chance to review your references, and you come highly recommended. I called both of them. You were with each of those employers for a number of years. Why did you quit the last employer, if I might ask?"

She hesitated and, just for effect, looked away before she answered.

"Her husband… her husband… let's just say it was best for me to move on, and leave it at that. Everything had changed in that household, and I no longer felt comfortable working there."

"I understand. Are you willing to do most everything a normal housekeeper does, like clean the stools, clean up dishes, make the beds, just the normal duties of a normal housekeeper? Are there things you don't want to do?"

"Not really, I can handle most all duties a housekeeper performs on a day-to-day basis."

"Great." Angelo, now apparently much more relaxed as he started to realize this was exactly the type of woman he was looking for, leaned back in his chair and clasped his hands behind his head. "There is one more thing. You understand, I assume, that whatever you see or hear in this house stays in this house. Is that a problem for you? I talked to both of your prior bosses, and they gave you a good recommendation in that respect. Do you have a problem with that?"

"Not at all. Nothing that happens here will ever leave here. Nothing that I see or hear will ever leave this house. Of that, you can be certain."

"When can you start?"

Kat was being interviewed in his office—the room with no security. As she talked, she looked around, trying to determine what she might do if she was hired.

"First of all, might I ask a couple of questions?"

"You may."

"I've read about you, Angelo, and what I've read hasn't been very positive. I hate to even bring this up, but have you been associated with issues of violence? Is it safe to work here?"

She could tell the question may not have offended him, but it certainly captured his attention. He lost his smile and moved forward in his chair.

"Don't believe everything you read, Catharine. I have never been convicted of a criminal offense, of *any* kind. I run legitimate businesses around Nashville, and I take pride in that. There are security cameras located around the property, and with only one exception, which involves a weekly off-site meeting, most of my employees are also in and around the property every day. You're safe working here. You're safe as far as my men and myself are concerned. The only issue you'll have while on the property is how to get your work done quickly and efficiently, nothing more, nothing less. Next question."

"I guess you told me what I needed to know. I was only concerned with what I asked you, and I'm satisfied with your answer. I can start Monday of next week, if that works for you. I assume the rate of pay was as advertised?"

Angelo stood and smiled from ear to ear. "It sure is. Wonderful, Catharine, wonderful. We'll see you early Monday morning. You can set your own hours each day as long as your work's done when you leave the house."

He extended his hand, which she shook as she stood.

"I'll see you Monday."

As she walked to her vehicle, she thought about the placement of furniture in the office, the bookshelves full of books behind Angelo's desk, and all the bookshelves on the opposite wall from his desk. As she started her drive home, she figured maybe a quick stop might be warranted.

An hour later, she found herself looking through home security systems in Home Depot, near the town of Hermitage, which was conveniently located on her way home. She definitely found a location in his office that was perfectly situated to film all she wanted to film, but the system and how it operated was extremely important.

She looked through all the systems available, finally locating exactly what she was looking for. It came with four small cameras, only one of which she would need. It was wireless and transmitted to a small box that could be situated up to 750 feet away. Kat had noticed electrical outlets in the bookcase. She may need to slightly rearrange the books to cover the plug-in for the camera, but that was certainly achievable.

She purchased the system and would become familiar with it during the next few days. It was exactly what she needed. Kat would need a location for the box, which stored the data, but she felt certain, with 750 feet to work with, that would not be an issue.

Upon arriving home, she immediately called Rosa.

"Rosa, you alone?"

"Yes, what's going on?"

"Got the job."

"Wow, that was quick. Does it look like it's going to work out?"

"Yes. He wanted someone so badly, I think I could have asked for the moon, and he would have given it to me. I could see nothing had been dusted, items were lying around that needed to be picked up, and I was actually afraid to walk in a bathroom. But it'll all work out, and I start Monday. I'll keep you updated."

"I'll say one thing, you got balls. I would have never ever walked into a tiger den like that."

"Let's just say I'm highly motivated, and leave it at that. Better go. Got a lot to do before I start on Monday. I'll talk to you after my first day."

CHAPTER 31

*A*ngelo had called a meeting of all the "boys," and they were just starting to arrive. He wanted not only his men who worked with him at the home property to attend the meeting, but *any* of the employees who worked on the property, whether it was on an occasional basis or full time. That would consist of eleven men. As he looked out his office window, he concluded most, if not all, of them had already arrived.

Rocco walked through his office door a short time later and said, "Boss, they're all here. Do you want me to bring them in, or what?"

Angelo, without ever turning around, said, "Ya, bring them in, Rocco."

Angelo was just taking a seat behind his desk as they started walking in the room. Rocco was the last one in. He shut the door behind him as each took a chair and quietly waited until the boss opened the meeting.

"Gentlemen, there are a couple of reasons why I called the meeting this morning instead of waiting until our scheduled meeting. First of all, have any of you uncovered any information concerning the whereabouts of Carsten?"

Each looked around at the other employees, but all of them finally shook their heads, indicating no one knew anything.

"Okay, well, I want you to look a little harder. It's imperative we find her *now* and blow her fuckin' head off. This trial starts in a few weeks, and I want her out of the way before it does. I don't think she'll be as an important a factor in this trial as Billy was at the prior trial, but I still want her out of the way. Obviously, someone knows where she is. Find out who knows, get the information we need, and get it done quickly. Now, for the next issue—I just hired a new housekeeper."

Rocco stood up and said, "I already told 'em, boss. They all know."

"Okay. She starts Monday. You guys need to keep your hands off her. She's good-lookin' and got a figure to match, but I wanna keep this one. So *no* one touches her, *no* one talks sex to her, and I mean no one. Let her do her job. No dirty jokes or patting her on the ass. In fact, don't even let her catch you eyeballin' her. To you guys, she doesn't exist unless she asks you a question. I wanna keep this one. Any questions 'bout that?"

No one said a word.

"Now, that said, although she has great recommendations, I'm not an idiot either. When you're around here, keep an eye out for her. Don't fucking *watch* her, but just keep an eye out, at least for the first few weeks. I don't think she'll ever create a problem, but just watch her for me for the first few weeks."

"Boss, who's gonna watch her when we have our meetings in Antioch on Wednesdays?"

"No one. I'm normally only gone a couple of hours anyway. There're going to be times when there's no one here with her, and that's fine. We're going to eventually need to trust her anyway. Her recommendations are exceptional, and that's one of the factors they address—how easy it was to leave her alone in the house. They all talk about her being trustworthy. But, regardless, let's just keep an eye on her for the first couple of weeks. Any questions?"

No one said anything. The meeting moved on to other mundane, banal subjects, finally concluding some ninety minutes later. Angelo had no time to stand around and visit. He needed to be in Rosa's office by eleven, and he didn't want to be late.

Angelo was seated in the reception area of Rosa's office at exactly 11:00 a.m.

The planning sessions with Rosa well in advance of actual trial preparation were imperative. Angelo hated surprises. He would rather pay Rosa double her regular fee, and have no surprise at the time of trial, than have something come up she knew about and just forgot to tell him. So the routine was always the same. Go over and over every small detail prior to every hearing, making sure he knew everything there was to know, *before* the trial started. That was the routine they used, and the routine that worked best for both of them.

June escorted Angelo into Rosa's office. He took a chair in front of her desk while she terminated a phone call.

"Morning, Angelo. How's your week going?"

"Well, as a matter of fact, pretty good. I just hired a new housekeeper. She starts Monday. That was probably the most important factor in my week."

"Great. You think she'll work out for you?"

"I sure as hell hope so. Her name is Catharine Ramey. You know her?"

Rosa looked down for a moment, in apparent thought, and replied, "No, don't think I know that name. Did she have recommendations?"

"Yes, she did. They were all good. I hope it works out. As you know, I really need someone. I just don't have time to wash dishes anymore, and it's like pulling teeth to get my men to do it. So, where are we today concerning the trial?"

"I made a copy of the indictment for you. June has it at her desk, and she'll give it to you as you leave. Look it over. Review the witness list. See if there's anyone on there you know other than Joni."

"This should be like shooting ducks in a barrel, shouldn't it, Rosa? They have absolutely no witnesses that seen me do this. How can they convict anyone based on that kind of evidence?"

"That's true, Angelo, they don't have an eyewitness. But if you think they've never convicted anyone in this country on circumstantial evidence before, you're badly mistaken. They have, and juries will continue to do just that. I don't want one of them to be you. Their witnesses will say enough to convict you if you aren't there to testify and explain your position."

"So you're still thinking I need to testify?"

"Yes." Rosa leaned back in her chair. "Angelo, one issue that we must really watch is selection of the jurors. You have a bad reputation in this community. You've been linked by the press to some nasty people, and while the jurors may all say they are unbiased, there will probably be a number of them that have an adverse opinion about you, but just won't admit it. We need to overcome that. The way I want to offset that is have you testify. I want you to make sure you can tell them where you were every minute of that time period, which includes the minute Stoney and Gail went missing until the minute they were found. Can you do that? Can you account for each minute?"

"I sure can. Other than when I was sleeping, I had someone that was with me every minute of every day they were missing, and they'll testify to that. Shouldn't be a problem at all, Rosa."

"Picking the jury will be vitally important. I made a copy of the jurors name list for you. Take it home and review it for me when you have a moment. Let me know if you know any of them and, if you do, what your association with them might have been."

"Okay. What about Joni? Did you ever find out where they had her stashed?"

"No. I probably won't. They're really being tight-lipped about her location, and since you didn't want any discovery taken, they didn't have to bring her here for her deposition."

The wheels were clearly turning. "Was that a mistake? Maybe I made a mistake. Any chance of changing our mind on that?"

"No. We waived it, and a trial date was set based on that waiver. You'll see her at the time of trial, but that's it."

"So you honestly believe it's *that* important I testify on my own behalf?"

"Absolutely. I'll have you well prepped, but you're going to need to get up on the stand and tell the jury you didn't do this. You basically have no prior record for the prosecution to hammer you with. I won't open up any negative areas during your testimony, which means the prosecutor can't cross-examine you concerning those types of issues, so that shouldn't be a problem. But, yes, I'm going to want you to deny, deny, deny when it's time for you to do so."

"Okay. Is that it? You just want me to pick up my material at the front desk and then set up a time for next week?"

Rosa stood. "Yes, that'll work. We can start going through your own witness list then, along with going through your testimony."

Angelo extended his hand. "Don't know what I'd do without you."

Rosa shook it. "Hopefully this will all turn out well for you, Angelo."

He picked up his paperwork and walked to his car. What a joke this was going to be. Easiest trial yet! This was all going to end up nothing but a small inconvenience—simply a bump in the road. It would take a moron to lose this case. He smiled. It will probably take more energy chasing that new housekeeper around the house than it will to win this case.

CHAPTER 32

*S*unday *night came too quickly. As Kat sat by the fire, very slowly* consuming a tall glass of her favorite Merlot, she wondered, again, if she was doing the right thing. She had thought about it all weekend, and now that she was but hours away from starting her new "job," she again considered whether she had jumped too quickly. Had she come to a conclusion to work this case based on an abundance of passion for the victims Bonaventura had harmed, rather than on a reasoned, rational approach to solving the problem?

She had started considering her "situation" while the sun had been completely absorbed in completing its journey, slowly sliding downward under a tapestry of darkening blue, and finally out of sight. The flames now lit up the face of the barn. The fields behind the barn were bathed in a soft glow only because of a waning crescent moon. She concluded a quick phone call was in order before she called it a night.

"Joni, Kat. Do you have a second?"

"Yes, certainly. For you, I have as long as you need."

"I start tomorrow. I'm, as you can imagine, somewhat apprehensive. Do you have any last thoughts about working for this man? Is there anything else we haven't discussed that I should be concerned about or that I should know?"

"Not really. I think you'll be fine, Kat, as long as he doesn't find out who you are. I never really had no problem with him. He didn't bother me physically, and he stayed out of my way. But, I got no doubt, he finds out who you are, if he finds out what you're doing, you'll have hell to pay. Kat make sure that don't happen, because if it does, you're gonna be in grave danger. That's one thing about him. Once he loses his temper, once he thinks you've one-upped him, he'll go insane. Nothing, absolutely nothing, will stop him if that happens."

Kat hesitated a moment, then responded, "He's not going to figure out who I am until it's too late. Thanks for your help, Joni. I'll let you know how it's going."

"Good luck, Kat. May God go with you."

"Probably going to need a lot of both, Joni. Thanks."

Kat terminated the call, then threw the small remaining portion of wine lying in the bottom of her glass into the smoldering embers. She stood, and walked inside to prepare for what would most likely be a short restless night. Tomorrow morning would be the start of a *work* week for her—first time in a long, long time.

Monday morning came a little too soon. Kat was actually more apprehensive than she really thought she would be. It wasn't just the nature of the individual she was working for that caused her so much concern, it was going back to work. She hadn't worked in years, and the thought of getting back into that type of routine, after the freedom she had enjoyed for so many years, was somewhat depressing.

She was out the door and driving down Interstate 40 at an appropriate time to arrive at the house a few minutes early. Probably not a good thing to be late the first day.

Upon arrival, she was immediately escorted into Angelo's office where he, along with three other men, were waiting.

Angelo stood as she entered the room.

"Catharine, these three gentlemen will be my most frequent guests."

He introduced them all, and they stood as they were introduced, the last of which was Rocco.

"Rocco will be the one most frequently here and the one to whom you will direct your questions. He's been with me many years and knows this place like the back of his hand. He's going to show you around this morning, and then you can go ahead and start. I would appreciate you taking care of the bathrooms first. As you can well imagine, they need cleaning the most."

Rocco showed her every room, every toilet, and every dirty dish that needed to be washed. She could hear Angelo in his office, discussing business with the men that were with him, and also making an occasional phone call.

The most important moment came when, once Angelo had left, Rocco pointed out all the books sitting on the bookshelves in his office. They contained row after row of classics written by the masters. Rocco told her Angelo loved to impress his guests by telling them he had read them all. He smiled and said Angelo was somewhat stretching the truth in that, in reality, he had read none of them. He told her Angelo hadn't removed any one of the books in years. For Kat, that small amount of information was, in and of itself, very important. As she pulled a few out, she noticed a plug-in located in the back wall, behind all the books. That was exactly what she had been looking for. Both the camera and the box needed for retaining the video could be conveniently plugged in without any problem whatsoever.

After the tour, she started in the kitchen. She cleaned it the best she could, but what she really wanted was to get in his office. Angelo waved good-bye as he walked out the back door later in the morning. Kat was ready to start cleaning the rest of the house, and while she wasn't alone—his men were everywhere—she knew now was the time to clean his office and take another look at how it was set up.

She walked in with all her dusting equipment, consisting of numerous rags, and one spray can of Dustall. She could feel the eyes of the men sitting in the living area as she walked in his office. As she started to dust his desk, she noticed an electrical outlet between one of the separated rows of books. She would need to extend one short end of books to cover the plug-in. The camera was small, really small. It would fit well between a book standing straight upright and a book leaning against another at the top, leaving a small gap between them near the bottom.

The box retaining the data was extremely thin and could be placed vertically, rather than horizontally, behind one of the rows of books without being seen. She would set everything up, and hopefully be able to review the flash drive to make sure it was working properly before next Wednesday. Maybe they would quit watching her so closely by then. Today, she could feel eyes watching every move she made.

"Everything okay in here?"

Rocco had walked in behind her while she was dusting and looking over the bookcase. Apparently she had stayed beyond the time he felt was necessary for dusting Angelo's office.

"Yes, all is well. This home is beautiful. I was just admiring all his great books. I'm an avid reader."

"Okay. I just wanted to make sure everything was all right."

"I'm done in here. I'll move on to the bathrooms now."

She brushed past him and walked to the bathroom feeling his eyes on the back of her neck. She had stayed too long. Good lesson. Remember who you are Kat. Remember, cleaning lady first, detective second. Don't get your ass in trouble the first day. At least wait a day or two, or until you have the camera in place.

Eight hours later, she was driving home, back down Interstate 40. For the most part, her first day wasn't as bad as she had anticipated. Cleaning those damn bathrooms was the worst part of the experience. She started with cleaning up the kitchen and making the beds, but then she had to move into the bathrooms. It was all she could do to finish cleaning each of them, and the thought of having to do it on a regular basis almost made her physically ill.

As she drove, she called Rosa and filled her in. She would take her time placing the camera and box in their appropriate location the first day everyone was gone. Rosa told her the trial was being fast tracked, and they had a trial date in about a month.

Hopefully that would be all the time she needed to gather the information necessary to put this guy away. He was so smooth, so accommodating. Kat knew though. She had been down this road with others like him before. On the surface, they were so accommodating and always a gentleman. But underneath, they were simply animals, impossible to deal with, impossible to satisfy.

As concerned her interaction with the boss and his associates, her first day couldn't have gone any better. Hopefully, as time went by and prior to the trial date, she would be able to be as successful accumulating all the data she needed to finish the job she was there to do, as she had been in dealing with the people she needed to deal with.

Wednesday morning, Kat again arrived precisely at 8:00 a.m. She carried with her the same purse she carried the first two days. It was larger than any of the others she owned. In fact, it was large enough she needed a shoulder strap to carry it. Normally it would contain a number of personal items she might need during the course of a day, but today, the majority of those items had been dumped. In their place, she carried a small camera and the box that retained its data.

They hadn't searched her the first two days. She figured if they did this time, she would tell them she had a use for the camera later in the day, and just carry it and her purse back to her vehicle. Hopefully they would leave her alone and, most importantly, leave her purse alone.

Upon walking through the front door, she could hear Angelo and some of the men in the kitchen area, located in the back of the house. There was no one in the living area or his office. She walked into his office, sitting her purse down on the floor between two chairs situated opposite Angelo's desk. Kat had worried during the night, concerned about how she would get the camera and box out of her purse and into his office without the security cameras picking it up. Leaving her purse in his office and removing the items there would alleviate that concern.

She worked in the upstairs bedrooms, cleaning everything in those rooms, until around nine thirty, when she thought she heard a door close. She walked to the staircase to determine whether people were coming or going. She heard nothing, absolutely nothing.

Kat walked down the steps and through the house. Everyone was gone. They had said nothing to her, most likely leaving her to guess about their return time. But she knew. Joni had told her where they went for a couple of hours every Wednesday morning. She didn't need to guess.

She walked to the kitchen, while still under the watchful eye of the security cameras, and picked up what she needed to clean Angelo's office. After she walked in his office door, Kat pulled the camera and box from her purse. She pulled books off the third shelf and placed the box, after turning it on, vertically, leaning up against the back wall of the bookcase. She then placed the camera, after plugging it in, between two books, one of which she leaned against the other at the very top, leaving a triangular opening large enough for the camera to hopefully operate effectively. The opening was located about seven feet above the floor and above level eyesight. Across the room, the camera was completely undetectable. She then extended the row of books on the same shelf as contained the plug-in, so the plug for the box became completely invisible.

Kat walked around the room. There was absolutely no way any of the apparatus could be seen. The only way it would be detected is if someone moved the books. Since she was the one that did the cleaning, and Angelo never read any of them, she felt she was safe. Even if the equipment was located, they couldn't prove she was the one that placed it there.

She smiled. Perfect! Just the way she had planned it. The smile lasted only a few short seconds. Only until she remembered she still had the shitters to clean before she left the house.

"Rosa, Kat. Got time to visit a moment?"

"Yes. I'm still at the office. Where are you?"

"Sitting out by the fire. Beautiful night. Stars shining, not a breath of wind, fire feels great. Just poured my second glass of wine. You should be out enjoying the night rather than cooped up in that office. Life's too short, Rosa, life's just too fucking short."

"You're right. That's exactly where I should be."

"You free this Saturday?"

"I'll make sure I am. What's up?"

"Why don't you just come on out. I'll fix us some supper, and we can sit around the fire. Maybe drink a little wine and talk about life."

Rosa hesitated. Finally she said, "I would love that. What time?"

"Around five. Drive your car in the barn. The door will be open. Best no one sees it here."

"Is everything okay? Did you get everything set up?"

"Everything's fine, but I'll tell you more Saturday. See you then."

Kat terminated the call and downed what was left in her glass. All in all, everything was working to perfection. She hoped everything continued that way. She figured if she got caught, her head would most likely end up in those same stools she was cleaning. One good thing about that—the stool would certainly be clean.

CHAPTER 33

*A*s *Rosa drove, she thought about last night. Again, she had dreamed, and again, she awoke in a sweat.*

Unfortunately, consistency was not her friend. Almost once a week, rather than the peaceful, dreamless sleep she normally enjoyed, she would dream of Stoney. The dream was never pleasant. It was always about his death. Last night, he told her he just couldn't understand why she wasn't there to help him, like he always was for her. She explained, numerous times, but he just didn't seem to get it. She finally awoke, but sleep was indeed difficult—in fact, virtually impossible the remainder of the night. Hopefully one of these days, the only memories that would remain would be the good ones, the good days, the good times she had with him and nothing more. But for now, the thoughts that would pop into her head on a random basis were of the way he died and how horrible it must have been.

She arrived at Kat's home a little after five. Kat had a small fire started in the pit and a bottle of Merlot on a small table between two large Adirondack chairs. The sun was hanging low under a perfectly blue Tennessee sky. It appeared late afternoon would segue into a beautiful evening, perfect for a fire and a glass or two of red wine.

Once Rosa arrived, she immediately drove her vehicle into the barn. Their chairs faced away from the roadway. Anyone passing by would see only a small fire and the backs of both chairs, which was exactly the way it was planned.

Once both were comfortably settled in their chairs, feet up on the stones surrounding the fire pit, conversation turned to the basic issues that first united them.

"So, how's work going—I mean, without Stoney around?"

Rosa said, "Nothing's the same. Everything has changed, from my personal life to the office, day and night. It's been hard moving on. I didn't realize how much I relied on him. Even now, last night, I had this frickin' nightmare about him, which really isn't unusual. I have one of those about every week. Unfortunately, you probably know all about this firsthand. Your husband was murdered, just like Stoney. It's not like we were as close as the two of you were, but we were pretty damn close."

"It's not easy. It's been the toughest time of my life. There was a period of time, right after he was killed, when I couldn't function at all. I was completely lost. Are you able to function on a daily basis? I mean, is it bad all the time?"

"No, and it's getting better. He's always in my thoughts, but I'm learning how to at least exist without him in my life." She turned away from Kat and watched the flames. After a quiet moment, she said, "Let's change the subject before I start to become emotional. Seeing me in an emotional state is not a pretty sight. What about you? How's the new job?

Kat poured herself another glass of wine. As she did, she smiled, and said, "Oh, just dandy. Can't believe I'm back to work again. Thought I had it all planned out so I wouldn't ever have to work, at least at something I really didn't want to do. But here I am, cleaning up whatever needs to be cleaned up. Yesterday morning, I had to clean up some asshole's vomit that nobody had cleaned up after their party. It's already been an experience I'll have little trouble forgetting."

"I'm assuming the house is as huge on the inside as it looks on the outside."

"It's a big house. I think half the rooms are bathrooms, and each and every one of them seem to be used. I just keep thinking of the ultimate goal rather than the moment-to-moment issues. That seems to get me through the day. I know I've gone through more bottles of wine this week than I did all of last month."

"What about Angelo? How's he to deal with? Has he been difficult?"

"You know, I've only seen him a couple of times all week. He doesn't seem to have much interest in what I'm doing. However, I do know he has his men watching me. They try to be inconspicuous while they're doing it, but they're pathetic at covering it up. I just continue to go about my work. Doesn't matter to me if they watch what I do. What about the trial? Is it still set for two weeks from Monday?"

"Yes. I'm in the process of getting as ready as I can, even though my heart isn't in it. But, we're on schedule, and I anticipate we'll start exactly when we're supposed to."

"Whatta ya think, Rosa? Do they have enough to get this guy?"

"They might. The jury could convict just because they can't help but have heard of him and what he does, who he is. But we wouldn't be doing this if I really had confidence they would find him guilty. No, I don't think they'll find him guilty, which makes what you're doing all the more important."

"Well, you need to know this is certainly no sure thing on my end."

"So what happened this week?"

"I got the camera placed where I wanted it. The problem is, they're all only gone on Wednesday, and then only for a couple of hours. I can't really do much other than when they all leave the house. Otherwise, someone is always watching. For some reason, they all left the house Friday afternoon. I have no idea what was going on, but I was alone for about forty-five minutes. That gave me enough time to transfer the accumulated data to a flash drive. I wanted to at least make sure the camera was picking up everything, including audio. I was able to retrieve the data and get out of his office before they came back, but I can't depend on those types of situations for getting to the camera. I just never know when they'll be gone. The only time I can depend on is Wednesdays."

"So did you have a chance to review the film once you got home?"

"Yes. It's perfect. I don't need to change anything. I was really glad it's working exactly the way it's supposed to. It's properly aimed to film everything that happens in the room. We're good to go, but I just hope the subject of the murders comes up. That's the only thing that bothers me."

"Was anything said about Stoney or Gail during the time you had everything placed in the room?"

"Absolutely nothing."

"Was anything discussed that might help us of *any* nature?"

"No, and that really worries me. We don't have much time. I just hope something comes up before two weeks from Monday, or all this planning and effort will most likely be in vain. He'll get off. And once he does, no matter what might come up after that, I assume double jeopardy is going to protect him."

"Yes, it will. So you're thinking the only time you're going to be able to retrieve the information off the camera is on Wednesdays, is that correct?"

"Yes, at least with any degree of certainty. I just have no idea when they'll all be gone other than Wednesday."

"We only have two more Wednesdays before the trial starts."

"What happens if something comes up that helps us *after* the trial starts but while it's still in progress?"

"I have no idea. I've never been down that road. Let's just hope we get the information we need to nail this guy before it starts, and we don't have to worry about that issue."

The sun had slipped down over the horizon. Rosa poured herself another glass of wine, and as she did, she said, "Is that the barn where you confronted that poor bastard Brakus, or whatever his name was?"

"That's the one."

"Got a light in there?"

"Does now, didn't then."

"Wanna show me what happened—how it happened?"

"You really want the tour? Does that interest you?"

"Yes, your story does interest me. Sure, show me what happened."

Kat pulled herself up out of her chair, poured herself a short glass of Merlot, and said, "Follow me, Rosa. You're the first and probably the last person I'll ever show around the barn and tell the story, but if you're interested, let's go."

The next hour consisted of two more glasses of Merlot for each, a spirited tale of an evil man, and how the battle finally concluded. Rosa decided to stay the night—too much wine. Each told stories until the early hours of Sunday morning, and as Rosa drove home later, she realized she had been missing out. Kat was a diamond in the rough. She only wished she had met her years ago, but as she drove in her driveway, she was certainly thankful she was getting to know her *now*, for more reasons than one.

CHAPTER 34

Marvin Jackson sat alone, at his desk, considering, again, if he had made a mistake. For five years now, he had reassessed, almost weekly, whether his career move had been appropriate.

He was doing fine where he was, before his move to Nashville. At twenty-four, right out of law school, he had gone to work in Chicago as a prosecutor with the Cook County attorney's office and had enjoyed a reasonable degree of success. But at twenty-nine, when Leon Kelmer, John Winstrom's predecessor, had offered him a job with Davidson County, Tennessee, he had jumped at the opportunity. Moving to Nashville seemed like the right thing to do, especially knowing he would work hand in hand with Leon, whom he so greatly admired.

But three years later, when Leon was bumped out of office, everything changed, and not insignificantly. Since the election, he had reconsidered his move many times, finding his work experience with John not nearly as rewarding as he had enjoyed with Leon.

He wondered if he should find employment in some other city. He certainly had the experience, and there were a number of opportunities available. But even though he had no wife and no children to consider, because he loved Nashville, he would move only if it became imperative.

His relationship with John was fine. That was it. It was fine, nothing more nothing less. If he had his choice, John would not be an individual he would choose to work with on a day-to-day basis. They didn't think, nor reason, in the same manner concerning anything. But since he had no choice, and since he didn't want to move or change jobs, he would continue to keep his mouth shut, do his job, and enjoy it, especially when he didn't have to work directly with his boss.

He had files, and parts of files, scattered all over the room. They all pertained in some form or fashion to one man—Angelo Bonaventura. They either involved cases that were tried in which he was the defendant or they were files that were started involving cases in which he was the major party of interest. None of them reflected a conviction. *Not one!*

In his deep baritone voice, kicking out words in his usual, slow methodical manner, he said, "Good morning, Rosa. Do you have a second?"

"Sure, Marvin. I just got to the office. I'm still trying to determine exactly what my schedule is today, but I always have time for you. What's going on?"

"You know, we only have about eleven days left until trial. You have anything for me on Bonaventura?"

Rosa laughed. "I wish I did, Marvin, wish I did. You know how I feel about him, and if there was something I had that could help you, believe me, I'd provide it, but as of right now, I have nothing. I've looked at your witness list. You know, even though my heart's not in representing Angelo, I still have to at least put on a good show. It appears to me you have the medical examiner, two cops, about five or six people indicating they saw Stoney and Gail together, five or six more individuals indicating they overheard Angelo say he would kill them if he found out they were involved, and, of course,

Joni Carsten. Are you going to add additional witnesses, and are you intending on calling all of those you have listed?"

"No, I'm not adding anyone else, and yes, I intend on calling all of them. I realize as concerns those people that will testify as to motive, I might have quite a few all saying the same thing, and that may be overkill, but it's all I got. I hope for once, maybe, *for once*, quantity rather than quality will be enough to convict."

"That's never worked out very well in the past, Marvin, but I hope you're right."

"Who you calling as witnesses?"

"I'm going to, of course, call him, and then a number of other witnesses who will testify as to his whereabouts during the time they were murdered. In addition, I've got about five witnesses who will say he talked about Gail having a relationship with someone else, but that it really was fine with him. He told me he was done with her anyway and that whoever was having a relationship with her was doing him a favor. That's about all I've got. Unfortunately, it may be enough. I'm just not sure you have enough to establish the guy's guilt beyond a reasonable doubt."

Marvin hesitated before he responded, "Not the best case I've ever had, but I have to go with what I have, and I didn't want to wait any longer. We tried waiting for additional evidence with two or three other major cases we thought involved Angelo, but they just became cold cases. I wasn't going to let that happen with this one."

"I think my first appointment just walked in the reception area. Marvin, I'll stay in touch with you all next week, and if anything comes up that might help you, I'll certainly be in touch."

"Thanks, Rosa."

A few minutes after he terminated his call, John Winstrom knocked on his open door.

"Got a moment, Marvin?"

"I do. Come on in."

"How's the Bonaventura trial coming? You ready to go?" He took a chair in front of Marvin's desk as he waited for a response.

"Pretty much. Witnesses are lined up and ready to testify."

"You have enough to convict?"

"I'm not sure. I think I do, but I'm really not sure."

"You know, Marvin, I let you run with this one, but I was really surprised when you decided to pursue it with no more evidence than you seemed to have. I trust your judgment, and that's why I never said anything, but I was surprised."

"Guess we'll see how it turns out. I just hope there's enough to convict."

"Have you considered any type of plea bargain?"

Marvin leaned back in his chair, and thought through that possibility, before he said, "No. This is a double murder. We've been trying to get this guy for a long time. I would rather end up with an acquittal than bargain this down."

"I want you to consider a plea bargain. I don't think you have enough to convict, and I would really like, for once, to get this guy on something, *on anything.*"

He stood to walk out. "I'm not asking, Marvin. I've looked over what you have for evidence, and I'm telling you to at least consider a bargain. I also want to be kept up to date on everything that's going on with the case."

"Whatever you say, John. You're the boss. I'll ask Rosa if she has any thoughts along those lines and let you know. You wanna try the case yourself, or second chair me?"

"No. I've got enough of my own going on. You handle it. Just keep me informed."

Marvin watched as he walked out the door. It took all he had to refrain from throwing the files on his desk at his boss's back as he walked out. Had he gone soft on crime? Why was he taking this kind of approach with this particular defendant?

He picked up his phone and punched in Rosa's number. After June had put him through, Rosa said, "Hi, Marvin. I actually have someone with me, but go ahead."

"Well, I guess I'm in the market for an offer. I was just told to bargain Bonaventura's case down if we could reach an agreement."

"Who told you to do that?"

"John."

"That surprises me. I'll discuss it with Angelo, but knowing him like I do, I'm thinkin' he won't even consider that. Does John's approach surprise you?"

Marvin took a deep breath. "If I hadn't been sitting in this goddamn chair, I would have fucking fell on the floor."

He was clearly under stress, with his voice reaching a new level of intensity he had never used with Rosa.

Rosa laughed.

"What's wrong? What's so funny? This isn't funny, Rosa. He wants me to try and bargain this out. That's just plain bullshit."

"Marvin, calm down, I understand, just calm down. I know you pretty well. You and I have known each other for quite a few years. You're clearly way stressed out. Can I ask you a question that's far from pertinent to the issues we've been discussing? Will that upset you if I do?"

"What?" he answered tersely. "What question? Depends on what it is I guess."

"Marvin, do you have any type of social life? Do you date? Do you go to movies and shows? Do you ever do any of those things?"

"What the hell does that matter? What does that have to do with anything?"

"Just stay with me here, Marvin. Do you do any of those things?"

"Well, I do go to an occasional show. I don't have anyone I'm seeing right now, I guess. Why are you asking?"

"You definitely need a change of pace. I've *never* heard you that stressed out, or ever use that kind of language before."

"I think John's getting soft on me. I can't believe he would suggest I bargain this case out."

"I don't have much doubt there will be no offer from Angelo, but I'll let you know. Now, my friend, you need a little social relief. Would you object if I lined you up with someone—with one of my friends?"

He hesitated for a second before he said, "I don't know, Rosa. Never had much luck with blind dates. I guess I could give it a try if you're the one setting it up."

"Let me talk to her first. I've got the perfect woman for you, Marvin. She'll settle you down. Believe me, she'll take your mind off your work."

"Whatever. Just let me know."

"Oh, I will. And when you first meet her, make sure and be familiar with what types of insurance you have, including the amount of coverages. That could be important."

"I'm sorry—insurance? Why?"

CHAPTER 35

They both lay quietly, staring at the ceiling. John had the sheet pulled up to his waist. Nothing but his heavy breathing would have indicated he had just, seconds ago, been involved in a sexual experience that curled his toes.

Rosa, just having experienced a hot flash, had kicked the sheet off her body to the bottom of the bed. The only physical indication that made it visually apparent she had just experienced sex causing that hot flash was the stimulated condition of both her nipples, pointing toward the ceiling like a couple of pop-ups in a child's book.

He continued to hold her hand. Both were wide-eyed and slowly catching their breath so each could function on a normal basis the rest of the evening.

It wasn't much past 6:00 p.m. John had driven from work to Rosa's home, intending to pick her up and take her out for supper. But after one sensual kiss, which led to another and then another, they just decided they would enjoy each other now, rather than having supper, and thinking about it all through the meal.

She finally said, "Whoa, okay then. Clearly we are compatible, at least in a physical sense. Not sure where we are as concerns the other 99.9 percent of our lives, but physically, we're pretty damn compatible."

He smiled, propped himself up with his arm, looked down at her, and said, "Oh, I think we're also just fine concerning that other 99.9 percent of life you're talking about. I haven't found many areas we aren't compatible."

He leaned down and kissed her.

She looked into his blue eyes and said, "Maybe we should discuss where this relationship is headed, Mr. John. Whatta ya think?"

"I think we do that over supper, not here."

"Well then, if we aren't going to discuss it now, what should we do? Shall we just lie here a moment and then go have supper? Or are you enough of a man to try this again, since we have the time and since we apparently aren't going to talk."

He winked at her and said, "Supper can wait a few more minutes. Now, let's just see if we can improve on perfection."

An hour later, they found themselves finally dressed and standing in line at a small sandwich deli near Rosa's home in Mount Juliet. She had been there a number of times. This was the first time for him.

They found a small booth near the back, where they could visit without fear of being overheard.

"Rosa, this food is incredible. Why haven't you brought me here before?"

"No particular reason I guess." She looked around and said, "It's not very romantic, but they do put out good food. I guess my outlook concerning eating out with you changes somewhat based on whether we have had sex before we eat or we wait until after we eat."

He grinned and said, "I agree. The emphasis is somewhat more on the food after you and I have spent time alone than it is if we haven't."

Between bites of a BLT and a large portion of macaroni salad, she said, "Tell me about Marvin. I've known him for years, but I feel like I don't know much about him. What's your take?"

"He's a little tight with personal information, but he's a good guy. He's a hard worker. I think sometimes he wishes he were the boss. I think sometimes he wishes he had my job instead of his. But Marvin is honest and hardworking. That's really all I can ask for. I'm glad he's with us. Why do you ask?"

"Does he have any kind of personal life?"

He was rapidly consuming a chicken portobello mushroom sandwich along with portions of southern potato salad, but he smiled and stopped chewing long enough to say, "Not to the best of my knowledge. He seems a little backward when it comes to dating, and things of that nature."

"Well, I'm about to set him up with my best friend, Nicki. We'll see how they get along."

"Is that your insurance friend?"

"Yes. I told him to be sure and have his coverages figured out, because that information would be a necessary part of at least the initial conversation between them."

"Definitely an interesting matchup. Now, speaking of Marvin, how's the case coming, the Angelo Bonaventura case?"

"What do you mean 'coming'?"

"How's it look to you? You gonna get him off? I told Marvin the other day his case looked weak."

"You know I can't discuss much of it with you because of confidentiality, but yes, I think we have a good case."

Rosa was hesitant. She would use the confidentiality issue as the reason not to tell John much about her case. It wasn't as if she didn't trust him, because she did, but Kat's undercover situation was Kat's business. No one would know about that until the appropriate time.

"Who do you have lined up for witnesses?"

"Oh, just some of his employees, and, of course, him… Angelo. They can explain where he was when Stoney and Gail were kidnapped. Angelo can deny it all. I'm hoping, with the limited evidence Marvin has, we have enough. How's your sandwich?"

"Good, good. I told Marvin the other day to visit with you about bargaining it down. Did he do that?"

"Yes, he did. How's that potato salad? Looks good."

"It is, it really is. What did Bonaventura say? Is he at all receptive?"

"Oh hell, I don't know. I presented it to him. He said he would think about it."

"I guess Marvin's best witness is probably Joni, that housekeeper. You know, law enforcement won't tell any of us where she's located. Couldn't believe that, but I'm sure they're concerned after what happened to the last witness they had in protective custody."

"Yes, that didn't end well." It was time to put a halt to this line of discussion. She had provided all the information about the case she felt comfortable providing. Time for this conversation to move in a new direction.

"Enough about work. Let's talk about something else—like you and I. That seems like an appropriate subject about right now." She reached over and placed her hand over his. "Where's this all headed, John? We just gonna have sex on an occasional basis, and sometimes an infrequent sandwich. What are your thoughts about you and I?"

He put his fork down and reached over, taking her other hand in his.

"No, Rosa, that's not the scenario I have in mind. I love being with you. I love making love to you. I love spending every minute we can break loose from our jobs and be with each other. Let's give this a little more time though. Let me figure out a few details, talk to my kids, and then let's see if you and I can make a plan for the future together."

She looked down for a moment, and then with a playful grin, she said, "Is that a proposal?"

"Not yet. Give me a little more time. Let's make damn sure this is really what we both want. Tell you what. Get that Bonaventura trial off your mind, let me work on a few issues of my own, and I promise we'll discuss it at length then. You okay with that?"

"Absolutely. I just wanted to make sure this—what we already did tonight and what we're doing now—isn't as good as it's going to get between us. I just wanted to make sure we were both on the same page. After our discussion, I can tell we are, and that's all I was concerned about."

Later that night, as Rosa lay alone, in a bed which now seemed way too big without him, she thought through the totality of her conversation with John.

He asked too many questions about Angelo. But then again, he was the one that would take the heat if Angelo got off, and benefit if he were convicted. He certainly had a vested interest in the out-come. She would not hesitate to discuss the case with him, but she would never breach Kat's confidence in any respect. There was too much on the line. If John knew, if he slipped up, if the wrong people found out, Kat's life would be in danger. Rosa just wasn't going to let that happen. If nothing came of Kat's undercover endeavors, so be it—end of story. If Kat did come up with something, hopefully her relationship with Rosa concerning the case would never surface. Either way, unless Rosa was pressed into divulging her relationship with Kat, nothing would ever pass her lips.

Now, to turn to the element of the conversation that brought a smile to her face. It was good to finally know that John was at least considering a future—a future with her... maybe kids... maybe a dog... maybe one of those houses with a frickin' white picket fence...

CHAPTER 36

*S*he watched as the rain intensified. Kat had every intention of sitting out by the fire tonight, relaxing with a glass of wine. Tomorrow was particularly important. Tomorrow was the last Wednesday before the trial began. Something needed to be on that flash drive this time. Nothing concerning the murder of Stoney and Gail had surfaced yet, and this would be the last opportunity to review the data before trial began.

As she continued to watch it rain, her line of sight carried her to those open barn doors. How different her life would have been if Mike had survived. Roy Brakus had changed all that. He had changed her way of life forever. Every time she remembered Mike, she remembered Brakus, and all he stood for. The two would be forever linked in her memory. Each time she remembered the battle with him, she seemed to develop an even greater resolve to do whatever she could to stop that type of person before they harmed another soul.

Every time she considered walking away from one of her self-created missions, she would have a moment like this. She would remember the misery, the pain that someone like that could inflict on another human being. She would remember firsthand, because that was exactly what Brakus had done to her. Those memories were always enough to rekindle that burn, that drive, to do all she could to help those women who were locked into that type of relationship. Tonight was no exception. She was anxious, concerned the flash drive would contain nothing that would help convict Bonaventura.

Even though sleep did not come easily, she arrived at work, on time, precisely at 8:00 a.m. Kat worked in every room of the home, other than Angelo's office, specifically planning to target it after everyone left.

She heard the front door close near nine forty-five and heard nothing from that area of the house thereafter. Kat walked to the window and saw Angelo and all his men piling in a couple of cars. They soon drove through the front gate and she, in response, walked into Angelo's office.

Kat knew she would need to clean his office at some point in time, so she carried all her cleaning supplies in with her, but her primary mission was certainly the camera. She quickly reached behind the line of books, removed the flash drive, replacing it with another. She dropped the drive into the bag carrying her cleaning supplies. As she turned to walk away from the bookcase, she heard the front door open.

Kat pulled out a dust rag and started dusting Angelo's desk at the precise moment he walked in his office door.

She looked up and immediately warned herself not to appear over solicitous.

"I thought I heard you guys leave. What's going on?"

Angelo walked behind his desk while she moved to the front and said, "My memory's getting as short as my... let's just say I forgot a few files."

He unlocked his desk drawer, removing a number of files apparently needed for his meeting.

After retrieving the files, he walked toward Kat and said, "You know, if you ever have a burning desire to initiate a relationship with me, just let me know. I might, I just *might*, be interested."

When he reached her, he ran his fingers down the side of her face. She stepped back as she said, "I'll let you know. I'm somewhat involved right now, but I'll let you know if and when I'm available."

When she backed up, she noticed a change in his appearance. Rejection clearly wasn't something he appreciated nor was it obviously something to which he had become accustomed.

He walked past her and, intentionally displaying a condescending smile, said, "That's fine. You be sure and let me know. I'll see if I can fit you in."

Kat took a deep breath. She should have waited a little longer. If there was a next time, if the drive contained nothing, and she needed to check the next one, she would wait a half hour or so before pulling it from the camera.

She started cleaning his office, anxious to have the day come to an end so she might review what had happened in his office during the week. Hopefully what they had been waiting for would be recorded, and she could end this charade.

Once she arrived home, Kat couldn't wait to shove the flash drive in her computer. She was able to fast-forward those times when Angelo was alone and not on the phone or when the room was empty. Those moments took up much of the space on the drive. It was when the office was filled with his men or he was on the phone with someone that was vitally important.

She was able to finish viewing everything by midnight. Unfortunately, there was absolutely no discussion during the week about the murder of Stoney and Gail. There had been some discussion with his men concerning what time they would need to be there to testify. But apparently the details of their testimony had already been discussed elsewhere, at some other time, because there wasn't a mention of that topic in his office during the week.

The next time she would have the opportunity to retrieve the data would be next Wednesday. The trial was scheduled to begin on

Monday. Would useful information even be relevant after the trial began? Should she just remove the camera equipment from his office when she could and send in her resignation? She didn't know what to do or how to proceed from here.

"Rosa, did I wake you? I'm sorry if I did, but we need to talk."

"You okay? Is everything okay?"

Rosa's voice was husky, and she sounded a little slow in her delivery, which was expected since it was a 2:30 a.m. phone conference.

"Yes, yes, I'm fine, but I just watched the data from beginning to end for this week, and there's nothing there, nothing that will help us. What the hell are we going to do? Should I continue to monitor? Can you still use anything if I come up with something after the trial has started?"

"Okay, just wait… slow down… hold on a second. Let me sit up and turn on a light. Hold on."

Kat could hear some activity at the other end of the line, the rustling of sheets and movement as Rosa sat up to continue the conversation.

"Yes. Evidence that pertains to the case, even though newly discovered, could still be used against him. I've done some research, and the only issue might be disclosure. It doesn't matter though. If you can get anything on that drive about the case, regardless of the time, we can use it up until the jury renders a verdict. It can be used one way or the other until he is found not guilty or is convicted."

There was a slight hesitation while Kat processed. "So you want me to leave the camera there and just continue working until the case is over?"

"Yes. I know that's probably not what you want to hear, but yes, that's what you need to do."

"Fuck what I wanna hear. I'll do whatever needs to be done to get this guy. I put in a new flash drive this morning. I won't be able to retrieve it until next Wednesday, but I'll let you know as soon as I do."

Rosa hesitated. "Tell you what. Let's *create* some activity in that office on our own."

"I don't understand."

"Let's *make* something happen. I meet with Angelo this Friday to go over everything one more time before we start picking a jury on Monday. I'll tell him the prosecutor has informed me they have additional new evidence concerning the crime scene that's going to break the case wide open. Certainly it won't be true. But I'm sure Marvin will back me, and when the evidence is never presented, I'll just tell them it wasn't as important as they thought it was. Hopefully, that will generate conversation in Angelo's office as concerns what Marvin may or may not have found."

"Great idea. If you tell him on Friday, that means either later in the day Friday or over the weekend, we most likely could pick up a little chatter. You know I can't get the drive until next Wednesday. Now, you're sure it can be used if the trial has already started?"

"Yes, but I'll do some additional research concerning the issue and make sure I'm right. I really don't want to provide it to Marvin before the state rests because I will be obligated to ask that the trial be continued, and I don't want that to happen. I'll set everything up on Friday, and we'll go from there."

"Great. Thanks. Let's talk Friday."

"Sounds good." Rosa never terminated the call. Kat could hear her still breathing.

"You gonna hang up?"

"You woke me up at two thirty. You started this conversation, you got my juices flowing, and then you expect me just to lie down and go back to sleep. Ain't gonna happen. Now, you talk and talk fast. I wanna know what you did today, what you had for lunch, how work was, and what you're doing this weekend. Start talkin', sister!"

Kat laughed and, through the laughter, said, "You got it. Well, listen to this. When I went to get that damn drive this morning, I thought they were gone…"

They talked until after 4:00 a.m. As Kat terminated the call, it had become clear that their relationship had changed. Two business associates had just become the best of friends, and that was more than acceptable to her.

CHAPTER 37

"Marvin, Rosa. Got a second to talk?"

"For you, yes, but my schedule overall is tight this morning. What's going on?"

"Angelo's coming in at ten. We're going through his testimony one more time before Monday. I need you to tell me something."

"What?"

"I need you to tell me you might have some new information acquired from the crime scene that could break this case wide open."

"I wish."

"No, I mean that. I want you to tell me that so I can pass it on to Angelo."

"Okay, what the hell's going on? I need to know a little more about what's going on before I lie to you and you lie to him."

"You wanna win this case?"

"Sure."

"Then just tell me you *might* have some new information, with the operative word being *might*. To me, that's not lying. You *might*, probably *won't*, but *might*. Can you do that for me?"

She could hear the wheels turning. Finally, he said, "Well, I guess I can. I suppose we *might* have some newly acquired information." Again, he hesitated, and finally he added, "Yes, I'm sure of it. We *might* have some newly acquired evidence that could blow this case wide open. Now, does that help you, because I sure as hell know it doesn't help me."

"Thanks. Yes, that's what I wanted to know. That's not good news for the defense team, Marvin. I'm really sorry to hear that you *might* have new evidence. I'll pass that on to my client."

"Could you tell me a little more, Rosa, or *might* that be a problem?"

"The only thing you need to know is that later this morning, I'm e-mailing you my friend Nicki Johnson's phone number. She knows you're going to call her. Just set up a time for both of you to get together over a cup of coffee. I think you two will get along well. Gotta go. Thanks, Marvin."

Rosa knew Angelo was waiting for her to get off the phone. She had closed her door for privacy during the call. It was time to set the trap.

"Morning, Angelo."

He walked in her door with an air of confidence that was overwhelmingly nauseating.

He took a chair, and as he developed an ever-broadening smile, he said, "Rosa, you look great this morning. You seeing anyone? You wanna catch supper with me sometime? We already know each other pretty well, how about taking that next step?"

Rosa felt sick to her stomach. The thought of having anything to do with this animal other than his legal work literally sickened her.

"I think I'll pass for right now, but thanks for the invitation. You ready for court on Monday?"

"Oh, I guess so. What a waste! What a waste of my time and yours, Rosa! They got nothin'. I just can't believe they're taking this as far as they are."

"Not to change the subject, Angelo, but before we talk trial, did you ever get a housekeeper?"

"I did, yes, I did. Thank God. That place was turning into an absolute shithole, if you know what I mean. She's working out well. She's somewhat standoffish, but she'll come around, she'll come around."

"I hope that doesn't mean what I think it means. Better keep your hands off her, Angelo, or you'll be looking for another house-keeper before long."

"Now, Rosa, you handle the legal matters. Let me handle the help."

"Whatever. You ready for Monday?"

"Sure. I've reviewed the jury list. There's only a couple people on there I might know, and that's only socially. They shouldn't be a problem. Everyone else seems okay to me. Should we go through the questions you're going to ask me when I get on the stand?"

"Yes. In addition, I want to go through the list of our witnesses and discuss their possible testimony."

For the next three hours, she reviewed the witness list and discussed his witnesses. She then grilled Angelo concerning his testimony, making sure he understood the process again, particularly cross-examination. She walked a fine line, and she knew it. But she had to create at least the semblance of a good defense, even though she hoped with all that was in her heart that she lost and he was convicted.

It was approaching noon when she finally felt he was ready for trial and that she had done all she could to adequately prepare him.

"Angelo, I think you're well prepared to tell them your side of this story. I don't think there's much else we can do based on the information we have."

"What does that mean 'based on the information we have'? Might there be information we don't have? I don't understand."

She leaned back in her chair and said, "No, I don't think so. However, I'm really not sure. I talked to Marvin earlier this morning, and he said there *might* be some additional evidence that came from the scene of the crime that could be relevant and important. I quizzed him concerning what it might be, and he said he would tell me if it turned into anything."

Angelo's whole demeanor turned on a dime.

"Well, don't we have a right to know what it might be prior to trial? I mean they can't just bring up this crime scene shit while I'm on trial, can they? I have the right to know about it beforehand, don't I?"

"Absolutely. Yes, they'll have to disclose it, and we can then ask for a continuance if we wish. But since you never killed them, obviously you don't need to worry anyway, do you?"

By now, he was perched on the front edge of his chair, clearly concerned about this "new evidence."

"No, no, you're correct. I don't need to worry. 'Crime scene evidence.' Wonder what the hell he's talking about. Guess we'll know soon enough."

Rosa stood, hoping he would too, which he did.

"Angelo, meet me at the courthouse around eight Monday morning. Meet me right outside the front door, and we'll find a conference room to settle in before the trial starts. If anything comes up before Monday that you think I should know, call me."

He turned around and gave her a wave of his hand as he walked out the door. He never said a word as he left. Clearly, the issue of "newly acquired evidence" had made an impact.

Later that afternoon, as Rosa was getting ready to shut everything down for the day, June informed her Angelo was holding on line 1 and that he needed to talk to her as soon as possible.

"Angelo, do we have a problem?"

"No, I don't think so. That's why I called you. Have you heard any more about the new evidence issue? I've been sitting here most of the afternoon trying to figure out what they might have."

"I never thought a thing about it. You told me you didn't do it. What could they possibly have, Angelo? You tell me. What could they possibly have?"

He paused before he said, "Of course. You're right. I was just curious. Thanks. See you Monday."

He had taken the bait—hook, line, and sinker. Now, she only hoped the conversation with his men involving the murders took place *in his office.*

"Hi, Marvin, Rosa. Before I get down to business, I just sent you Nicki's information along with a few of my thoughts about her."

"I know. I was just looking it over. Are you sure about this? I'm not very good at this dating game."

"You'll be perfect for each other. I have a question. If there happens to be some newly discovered evidence that needs to be introduced at Angelo's trial, if it comes to your attention after the state rests, can you still get it in?"

"What kind of evidence?"

"Doesn't matter. Let's just say extremely relevant and important for the jury to hear."

"No. Not unless it goes in as rebuttal. I could use it to rebut whatever the defendant might testify to, *if* he testifies, but other than that, once I rest, I think newly discovered evidence is out."

"That was exactly my thoughts too. So if Angelo gets up on the stand and says he didn't kill them, and you have newly acquired evidence that could be used on rebuttal, you would have no obligation to disclose it to me. You could use it against him at that time, is that your thoughts?"

"Exactly. Do you have anything? Anything at all?"

"No. Nothing. But I just wanted to make sure that if something did come up, you could get it in."

"I suppose if he testified he didn't kill those two, and I had newly discovered evidence establishing that he did, I could use it at that time. Are you planning on having him testify he didn't do it?"

"You bet your sweet ass I am."

"Do you have something for me I can use to rebut that?"

"Not yet, Marvin, not quite yet."

CHAPTER 38

Saturday morning! Normally, especially as tough as the prior week had been, she would have done nothing, gone nowhere, talked to no one. But Nicki had called last night in a panic about her "new man," Marvin. He was now her "new man." At least that was what she was calling him at this stage of the game.

She wanted to meet with Rosa and discuss him, so they decided to meet this morning at the coffee shop in Mount Juliet.

Rosa had been seated for about thirty minutes when Nicki sauntered in and walked up to the counter for the first of what Rosa figured might be many cups of coffee.

"Glad you could make it."

As she took a chair opposite Rosa, Nicki said, "I'm not late. I told you eight."

"Okay, so why weren't you here then? I was."

"Oh, what time is it? I left my watch somewhere. Can't find it. I thought it was about eight."

"It was—*a half hour ago.*"

"Sorry. I just lost track I guess."

"So what's on your mind? You were obviously having issues last night when I talked to you. What's your problem?"

"Well, you set me up with this guy, this guy that sounds like Scotty McCreery on the phone. You know, that singer? He's got the deepest voice I ever heard. I know nothing, absolutely nothing, about him."

"So are you saying it's somehow different than all those so-called clients you're sleeping with? At least I know a little about this guy, about his background, his history. That's more than you've told me you know about these guys you sleep with while you're selling insurance to them. At least Marvin comes with a recommendation—*mine*. What are you worried about?"

"Yes, but with those 'other guys,' at least I have something in common—*insurance*. I don't have anything in common with this guy. Tell me about him. I'm really worried about this."

"When's your date with him? You never told me."

"Yes, I did. It's tonight. We're just going out for supper, but what should I know about him? Should I try to sell him some insurance? Would that be the smart thing to do? Whatta you think?"

"Well, first of all, as you well know, I'm not the best person to discuss issues involving love or relationships. You're not talking to someone with the best track record when it comes to dating. But, if you really want my advice, I would probably leave the insurance issue at home, at least as concerns selling to him. Now, if I were you, the first thing I would do is relax. Good god, you're wound up tighter than a violin. Relax! He's only human. You act like you haven't been out with anyone since you were ten years old. Just be yourself. That's why I lined you two up in the first place. I know both of you. You're a perfect match. Just be yourself, Nicki. You'll be fine."

"This is really the first legitimate date I've been on in a while. I guess maybe I have gone a little overboard, maybe just a little too uptight about it."

"Ya think! And another thing. Don't take him to bed right after supper. Find out if the two of you like being with each other first. Try something new. Don't take that thong off before you at least know you like him. No insurance involved this time, Nicki. It's just you and him. Take your time. He's a great guy. He's a little backwards when it comes to the dating game, so don't scare him off the first day by ripping all his clothes off. Try something new. Play it slow this time, and see what happens."

"You say he's a little backward when it comes to dating?"

Rosa smiled. "Maybe backwards was a little harsh. He wraps himself up in his work. He just hasn't taken time to date much. Marvin is really smart and a great prosecutor. I told him he just needed to unwind a little, and I knew the perfect person to help him do that—*you*."

"You didn't set the bar too high, did you? *Did you set the bar too high?* I think that's what you did. After what you've told him about me, when I actually meet him, I'll probably be a disappointment."

Rosa couldn't help but laugh. Nicki was so distraught over absolutely nothing.

"Just try him one time. If it doesn't work, I'll smooth it over. You have nothing to lose, Nicki. Just try one date with him, and you can move on, either with him or without him. Your choice."

Nicki looked away for a moment while she considered Rosa's remarks.

Finally, she said, "Okay, okay, we'll see where this all goes I guess. I'm obviously somewhat concerned, but I'll try him out and see what happens. Now, let's move on. What about you? How's the case coming?" She moved closer to the table, and her voice dropped a level or two. "How's Kat getting along?"

"I'm really concerned about her." Rosa's volume also dropped noticeably. "Each day she's in his house, the risk increases. I'm so concerned one of those guys that work for Angelo might somehow find out who she is, or who she isn't. I worry about her every day."

"When does his trial start?"

"Monday, and that's not soon enough for me."

"How do things look? Is he going to get convicted?"

"That's the sixty-four-dollar question. I just don't think Marvin has enough. In addition, Kat is having a hell of a time getting any information out of that house."

"When can she quit and get out of there?"

"If we don't have something by the time I start presenting the defendant's case, I'm afraid we're done. I'll get her out of there then. We tried something new yesterday, but we aren't going to know if it worked until next Wednesday. We're both just keeping our fingers crossed. If it works, I'm telling her to get her ass out of there immediately."

"Is this man really that bad? Would he hurt her if he found out what she was doing?"

"I think, if he's able, if he's not locked up, he would have her murdered in the blink of an eye. If he's in prison, I think his whole operation will fall to pieces, but until he's put away, Kat's in real danger if they discover what she's trying to do."

"I haven't seen her or talked to her since this all started."

"I've been with her a number of times since it started. I really like her. We've become close since this all began. We have a lot in common. The three of us will need to get together once this is all over."

"What about you and John, Rosa? Is that all going to work out for you? You haven't said much about him lately."

A sudden change in the conversation's content brought a quick smile to Rosa's face. "We're doing well. This may be it for me, Nicki. He may very well be the one. I don't talk about it much, but I guess I'm afraid I may jinx us. Like maybe I'll wake up, and this will all have been just a dream. We're starting to make some long-term plans, and if all goes as it has been, I'm thinking we'll maybe have a fall wedding. We're a lot alike. We have many of the same goals. We'll see. If it all comes about, you'll be the first to know. How's your work going? Still doing about two or three guys a week for a sale? How's that all working out for you?"

She looked down at her coffee cup for a second before she said, "You know, sales have been slow. I'm down to just a couple of guys a week. Been trying to cut back. You know, I've been thinking maybe I'm not cut out to be a salesperson, at least as concerns insurance."

"I have to admit, your approach to selling is a novel one. I'm really not sure, if I were you, that I would share that approach with your fellow salesman. You know, if you were called to speak at an industry-wide meeting, I'm just not sure I would discuss and recommend your approach to your colleagues."

Nicki smiled. "Smart-ass."

Rosa could see the wheels turning. Finally Nicki said, "Holy crap, I suppose if something good did come out of this date tonight, I would have to stop that method of selling completely, wouldn't I? I don't think Marvin would approve."

Rosa sat back in her chair and laughed.

"No, I agree, Nicki. I have a feeling your sales method would need to change, and in a big hurry. Marvin would never go for that I'm sure, no matter how much money you were bringing in."

"Good god, I'd probably have to change professions. What the hell would I do? I don't know anything else."

"Nicki, if I were you, knowing how you operate in the business of sales, especially when it comes to men, if you want to preserve your marriage, I would definitely suggest a future in sales of woman's makeup or working on an assembly line. I'm thinking working in those two areas might be the only way you could preserve your marriage."

As Rosa drove home, she had to smile while considering her intense conversation with Nicki. She had no doubt, if Nicki and Marvin hit it off, there would need to be numerous discussions between herself and Nicki concerning the mixing of marriage and her occupation.

But at this point, her thoughts concerned one issue and one issue only—Kat. Having her in Angelo's house couldn't end soon enough. Her only hope was that this process ended successfully, and Kat got out alive. Perhaps the three of them would then have the opportunity to enjoy life together, as friends, after the issues involving Angelo were finally over.

CHAPTER 39

*S*hould he wear his black shirt with no sweater and gray slacks? Or maybe he should wear his white shirt with black slacks and a sweater. It could be chilly tonight. He needed to wear a sweater. But would a sweater be too hot in the restaurant? So many decisions, so little time. It was already 6:00 p.m., and he was to meet Nicki at 6:30. He was nervous, really, really nervous. He hadn't been on a real date for well over a year, and that one had ended in disaster.

Marvin finally settled on a gray V-neck sweater, white shirt, dark slacks. They were to meet at Union Common, a small restaurant located in west Nashville. He wanted to arrive somewhat early and be seated when she walked in the door. He put on just a touch of cologne before he left his apartment, a touch he hadn't found important in years.

Marvin hadn't dated since he moved to Nashville, at least not to any extent. When he first arrived, he knew no one. Since his arrival, he had had an occasional date, but work always seemed to interfere. Well, maybe it didn't interfere—maybe it was simply a matter of priorities. But for whatever reason, his social life had been nonexistent since his arrival in Nashville.

During high-pressure situations, as was the current situation with his handling of Bonaventura's case, he normally never had a social life of any type, opting to spend all his time, all his mental energy, on prosecuting. But Rosa was a good friend, and he respected her judgment. She felt he and Nicki would make a good couple. He would respect her opinion and proceed from there.

Marvin arrived at the restaurant shortly before six thirty. They had a table ready, and he took a seat, ordering bourbon and water while reviewing their menu.

He knew as soon as she walked in she was the one he was waiting for. She was as Rosa described her—perky, short, cute figure, smartly dressed.

She walked to his table as he stood.

Nicki extended her hand, and he shook it as she said, "You must be Marvin. Rosa has told me so much about you. Please sit, sit."

He helped her with her chair, sitting down opposite her, as he said in his slow, deep voice, "You're exactly as Rosa described. Glad we both had the evening open."

"Me too, yes, sir, me too. So you're an attorney, are you? How's that all working out for you? You enjoy the job? Is it hard? Your job I mean."

He thought *he* was nervous. He didn't hold a candle to her. She spoke in short, choppy sentences, clearly operating her mouth before she engaged her brain.

"Yes, I enjoy the job, and yes, it's difficult. Now can I order you a drink? Would you like a glass of wine, or something else to drink, before we eat?"

"You g'tting' one? Oops, you got one. Sure. Sure, I'd like something before you and I, you know, have supper. Sir, sir, I'd like to order something before supper. Sir, do you have a minute?"

It was obvious this wasn't the same person Rosa told him about. He needed to make her feel at ease. Not that he was much better. It was clear, both needed to relax.

Nicki ordered a glass of the house pinot noir and waited quietly for them to bring it. Once delivered, she drank half of it immediately, then visually studied the glass as she set it down carefully on the table.

He said nothing, waiting for her to comment on the wine, or initiate conversation concerning something—anything, at this point. Finally she said, "How are your insurance coverages? I sell insurance you know. Have for a long time. Always want to make sure my friends are covered. You covered?"

Marvin started to smile. This had gone on long enough. He reached over and placed his hand over her hand, which was securely wrapped around the base of her wine glass.

"Nicki, Rosa has told me so many wonderful things about you. So far, the Nicki I've seen tonight isn't the Nicki she described. I haven't dated much in the past few years. I've made my occupation my priority. It's consumed every day and most nights. I'm ready to break that trend and start enjoying life a little more than I have been. Obviously you're nervous about this date. So am I. Let's just start over. Let's both just take a deep breath and start over. How does that sound to you?"

She just looked at him, but said nothing.

"Nicki, what the hell do we have to lose? If this doesn't work out for one or both of us, we owe each other nothing. We walk out of here tonight and go our separate ways. We'll both simply enjoy a good meal. If we get halfway through the meal, and both of us have had enough, we can throw what's left of our meals at each other and walk out the door. Whatta we have to lose?"

She took a deep breath, looked down, rolled her hand over in his, and squeezed it.

"You're absolutely right." Her voice had returned to what appeared to be its natural tone, and her rapid rate of speech also returned to a more normal manner of speaking.

"I'm sorry. Rosa has told me so much about you. She really feels you're a good friend. She highly respects you, and believe me that's a compliment. There aren't many people she respects. Both issues—the fact she thinks so very much of you, and that you're an attorney—did tend to make me a little nervous about this date. But you're absolutely right. Neither of us are obligated to enjoy the other's company. We can spend some time together tonight, and if it doesn't work, it doesn't work."

"And if it does, it does."

Nicki smiled. She took another drink, then said, "Now, can we talk for just a moment about your insurance coverages?"

That was the beginning of a four-hour meal, during which time they enjoyed a shared, small plate of smashed fingerling potatoes, prime beef, and one of the house specialties—a shared dessert of apple crisp. It wasn't the first time Marvin had eaten at Union Common, nor would it be the last. The restaurant was pricey, but the service and the food served was as good as any restaurant in Nashville.

About halfway through dessert, Nicki said, "Rosa has me a little worried. She seems really wrapped up in this case. Much more so than others. I've known her a long time, and I've never seen her wound as tightly as she seems to be right now."

"She's in pretty deep, I would agree. But Rosa's a very competent attorney. She knows what she's doing. This guy she represents is an animal. I only hope I can get the jury to convict him."

The evening ended with a short kiss as she was waiting for a taxi, which he had called for her. They agreed the date was a success, and he was to call her in a couple of days. They would then figure out their next date together.

But as he walked home, it wasn't Nicki he thought of. She was obviously worried about her friend Rosa, and to be perfectly honest, he too was worried about her. She was standing on thin ice. Her client would stop at nothing to get what he wanted, and he wanted an acquittal.

The next morning, he called Rosa. It was Sunday, but he knew where she would be—at her office.

"Rosa, Marvin. Figured you'd be working, getting ready for tomorrow. But that's not why I called. Thanks for lining me up with Nicki."

"I was hoping everything went well. How did it go?"

"I enjoyed every minute I was with her. We're getting together again sometime this week. We had a great evening."

"To be perfectly honest, she called me last night and talked until two. I took it by her conversation you two really hit it off, so I'm glad you felt the same way. You were meant for each other."

"Time'll tell, Rosa. You know, she's really worried about you. She thinks you're in this Bonaventura case pretty deep. Is everything okay? Should you be getting out of it? Perhaps have someone else represent him?"

Rosa laughed. "It's a little frickin' late for that, Marvin. No, I'm right where I wanna be. I'll be fine. Thanks for your concern though. I'll make it through just fine."

They talked for a few more moments, and then terminated the call, agreeing to meet to discuss a few additional scheduling matters concerning the trial, at the courthouse before the commencement of evidence tomorrow morning.

But as Marvin terminated the call, he knew Rosa well enough to know this case was different. It was clearly affecting her. For him, it couldn't end soon enough, and he had no doubt Rosa felt the same way.

CHAPTER 40

Davidson County Courthouse
Trial, Day 1

Angelo, *pursuant to instructions, was exactly where he was sup-posed to be,* and on time. They walked through the metal detector together and located a conference room where they then agreed to meet on a daily basis prior to commencing each day's trial session.

They went through the details of jury selection one more time. Rosa didn't believe the trial would proceed much further today than just jury selection. With Angelo, she would review the appropriate details of each day's proceedings *on that day*, so as to avoid confusion.

Again, he brought up the issue of "new evidence." He wanted to know if there was any, and if there was, what it was. Again, Rosa put him off. She told him she would let him know as soon as she knew. Obviously, the issue concerned him. She only hoped those concerns were addressed in his office, and that on Wednesday, Kat would provide her with some good news.

Rosa walked into chambers just ahead of Marvin. Judge Beason had been assigned the case. He was already deep in thought as he reviewed the file prior to selection of the jury.

The judge looked up only long enough to say, "Good morning. Have a chair," and then again, he turned his attention to a review of the pleadings along with additional materials contained within the court file.

Both attorneys took a seat before the judge's desk, waiting for him to look up and start a dialogue concerning the case, neither wanting to interrupt the intense scrutiny he was giving the paperwork in front of him.

Finally, the judge leaned back in his chair, looked at Marvin, and said, "Doesn't look like you got much evidence, Marv. You might have enough to get past a motion for judgment of acquittal, but I guess we'll just need to wait and see how it all comes in. Is that a fair assessment concerning what evidence you have to present?"

"Yes, Your Honor, it is. The sad fact is that's all there is, plain and simple. But I just wasn't going to let this case become another one of his cold cases. We'll try this one and see where the chips fall."

"Looks like that housekeeper is pretty important to all this. Think you can keep her alive long enough to testify?"

Marvin smiled at the question, but certainly not the issue. "Yes, judge. I think we got it covered this time. She'll testify, probably on Wednesday."

"How long's this going to take? Any idea?"

"It appears to me about two weeks. Rosa, you think that's a fair assessment?"

"That's probably about right if the judge doesn't throw it all out at the conclusion of the state's evidence."

"Okay, folks. Whatta ya say, we all go in and pick ourselves a jury. You both ready to proceed?"

Both nodded affirmatively.

"Okay, I'll see you in there in about fifteen minutes. Need to make a bathroom stop first."

Both attorneys left chambers, Rosa to make her way, reluctantly, to the conference room, and Marvin to his council table in the courtroom.

Fifteen minutes later, they started selection of the jury. The selection of twelve people and two alternates went smoothly with few issues.

Trial, Day 2

The following day, the attorneys and the judge worked on jury instructions most of the morning, not bringing the jury back in until 1:00 p.m. When they were seated in the jury box, the court provided them with some general information concerning their conduct during the time they served as jurors, and opening statements were made by both attorneys.

The medical examiner's testimony took the rest of the afternoon, explaining the gruesome details concerning cause of death of both victims. There were a couple of times Rosa, hearing the specific details concerning her friend's murder, thought she was going to lose it, both emotionally and physically, but she hung in and made it through without drawing attention to herself.

The schedule called for Joni to testify tomorrow morning. Everyone directly involved in the case was waiting to hear her story.

Trial, Day 3

Joni Carsten had just been sworn in. Marvin's deep voice, slow and deliberate, led her through all the preliminary information defining who she was, who her employer had been, and what her duties were before getting down to the facts of the case. He was now ready to introduce her knowledge concerning the specifics of the case to the jury.

"Now, ma'am, did you know Gail Harper?"

"Yes. She was Mr. Bonaventura's girlfriend and a good friend of mine."

Rosa thought about objecting to her answer. It wasn't responsive to the question asked, but she just decided to make her points on cross, rather than objecting to something Marvin would eventually get into evidence anyway.

"Did Ms. Harper live there, at his house?'

"Yes."

"Were you aware of the relationship between Gail and Bill Stone?"

Joni looked down for a moment, considering her response, and finally said, "I knew something was going on, I just didn't know how involved they really were."

"Did Angelo know?"

"I don't know if he knew, but I know he strongly suspected it."

"How do you know that, Ms. Carsten?"

"Because I heard him say many times if he determined without a doubt they were involved, he would kill 'em both."

"Did he have his men checking into their relationship?"

"Objection, leading."

"Sustained."

"Let me rephrase. Do you know if he was doing anything to ascertain whether or not they were involved?"

"Yes. He was having his men check into their relationship."

"Do you know whether or not they ever uncovered anything linking the two of them together?"

"All I know is that they had a meeting one day, with all his men, and one of them said to me someone had just seen the two of them together. They were both found dead a few days later."

"Objection. That whole answer was based on hearsay. Move to strike."

"Your Honor, that statement was not intended to prove whether or not they actually *were* together, but only that the statement was made and the defendant *thought* they were seeing each other—state of mind. It falls within an exception and clearly is not testimony which should be excluded based on the definition of hearsay."

"Overruled. You may continue."

"Your Honor, we have nothing further."

"Council, you may cross."

Rosa stood and slowly approached the witness, stopping a few feet away.

"Did you ever see the two of them together?"

"No, of course not."

"Did anyone ever tell you they had in fact been seen together?"

"No."

"Did Gail ever tell you they were actually involved?"

"No. I knew something was not right, but—"

"Please stop, Ms. Carsten. You can answer with a yes or no, and you did that. Now, did anyone ever tell you the defendant murdered the two of them or had them murdered?"

"No."

"As I understand the situation, all of your testimony is based on hearsay, comments made by the defendant you overheard, and supposition. Is that correct?"

"Objection."

"Sustained."

Rosa returned to her chair at the council table.

"Okay, Ms. Carsten, you tell me what *you* saw, what the defendant said to *you directly*, or what anyone else might have *said to you* that confirms the fact the defendant murdered Ms. Harper or Mr. Stone. Let's hear it."

The witness said nothing.

"That's all I have, Your Honor."

"Redirect, Mr. Jackson."

Marvin cleaned up Joni's testimony the best he could. It was clear at this point his case was extremely weak. Rosa knew Marvin would present a string of witnesses that would all testify to the same set of facts—that Angelo was going to murder both Stoney and Gail if he found out they were involved.

Marvin had made his point today. Joni probably said enough to keep the case in court and survive a motion to dismiss, but Rosa still didn't feel there was enough to convict. Hopefully Kat found out something that would help finish the state's case, because without more than the state presented today, this case appeared to her to be going nowhere fast.

Rosa's thoughts the rest of the day weren't based on what she was doing, but were centered upon what Kat was doing. She knew today was important. Even with Angelo in court, and not available for the meeting, hopefully all of his men would leave the house for their meeting and the information they needed to put this guy away would be on that flash drive.

She hesitated to call Kat. She knew Kat couldn't call her while she was in his house, and she had no knowledge as to when Kat might have been able to leave the house for the day. So she waited for Kat to make the call to her.

It was now near 6:00 p.m., and Rosa was just getting up from her desk to leave the office. Her cell rang, and caller ID identified the caller she had been waiting for all day.

"Rosa, Kat. Can you talk?"

"Yes, go ahead. What happened?" Rosa sat back down and held her breath.

"Nothing. Nothing happened. Those bastards stuck around the house all day. From what I understand, Angelo had told them to stay put in case he needed them at the trial. There were six of them around the house all day. I couldn't get in his office alone. I don't have a fuckin' thing for you."

Rosa said nothing.

"I'm sorry, Rosa. I don't know what to do. I know there's no way to get that drive with them all here. What do you want me to do?"

Rosa thought for a moment.

"No matter what we do, we can't press the issue. We need to take what they give us. If you get caught, we're done. We just can't take a bigger chance than we already are, no matter what the factual situation might be. Let me think about this a day or two. Just keep doing what you're doing, and if at some point they all leave, get the drive. If that doesn't happen, we'll figure something else out. Let's just be patient for a day or two, and see what happens."

"I'm sorry, Rosa."

The disappointment was evident in her voice.

"Hang in, Kat. It'll all work out. We need to be patient. It'll all work out."

The call ended shortly thereafter.

Rosa could only pray it would all work out. She knew something positive was going to need to happen, and quickly. Because based on today's evidence, if Marvin had nothing more than he had presented, Angelo would surely walk out of that courtroom a free man, *again*.

CHAPTER 41

Davidson County Courthouse
Trial, Day 8

T he days moved slowly, as Marvin presented witness after witness, all basically testifying to the same set of facts, to wit: If Angelo determined Gail was involved with someone else, once he found out who it was, he would kill them both. The testimony concentrated only upon the issue of motive. Every item of evidence and every witness that testified presented basically circumstantial evidence but, unfortunately, most likely not enough to convict. Rosa knew if she didn't come up with additional facts, additional *specific* facts, Angelo would never be convicted. Hopefully today Kat would come up with something from the camera.

Approaching 3:00 p.m., Marvin presented his last witness, and the state rested. The judge dismissed the jurors for the day asking them to be in their chairs ready to proceed at nine the next morning, when the defense would start presenting evidence. As soon as the jurors left the room, the judge turned to Rosa and said, "Do you have motions to make?"

Rosa stood and said, "We do, Your Honor."

"I figured you would. Let's take a break. I'll see both attorneys in chambers in a few minutes."

The judge stood and left the courtroom. Rosa and her client walked out the back door of the courtroom, into the hallway. They proceeded to the conference room they had used for the last week, and as they entered the room, Angelo said, "That was literally the biggest waste of time I have ever been through. They have nothing on me. Will the judge dismiss it? I assume you're going to make your standard motion to dismiss. Will he dismiss it?"

All three of Angelo's right-hand men were waiting in the room for them to return. Rosa had told Angelo she might need them to testify today. Rosa had taken matters into her own hands. She wasn't going to wait and determine whether there was or wasn't a meeting that would pull them out of Angelo's home office. Their presentation of evidence today wasn't going to happen, but she wanted them out of that house, and this was the only effective method she could think of. Hopefully, their removal would leave the house empty so Kat could retrieve the drive. She had no idea whether he would replace the guys that normally hung around the house with others, or just leave it empty, but it was worth a try.

"I doubt it, Angelo. I'll make the motion, but I doubt it. They normally let the jury determine these kinds of cases. Besides, I really feel if we offered no evidence, and just rested now, the jury *could* find you guilty. I'm not saying they would, but they *could*, and that's normally the standard this judge uses. I'll walk back to chambers, and we'll see what happens. It'll probably take up to an hour. Just wait here."

Rosa walked into chambers. Both the judge and Marvin were already seated.

Rosa handed both men copies of her Motion for Judgment of Acquittal, which she had filed with the clerk of court on her way to chambers.

"Gentlemen, the motion is self-explanatory, but I can paraphrase most of it for you if you wish. By the way, judge, the defendant's presence is waived."

She turned to look at the court reporter recording the hearing and said, "Please note the defendant has specifically waived his presence concerning this hearing."

"Judge, the evidence just isn't here. It's all circumstantial. There are no eyewitnesses that can tell us what happened. There's no weapon. There's no ballistics testimony. There's no DNA. All we have are a group of people indicating *if* the defendant ever found out Gail was having a relationship with someone else, he would kill them. There's no indication he ever found that out, and certainly no evidence he killed them, or that any of his men were involved. The case needs to be dismissed."

"Marvin, your response."

"Your Honor, we feel there is more than enough evidence to submit the case to the jury. True, most of it is circumstantial, but men have been convicted of crimes based on circumstantial evidence for years. This one is no exception. We feel there is certainly enough evidence to move beyond the defendant's motion and let the jury decide."

Rosa's stomach was in knots. She knew this precise moment was pivotal. She had no choice but to present the motion, and argue it as well as she could, or if he were convicted, her incompetency in that respect would definitely be an issue. She held her breath as the judge listened to Marvin and studied the motion in his hands.

After a long five minutes, the judge looked at Rosa and said, "You know, Rosa, this is a close call. You're correct in that everything is circumstantial, but you've been involved in this type of case before, and you certainly know that circumstantial evidence can be used to convict. It just seems to me, this is one case in which the jury should be allowed to decide the issue. I really believe if the defendant doesn't testify, or in the event you put on no evidence, they could convict him, and the conviction would be upheld."

Again, he studied the motion before he said, "I'm going to overrule the motion. I could be wrong, I really could, and I'm sure if he's convicted, Rosa, you'll ask the Supreme Court to determine whether I was or wasn't correct. But at this point, if I'm wrong, I'm going to be wrong *overruling* the motion rather than *sustaining* it. Your motion is overruled. Now if neither of you have nothing else, I want to review these instructions before I go home tonight. Anything from either of you?"

Both attorneys indicated they had nothing.

"Then I'll see you both tomorrow morning around nine. Rosa, will you be ready to present testimony?"

"Yes, judge. I'll probably have the defendant testify first thing, and then go from there."

Both attorneys left chambers and walked into the hallway.

"Don't mind telling you, Marvin, I was really afraid he was going to sustain my motion. Thank God he didn't," Rosa whispered.

"I was worried about it too. At least this way, the jury can review everything, and I have a chance at a conviction. I assume you have nothing new for me."

"Nope. I'll know more later today."

She walked down the hallway, dreading the prospect of telling her client and his employees the news she needed to tell them.

She walked in and took a chair.

"He didn't dismiss, did he?"

"No, Angelo, he didn't. We need to start presenting evidence in the morning."

Angelo shoved his chair backward, rising up in obvious rage. The look on the faces of each one of his men told her they had been in this position before. This wasn't the first time they had seen him this way. They clearly were not surprised at his response.

"That rotten son of a bitch. They have absolutely no case."

He started pacing around the room running his fingers through his hair.

"What a waste! What a waste of fucking time *and* money. They have nothing." He stopped, looked at Rosa, and said, "What happened to all that *new* evidence they supposedly had? Where the hell did it go?"

"I have no idea, Angelo. Apparently it wasn't enough. Apparently it wasn't sufficient to even discuss."

He started pacing again.

"So what now? We just move forward, present our witnesses, and hope they find me not guilty?"

"Yes. I really don't think based on the evidence that's been presented, they could possibly find you guilty. But you'll need to remain calm, make a good appearance when you testify tomorrow, and make sure the jury understands you could never do something like this, that it just wasn't you. It's all up to you now, Angelo."

"Are you going to have these guys testify after me? You know, have them tell the jurors I wasn't around while this was going on?"

"Yes."

"Okay. Guess I'll just handle the situation myself. I won't have any problem on the stand. As you know, I can be pretty convincing when I need to be. And certainly that prick Marvin what's-his-name don't bother me. I'll handle him."

"Oh, I have no doubt you'll handle yourself just fine, Angelo." She rose to leave as did he.

As she sat at her desk an hour later, she only hoped she heard from Kat tonight. Hopefully, making sure his men left the house had worked. Time was short. Rosa probably had enough testimony to last a couple of days. She doubted Marvin would put on any rebuttal, and she estimated the jury wouldn't take a full day to acquit. They had little time left. If nothing happened in the next couple of days, Angelo would again be free to roam the Nashville area, inflicting his own method of justice on anyone that dared resist.

CHAPTER 42

*R*osa remained at her office until well after six. She had heard nothing from Kat, but she wasn't sure that meant anything. She knew Kat had to leave work, travel home, and then view the data, if she was even able to retrieve it. She would be watching footage, which included many hours, indeed many days, of activity. While much of the footage would most likely consist of an empty room, there would also be hours of conversation, irrelevant and hopefully relevant, she would need to listen to, word by word.

She finally decided Kat would reach her no matter where she might be, so she closed the office, drove through the drive-in window at Wendy's, picked up a burger with fries, and drove home for the night.

Rosa kept watching her phone, as if somehow that might make it ring. Nothing had happened by eleven, so she decided to try to get some sleep. She lay in bed for an hour trying to sleep, and finally sometime between midnight and one, she fell into a restless, shallow sleep until a few moments before two, when her phone rang.

"Rosa, Kat. You awake?"

Rosa hesitated. Finally she said, "First of all, I know who you are. Secondly, what the hell do you think? It's two *in the morning*! Hell no, I'm not awake. Now, what's going on?"

She giggled. "You need to come out?"

"Okay… sure… come out? Come out where… when?"

"Here! Now!"

"Why… I mean *why*… why now, why there?"

"Got something you need to see."

Rosa sat up in bed. Her heart skipped a beat.

"Is it worth the trip—worth a drive at two a.m.?"

"It's worth your time all right, or I wouldn't have bothered you."

"Be right out."

Rosa terminated the call, throwing on a sweatshirt along with a pair of old jeans. Upon her arrival, she noticed every light in Kat's house was on. Rosa never even bothered to knock. She found Kat in her living room, still looking at footage.

"So whatta ya got that necessitated me driving out here at two, waking me up before a tension-filled day, and ruining what was just starting to become a restful night?" Rosa asked.

Kat never turned away from the screen as she responded, "You told those guys they needed to be in court, and that was all I needed. No one was in the house today. Wait till you see what happened the day you told Angelo the state had new evidence. I've been watching this since I got home. Let me go back."

Kat rolled back time, and the footage finally stopped at a point where Angelo was seated in his office alone. As the footage started to again move forward in time, Angelo's men—Rocco Nelson, Danny Moss, and Andrew Gross—walked in the room, shutting the door behind them.

"Sit down, all of you, sit down."

Each of them took a chair as Angelo said, "I understand the state may have some new evidence they acquired at the scene where you guys dumped those two bodies. Do any of you have any idea what it might be?"

Each of them looked at each other. Finally Rocco said, "Boss, it can't be nothin'. We left nothin' there. We all used gloves. There was nothin' we left there but the bodies. No one saw us. Both of them, Stone and Gail, was dead. Had been for a couple of hours. There can't be a damn thing at that scene they can use against us. Did they say of what nature the evidence might be?"

"No. Only that something was left at the scene that might affect the trial. That was all she told me. Rosa don't lie. There's something goin' on. I know it was dark, but did you all look around good before you left?"

"Fuck yes," Rocco said. "Boss, there can't be anything we left there except both them dead bodies. There was no one around anywhere. It was about two hours after we finished them off, which made it about three a.m. when we dumped them, dark as hell, and no one around. They can't have a damn thing. That's a bunch of bullshit."

Angelo thought for a moment. He looked at Rocco and said, "If I find out one of you screwed up, and left something out there, something that implicates you guys or me in killing those two, I'll cut your nuts off, and feed them to you a nut at a time—raw, not fried. Now, you guys got any questions?"

They each shook their head negatively.

Angelo leaned forward in his chair and said, "Good. Now get out."

Each man hurriedly rose and walked out the door. Rocco was the last one out. As he reached the door, he turned and said, "Want me to shut this, boss?"

"Whatever, sure, sure, shut the fucking thing!"

Kat stopped the drive.

"Will that do it for you?"

Rosa got up out of her chair and walked toward Kat, who was seated cross-legged on the floor.

"Get up."

"Why... what's wrong?"

"Get up."

Kat slowly rose up, and as she did, Rosa put her arms around her, embracing her.

"I love you. I love your courage, your strength, your resolve. I'm so incredibly proud of what you've done. And yes, that will do it for me."

Kat embraced her for a moment, leaning her upper body back to look at Rosa as she spoke. When she was finished, she simply said, "All just part of the job, Rosa, just part of the job. How 'bout a short glass of wine?"

Rosa laughed and said, "Why not. I'm wide awake. Why try to sleep now? It's only a couple of hours before I get up to go to work anyway."

As Kat poured the wine, she said, "How's Marvin gonna get this into evidence?"

Rosa took the half glass of wine offered by Kat and said, "He and I really haven't discussed that much, because we were never sure whether or not we would come up with anything, but I think he's just going to offer it as rebuttal. And I think I'll wait and tell him we have it only after Angelo testifies he didn't do it. Which by the way is only a few hours away."

"Is he going to testify today?"

"Yes. What's your position now? Whatta you gonna do, continue working or quit?"

"I don't know. What are your thoughts?"

"I think you should continue. I wouldn't quit yet. Let's get to the point where he's denied killing them, and they're ready for the state's rebuttal. When we get to that point, I think it's time you get out. What about the camera? You gonna just leave it there?"

"Probably. Hell, no one will ever find it anyway. No one reads any of those books."

"Did you make more than one copy of the data?"

"Yes. I'll give you this one and keep the other one."

"Okay, great. Once Angelo and his men are done testifying, which will probably take a couple of days, I'll get together with Marvin, show him what we have, and go from there. You know you'll have to testify. You'll have to tell them how you got this video, so I hope you're prepared to do that."

"Absolutely. Been there, done that. Not a problem for me."

"I can't believe we finally got him."

Kat hesitated. "There are some other issues with other people that came and went out of that office. We'll need to discuss them and what you want to do in that respect, but we can do that at a later date. I really think we just need to focus on Angelo and put this bastard away first."

"That sounds great to me."

They didn't stop with that short glass of wine Kat initially poured. About five thirty, they fixed up a batch of scrambled eggs and bacon. With it, they had another half glass of wine, while continuing to celebrate the acquisition of the information they needed.

Rosa finally made it home just before six thirty. She quickly showered, got dressed for a short trip to the office and her subsequent drive to the Davidson County Courthouse.

She would call Angelo to the stand first thing, then call his three men, knowing each of them would lie not only because that was just who they were, but also to save their own lives.

At this point, it didn't really matter. If they could find a way to get the flash drive into evidence and get it in without anyone knowing Rosa was somehow involved, that would clearly be enough to tip the scales and put the murdering son of a bitch away once and for all.

CHAPTER 43

Davidson County Court House
Trial, Day 9

*T*he sound of the gavel striking the sounding block could have been heard in Galveston, Texas. The judge wanted order in the courtroom. The jurors were all visiting, Rosa was talking with Marvin, and Angelo was trying to explain to Rocco, again, exactly how he and the men were to testify once they were called.

The judge first tapped it softly, but no one responded. This time he left no doubt what he wanted. He wanted this show to move along, *now*.

As everyone returned to their appropriate spot in the court-room, the judge said, "Ms. Norway, you ready to proceed on behalf of the defense?"

Rosa stood. "We are, Your Honor."

"Remember, all witnesses are to be sequestered. I see your client talking with someone before we start this morning. If he's a witness, he must leave the courtroom before testimony begins."

Rosa frowned at Angelo. He knew the rules. Rocco had just taken a seat in the front row of the spectator's area.

Angelo turned around, flicking his fingers at Rocco, as if he were dispensing with a small piece of dirt that had stuck to one of his appendages. Rocco immediately rose, walking hurriedly out the back door of the courtroom.

"Please proceed, Ms. Norway."

"The defense calls Angelo Bonaventura to the stand to be sworn and seated."

Angelo slowly rose, adjusted his tie, smoothed out his thousand-dollar suit coat, and walked leisurely to the witness stand. He was sworn in, then took his seat.

Rosa had determined she would limit his testimony to only the bare essentials. His testimony would be short and sweet. If Marvin wanted to expand the scope of his testimony, she would, within reason, let him do so; but otherwise, she would have him testify he didn't do the crimes for which he was charged and get him off the stand.

After having Angelo testify as to a number of foundational issues including his name, address, and occupation, she moved on to the merits of the charges against him.

"Now, sir, did you know the victims in this case?"

"Of course, I knew Gail, but I didn't know Mr. Stone."

"Never met him?"

"No."

"How did you know Gail Harper?"

He dropped his head and hesitated a moment before he responded. Rosa knew it was strictly for effect, but Angelo was pretty good at what he did, and to the unknowing, it would clearly have an effect.

"We lived together for a number of years."

"Never married?"

"No, not yet. We had planned a wedding for later this year"— again he dropped his head— "but she never lived to see it happen."

"Did you kill her?"

Everyone looked at Rosa, expecting her to lead up to the events of that day. No one expected the question that soon or so directly.

"No, I didn't kill her," he said softly. "I loved her."

"Tell us what happened that day."

"She left while I was away, and just never came back. I think she said something about going shopping for the morning, and she just never returned. I never saw her again"

"Did you think she was seeing someone else? There's an abundance of testimony that she might have been seeing someone else, and you were upset about it. Is that true?"

"Yes, that's true. I felt she might be seeing someone else, but I wasn't sure. I admit I was upset. But I've been upset with her before, and she with me, but neither of us ever killed anyone then, and I didn't lay a hand on her this time. It was frustrating. I just wanted to know. I wanted her to tell me if she was seeing someone else so we could each just go our own way. I loved her then, I love her now. I said some things I'm sorry for, but there's no way anyone can prove I killed her—because I didn't."

"Did you have someone else kill her?"

"No."

"Were you trying to determine if she was having a relationship with Mr. Stone or anyone else?"

"Yes. I asked around, and I told my employees to let me know if they heard anything. But that was it."

"Who do you think did this, Mr. Bonaventura?"

"I'm assuming it was someone that was upset with a job Mr. Stone did or was doing for them. He was a private investigator, you know. He could have pissed off any number of people." He quickly turned and looked up at the judge. "Oops, sorry, Your Honor, if that wasn't the proper term to use. I won't do it again."

"Again, did you kill these two victims, Mr. Bonaventura?"

"No, I didn't. You know, even if I had determined they were involved, which I never did, I would have just terminated our relationship and kicked her out of my house, but I never would have killed her, under any circumstances."

"Your witness."

Marvin stood. "Your Honor, may I approach?"

"Certainly."

Rosa had seen Marvin use this tactic before. He wanted to get in Angelo's face and intimidate him with that booming bass voice, hoping to wear him down. She knew he was barking up the wrong tree with that tactic. Angelo would never waver under cross-examination, no matter how much pressure Marvin created.

After two hours of reexamining Angelo's prior testimony involving everything *but* the ultimate issue, he said, "Mr. Bonaventura, you knew she was having a relationship with Mr. Stone, didn't you?"

"No, I never—"

Marvin moved close. "Sure you did. You knew they were having a sexual relationship, and it drove you crazy, didn't it? Knowing she was rejecting you for another man absolutely infuriated you, didn't it?"

"No, it didn't and—"

"So you just took matters into your own hands, didn't you?"

Marvin was now only a foot away from Angelo. It was obvious to everyone in the courtroom Marvin was involved. This was personal. The judge finally said, "Mr. Jackson, please move back. I don't mind you approaching, but I don't want you in the same chair with him. Move back."

Marvin looked at the judge, suddenly realizing what he was doing. He took a few steps back and changed his approach.

"How many others have you murdered, Mr. Bonaventura? There have been others, like for instance your son-in-law. How many others have—"

Rosa was on her feet immediately.

"Objection. Beyond the scope of direct, Your Honor. I never went there with this witness."

"Yes, yes, Mr. Jackson, watch what you're doing here. You're way beyond the scope of direct, and you know it. Don't go another step down that road."

"Sorry, Your Honor. Sir, did you tell anyone—in fact, did you tell a number of people that if you determined Gail and Mr. Stone were involved, you would kill them? Did you say that not only once, but many times?"

"I might have, yes, but—"

"Stop right there. Just answer the question I ask."

Rosa stood again. "Your Honor, surely the witness should be allowed to respond, to explain his answer."

"Let him finish his sentence, Mr. Jackson. Proceed, Mr. Bonaventura."

"Yes. I was upset. I agree I was upset. But I could never kill someone like Gail, someone who never hurt anyone in her life. I would never touch a hair on her head. She was special, to me, and to many others. In the heat of the moment, I probably made some stupid statements, but I didn't kill her. I swear on everything that's holy, I never killed her."

"I believe you mentioned you weren't around that night. Where were you? Where were you the night she died?"

"I had a meeting with my men. I was with them until late into the night. They'll tell you. They'll tell you I was with them when she was murdered. You can ask them yourself."

"Oh, I will, Mr. Bonaventura. I will."

Marvin had had enough. He knew he could never break Angelo. The facts presented during the state's case were going to need to be enough to convict. The jury would just need to accept the state's case on blind faith because Angelo was never going to convict himself.

Marvin took his seat, looked over his notes one more time, and said, "Your witness, Ms. Norway."

The judge looked at Rosa and said, "Any redirect, Ms. Norway?"

"None, Your Honor."

"Ladies and gentlemen, it's time for us to break for the day. Please remember the admonition I gave you concerning not discussing this case with others, and I'll see you all tomorrow morning, seated, at nine a.m."

Trial, Day 10

Court reconvened at precisely 9:00 a.m. During the course of the morning session, Rosa introduced testimony from all three of Angelo's closest employees. They all testified to exactly the same set of facts. They all testified that Angelo and his three men were together well into the night, until around 2:00 a.m., the night Gail and Stoney were murdered. None of them could have been involved because they were all discussing whether to purchase a business in Nashville.

They all testified as to precisely the same set of facts, and after the second one testified, Marvin quit trying to break them. It was wasted effort, and he knew it.

They all had their stories down pat, and Marvin, as was the situation with Angelo, wasn't going to trip them up no matter how long he cross-examined them. They were well rehearsed and good witnesses for Angelo.

Court recessed for the noon break, but immediately prior, Rosa rested. The judge indicated they would dismiss for the day. He had a couple of other matters to handle during the afternoon hours. Judge Beason indicated he would meet the attorneys in chambers for a few moments prior to their departure. Rosa immediately renewed her motion to dismiss. She figured if the judge had overruled it at the conclusion of the state's case, he would remain consistent and over-rule it again, which he did.

The judge asked Marvin if he wanted to offer any rebuttal to the defendant's witness's testimony, and Marvin indicated he wanted to review his notes again. He would let him know first thing in the morning.

As Rosa started her drive toward Mount Juliet, she punched in Kat's number.

Kat didn't answer. Rosa knew she would be working, and only hoped she would return her call.

About fifteen minutes later, she did.

"Kat, can you meet me at my office tonight, maybe about six?"

"Sure, what's up?"

"Just meet me. I'll tell you then."

She then punched in Marvin's number.

"Can you meet me in my office about six-thirty tonight?"

"What for? No, I can't. I need to figure out what I'm doing tomorrow after your client's testimony about sunk my ship today. No, I can't."

"Let me change my approach. Meet me at my office at six-thirty, understand?"

Marvin hesitated for a second before saying, "Must be important."

"It is."

"See you then."

CHAPTER 44

As Marvin approached Rosa's office, he noticed the reception area was completely dark. Only a faint ray of light pierced the darkness, apparently emanating from a back office. The front door was unlocked. He walked down the hallway, and as he did, he said, "You here?" his deep baritone voice echoing off the wall at the end of the hallway.

He was near her office door when she replied, "I am. Just keep walkin'."

He took a seat in front of her desk, smiled, and said, "Okay, what's so damn important?"

"I have someone I want you to meet. She isn't here yet, but you need to visit with her about our case."

He said nothing for a moment, trying to fathom exactly which case. "You mean our Bonaventura case? Which case? We have about ten that are pending which involve the two of us."

"Yes, Bonaventura."

"I don't understand. What's this all about? Why do I need to visit with anyone about that case?"

As he finished his sentence, he heard the front door open.

Kat Rickter walked into Rosa's office, and both stood.

"You're early. Marvin, this is Kat Rickter. You might remember her from the newspaper articles surrounding the death of her husband, Mike, who was a cop in Nashville. She has some information concerning Bonaventura you might be interested in."

Marvin extended his hand and said, "I remember Mike's death well. I've never had the opportunity to tell you how sorry I was about what happened."

She shook it and said, "Thank you. I think I might have a little information you may want to review concerning Bonaventura's case."

"I've taken the liberty of setting up a computer in Stoney's old office across the hallway for you to use. I don't want anything to do with this conversation. I'm gonna walk over to the coffee shop across the street while the two of you visit. Kat, when you're done and Marvin's left, give me a call, and I'll walk back over."

Rosa got up and left as Kat started explaining.

"Marvin, since Mike's death, I've tried to help women that have been involved in difficult domestic situations. Gail Harper was certainly involved in a bad relationship, and it got her killed. I decided I wanted to see if I could help bring the man to justice that committed the murder, and for the last month or so, that's exactly what I've been doing."

"Please explain. Exactly *what* have you been doing?"

"I set up a fake identity and went to work as a housekeeper for Bonaventura. I was finally able to place a camera in his office, and the past few weeks, I've been filming everything in that room."

"You're kidding. Did you do this with the assistance or under the authority or control of any law enforcement agency?"

"Absolutely not. I did it on my own."

Marvin sat back in his chair to consider the situation, not only factually but legally.

"Well, I can't think of any law you broke, I guess. The criminal code provides for 'intercepting' telephone signals and things of that nature, as being criminal in nature, but this seems to me totally different. You had a right to be in the house, and you technically 'intercepted' nothing. Besides that, I can't imagine anyone in the Davidson District Attorney's office prosecuting you for anything that might be used to establish a murder." Again, he was quiet for a moment, then said, "Law enforcement wasn't involved, so there's no issue concerning a right to privacy or entrapment. You might be subject to civil litigation for an invasion of his privacy." He hesitated before throwing out the next question. "Did you come up with anything?"

"Let's go take a look."

Together, they walked across the hall. She shoved the flash drive into the computers port. As the scene in Angelo's office started to unfold, all Marvin could say was, "Oh my god... oh my god!"

Once Marvin had viewed the pertinent portions of the drive, he looked at Kat and said, "I need you to testify. Do you have any concerns about him suing you for invasion of privacy? Can you meet me at the courthouse Monday morning? Are you available?"

She smiled and said, "Let the fucker sue me. No, I'm not concerned about that issue, and I've already made arrangements to be there."

Marvin rose and started to pace the room. "I think we can get all this in on rebuttal. Why don't you meet me there early, say around eight, and I'll find a vacant conference room for you to remain prior to the hearing."

"Actually, I had already made plans to meet Rosa there, and she said she would take care of the conference room issue. But at this point, I think it would best if you just handled everything from now on. I'll plan on meeting you there early, maybe seven would be better just to make sure we are there before anyone else shows up. Does that work for you?"

Marvin smiled. "Absolutely. I'll plan on meeting you on the second floor around seven."

"I'll be there."

Marvin moved toward the door. "You cannot believe how much this means to the state, to me personally. This could be the evidence that turns this case on its ear and puts this man away forever. Thank you."

"See you Monday morning, Marvin."

Trial, Day 11

Marvin was in the hallway when Kat arrived precisely at seven. He escorted her to a conference room that was available, where she could remain until needed.

As soon as the judge arrived, the court reporter sought out Rosa and asked her to join the judge and Marvin in chambers.

As she walked in the door, she noticed Marvin had set up a large screen computer, and the court reporter, no doubt at Marvin's insistence, was ready to report the hearing that was about to take place.

"Well now, what's happened overnight that demands such attention from the court this early in the morning, Mr. Jackson?"

"Judge, I received some information last night which I wanna use as rebuttal today, but I want you to review it first, and I want Rosa to see it at the same time. This is a video of events in the defendant's office, which were taken by a woman who was hired as the defendant's housekeeper."

"Now wait a minute, Marvin. Is this someone hired by you or any other law enforcement agency?" Rosa knew she had to continue to play her role at every stage of the proceedings, and do it convincingly.

"No, Rosa. She did it completely on her own. She wanted to help try to put this man away, and what she did was done without the involvement of any of other person or agency. Incidentally, Rosa before you ask, I called one of our techs *and* an independent tech I was able to locate last night. I had them both check the drive. It's *not* been altered in any manner."

"Okay, okay, before we go any further, let me see the video," the judge said. "Let me at least take a look at what you have before we argue about it."

Marvin inserted the flash drive, and all three watched in complete silence.

Once the appropriate portion was completed, the judge said, "Well, that bit of evidence certainly popped up at an opportune time. What do you intend to do with it, Marvin, use it as state's rebuttal?"

"Absolutely."

"Rosa, what are your thoughts?"

"Obviously, I'm going to object to its use. We should have been given notice and had a chance to examine it. Regardless of the state's statements that it hasn't been altered, we should have the right to examine it with our own experts. We need, at a minimum, a continuance. And how do we know this wasn't all set up by law enforcement? This is a complete infringement on my client's right to privacy. Those objections are just for starters, judge."

The judge leaned back in his chair, deep in thought, and turned to look out the window. He finally turned to face both attorneys. "You know, this is rebuttal... the state has no obligation to provide the defense with evidence they might use as rebuttal because they have no idea what evidence the defense is even going to present during their portion of the testimony. I'm not going to continue this trial—for any reason. We're here—we're going to finish it. I'm going to let her testify. Rosa, if you want one of the techs to testify as to the authenticity of the video, feel free to call the individual as your witness. I wanna hear what she has to say, and if the defendant wishes, he can then respond. If law enforcement was in no respect involved, I can see no constitutional issue here. I don't really believe, the way she handled it, that it violates any of the criminal statutes concerning privacy either. If she isn't worried about the civil ramifications, she can testify as long as she wishes, as far as I'm concerned. Is that the only witness you have on rebuttal, Marvin?"

"Yes, Your Honor."

"Rosa, when he's finished, you can put your client back up on the stand and let him refute everything, but Marvin's witness is going to be allowed to testify, and the jury is going to be allowed to see this video. Now, if neither of you have anything else, I wanna review a few more matters before we start this morning. Be seated by nine, and we'll get started."

Both attorneys rose to leave the room. Once in the hallway, Rosa turned to Marvin, smiled, and said, "Give me five," at which time Marvin grinned and slapped hands with her, resulting in a resounding sound that echoed off both ends of the courthouse hallway.

CHAPTER 45

"**We** *have a problem.*"

Angelo was sitting with Rocco deeply involved in discussing issues, which apparently required hushed voices. Shortly after Rosa entered the room and turned to shut the door, that discussion ended in its entirety.

Angelo turned and said, "What kind of problem? Whatta you talkin' about?"

"You know that housekeeper you hired?"

"Ya, what about her? She's home cleaning the stools."

"Not today. She's here, and she seems to have acquired a video involving conversations in your office concerning the murders."

"Bullshit." He swiveled around in his chair, so he now faced her.

"You're going to watch it because the judge just allowed it into evidence. I'll be watching it too, but when you watch it, you can't show any emotion. Sit quietly and let me do what I can to keep it out of evidence. We'll talk about what we're going to do to offset it after it's played to the jury. Now, do you understand? Just sit quiet."

"There were no conversations in my office concerning those murders because I didn't do them. If there's a tape, it's been fabricated. There's no way."

"Time to resume. Let's go see what they've got."

They walked out of the conference room and across the hall into the courtroom. Once seated, Angelo turned around, looking over the bench seats behind him. He saw Kat seated in the far back row. He turned to Rosa and said, "That's Catharine. I don't get it. First of all, why the hell is she here? And secondly, if she's here, who the hell's cleaning my house?"

"I think you're going to get an answer to the first question sooner than you want, and I'm afraid the answer to the second question is, no one."

The judge walked in shortly. The jury was seated, and with all the appropriate parties now where they were supposed to be, the judge looked at Marvin and said, "Mr. Jackson, do you have any rebuttal on behalf of the state?"

"Yes, Your Honor, I do. The state calls Kat Rickter to the stand to be sworn."

Angelo whispered, "Her name's not Kat Rickter, it's Catharine, Catharine Ramey."

"Apparently, Angelo, you're mistaken," she whispered.

"Please state your name."

"Kat Rickter."

"Occupation?"

"Up until today, I was the housekeeper for the defendant. Today I'm unemployed." She turned to the defendant and said, "Mr. Bonaventura, I quit."

Everyone turned to look at Angelo.

He turned to Rosa and whispered, "What the hell's going on here?"

Marvin examined her as to a number of factual foundational issues and then said, "What did you do for the defendant?"

"Cleaned his house, but while I was there, I installed a camera in his office so I could film his conversations. I wanted to know if he killed Mr. Stone and Ms. Harper."

"Were you able to come up with anything?"

Rosa stood. "Wait a minute, just wait a minute. Might I voir dire the witness, Your Honor?"

"Proceed."

Rosa started walking toward the witness. "What's your occupation, ma'am?"

"Nothing. I'm unemployed. I'm independently wealthy. Don't need employment. I do, in my spare time, however, work to help women that are in trouble getting them out of their 'situations,' if I can. Gail Harper was just such a woman, and she was murdered by the defendant. So I wanted to help bring him to justice, which is why I'm here."

"Who do you work for?"

Rosa stepped closer. *"Who do you work for?* You didn't do this on your own. No one's that crazy. What law enforcement agency employs you?"

Kat calmly looked at Rosa and said, "My husband was Mike Rickter, a cop with the Nashville Police Department. He was murdered by a man who was in many ways just like the defendant. I swore after his death I would do all I can, on my own, to rid the world of people like him, which is why I did what I did."

The silence of the jurors was suddenly broken by their soft whispers when the jury put two and two together and figured out who she was. Most everyone in Nashville had heard the name Mike Rickter after his well-publicized murder.

"Why are you just coming up with this now? Why didn't you provide the information prior to commencement of this trial?"

Marvin stood and said, "You know, Your Honor, I believe the purpose for voir dire is over. She's asking questions which I believe are appropriate only for the attorney that called her, and that would be me. I would ask that the court terminate this line of questioning and allow me to continue with the state's rebuttal."

"I agree. Ms. Norway, be seated. Let the state continue. You'll get your chance to actually examine the witness when he's finished."

Rosa turned and walked back to her seat. As she did, Angelo said, "What the hell is happening here? Do you know what's on that video?"

"Be still, Angelo. Let's see what happens here. I need to listen to what's going on from the stand, not from you. Now just be still for a moment."

Marvin said, "You were saying you were able to set up a camera in his house? Where was it located?"

"In his office."

"I assume you filmed something that was pertinent to the case?"

"Yes."

"Why are you just coming forward now?"

"Because I was just able to retrieve the drive. I just watched it myself. I would have been here sooner, but the drive only became available to me, and I contacted you as soon as I watched it."

"But I'm still not sure I understand your motivation. You went undercover for the sole purpose of trying to help convict this man? Is that what you're saying?"

"Yes."

"Has this drive been in your possession and control since the video was made?"

"Yes."

"Have you had it altered, or would anyone have been in a position to have altered it without you knowing?"

"No."

Marvin turned his attention to the judge.

"Your Honor, I need to make a professional statement."

"Proceed."

"Your Honor, I only saw this video for the first time last night. I called one of our techs, and he along with an independent tech

I contacted both examined the flash drive she used. They've both determined it was not altered in any way. It's an original, and the contents it contains are legitimate."

Rosa stood immediately. "Your Honor, we have the right to inspect and to determine that ourselves. We shouldn't have to rely on self-serving statements of the state's attorney."

"Remember now, Ms. Norway, this is rebuttal, and the rules on rebuttal aren't quite the same. Let's play the video. Overnight, I'll allow you to contact anyone you wish with a copy of the drive and let them determine its legitimacy. Is that acceptable?"

"Do I have any other options?"

"No."

"Then I guess it's acceptable."

Rosa sat back down, and Marvin continued.

"Mr. Bailiff, please bring in that large-screen computer I have in the hallway."

The bailiff nodded and walked into the courthouse hallway, returning with a computer containing an oversized monitor.

"Please place it facing the court and jury so all can see. Perhaps the defendant and his council can slip over alongside the jury box and watch from there."

The bailiff placed the computer where directed. The judge had the drive marked as an exhibit and directed Marvin to make a copy available for Rosa.

"Please insert the drive, Mr. Bailiff. Let's see what we have."

For the next few minutes, everyone sat spellbound, while the drive gave up Angelo's secret. No one moved. Everyone remained glued to the screen until all the parties, except the defendant, had left Angelo's office.

"Turn it off, Mr. Bailiff."

Kat sat motionless, still, in the witness chair.

Angelo finally broke the silence, slamming his fist down on the jury box.

"Goddamnit, that's not me!" he screamed. "That thing's been doctored."

"Mr. Bonaventura, return to your chair. Let your attorney handle this. One more outbreak like that, I'll place you in another room. You can watch what's going on from there."

Both Rosa and the defendant walked to their table as the judge said, "Ms. Norway, your witness."

Rosa again stood. "So you're working for no one, is that your story?"

"Yes."

"No one from law enforcement helped you or was involved in this in any way?"

"No." Kat remained cold, indifferent, as if this was simply another day on the job. "I decided this man should be put away, and I needed to help if I could. I had a fake ID set up, Angelo hired me, I set up the camera, and Mr. Bonaventura and his men provided the entertainment."

"Did anyone else know anything about what you were doing?"

"No."

Rosa knew that answer was incorrect, but she also knew Kat would do and say whatever was necessary to keep both she and Joni out of the mix. That was just the way it had to be—do and say whatever was necessary to make sure the drive, and the information contained on it, remained the focal point.

"Your Honor, my client has a right to privacy in his own home. We object on that basis also."

"You're probably a little late with the objection, but it doesn't matter anyway. She wasn't working for any state agency or law enforcement agency of any kind. She was in the house legitimately. She was his employee. I see no criminal issues. Now, he may have a right to sue her personally, but that doesn't affect these proceedings in criminal court. No matter when you made your objection, it would have been, and is, overruled."

Rosa turned and sat down. "Judge, I have nothing more at this time. But I reserve the right to recall this witness after I've had a chance to have the drive examined by our own experts."

"Noted. Folks, let's take a break and reconvene tomorrow morning. I wanna give council a chance to have the drive examined. See you here, in your seats, at nine a.m."

The judge slammed down his gavel. Kat got up from the witness chair and met Marvin, who had started walking toward her. Rosa told Angelo to meet her in the conference room in a moment. She needed to discuss the rest of the proceedings with Marvin when he was done with his discussion with Kat.

Angelo and his men left the courtroom, and as he did, Rosa motioned to Marvin. He walked toward her, leaving Kat alone, and said, "I thought that went quite well."

Rosa smiled. "I would say it did. Are you going to place her in protective custody tonight? He'll be looking all over for her. She's not safe."

"That's already been discussed. She's reluctant, as you can imagine, but she's agreed to stay where I put her, under protection, at least for tonight."

"Good. I better go meet with my client. Well done, Marvin, well done."

"Thanks," he whispered. "Couldn't have done it without you."

She turned to walk into the lion's den. Rosa only wished she had someone that could help her with this meeting. She knew how it was going to go. It wasn't going to be pretty. People would, without doubt, be able to hear him yelling at her all the way to Chattanooga.

CHAPTER 46

"*Sounds like you had an exciting day.*"

"Not sure I would describe it as 'exciting.' More like disastrous."

They sat in the back of a small sandwich shop in Mount Juliet, each with a refreshed cup of coffee. A small plate, once containing a large piece of chocolate cake, drizzled with caramel, and covered in whip cream, pushed off toward the wall, now sat empty with nothing left to fully substantiate what once adorned it.

John said, "Did you know anything about this woman before today?"

"Hell no. She was as much a surprise to me as she was to everyone else. I'll tell you one thing though, she's good—she's really good at what she does. For her to go into his house, undercover—well, all I can say is wow. She's got a lot more courage than I have."

"Marvin said she was very convincing."

"She was very believable, yes, but the video told the tale. *If* it's authentic, which I'm thinking it probably is, Angelo is in it up to his neck."

"Are you having it authenticated?"

"As we speak. I told them to run every test they could think of and to work all night if necessary. They need to conclude it's been altered, or we're cooked."

"Do you have nothing else to offer?"

"Just him. Just him saying it's all doctored up, but if that's not what the experts say, I have no idea where we go from here."

"Where is she from anyway? Sounded like there was so much confusion today, no one ever mentioned her address. Is she from around here, or from Nashville? I, of course, along with everyone else, know the story of her husband, but nobody seems to know where she actually lives now."

He was asking too many questions about someone else's business. She swore she would keep the details about Kat private until Kat disclosed whatever she wanted to disclose. It just wasn't Rosa's business to disclose Kat's business.

"I don't know. Guess it doesn't matter much now anyway. The drive is the issue, not her."

"True. How did Angelo take it?"

"I actually thought he was mad enough to strike me. He was insane. You can't ever one-up him, you know, and that's exactly what she did. He was all over the conference room yelling and screaming about the video being altered. I finally just said we need to go. We walked out together, but he said nothing as he left me. I'm thinking he had other things on his mind. Most likely things he wanted me to know nothing about."

"So what's your position now? Are you just going to put him back up on the stand and let him deny everything?"

"Not much else I can do."

Rosa took another sip of coffee. As she returned the cup to the table, he reached over and took her hand.

"Actually, I didn't set up this date with you to talk about him. Can we talk about us for a moment?"

"Sure. What about 'us'?"

"Do you love me?"

"Absolutely."

With his free hand, he pulled a small box out of his pocket and laid it on the table.

She looked down at the box and then at him. He smiled but said nothing. Again, she looked at the box and back at him. Again, he said nothing.

"What… is… that?"

"Do you love me enough to wear this?"

She grabbed the box and opened it. Inside, she found something she never expected to see during her lifetime. She found a silver band with a single diamond, at least a karat.

"Will you marry me?"

She couldn't get the words out fast enough.

"Yes yes yes!"

She put the ring on her finger, and through the tears, she grabbed his hand, pulling him to his feet. She wrapped her arms around him and kissed him. She didn't care how many others were watching or where she was or what tomorrow might bring in that courtroom. All that mattered was him, and now, and him.

She leaned back. "Why now, why here, of all places?"

"You're having a tough go of it with this trial, and certainly the past few months have been difficult for you. I just thought it was time to brighten your spirits. I knew it was going to happen anyway. It might as well be now, while I had the opportunity. I figured you'd go back to work when we left here. I was just feeling it tonight. Honestly, I was a little concerned about your answer. Thank you. You've made my day—my month—my life. I love you."

He kissed her again.

She returned to the office a few minutes later. She was literally on top of the world. She figured that would last only a few more hours. She would need all the strength she could muster to travel from one extreme to the other in such a short time. She would proceed from being on top of the world with John to controlling the monster she was representing, in but a few short hours.

Trial, Day 12

One could cut the tension in the courtroom with a knife. Everyone was seated, ready to proceed.

"Ms. Norway, have you had an opportunity to have the drive examined?"

Rosa stood. "Yes, Your Honor, we have. They concluded it was authentic and had not been altered."

"So be it. The exhibit was already admitted into the record subject to your examination, but I'll now revise that to show that it is an exhibit and is to be made a part of this record no differently than any other exhibit. Are you wanting to present any surrebuttal?"

"Yes, Your Honor, the defendant has decided to respond."

"Please proceed."

"Angelo, please take the stand. Remember, you're still under oath."

The defendant rose, smoothed out his suit, and proudly sauntered to the witness stand, where he took his time sitting down and making himself comfortable.

"Mr. Bonaventura, you had the opportunity to review the video just as we all did, did you not?"

"Yes."

"What's your response to what you saw?"

He looked toward the back of the courtroom, where Kat was seated. He slowly raised his arm and pointed his index finger toward her.

"That woman is a lying bitch. That video was fabricated. I don't care what anyone says, that's not me." His voice continued to increase in intensity and volume as he proceeded. He rose from his chair. "Somehow she's found a way to alter that video without anyone figuring out how. I did *not* commit those murders! She's a lying, fucking bitch. That's what I got to say!"

Rosa turned to look at Kat. She had a grin from one side of her face to the other.

"Your Honor, Your Honor, I would ask that this witness be admonished from using that kind of language. That he be ordered to return to his seat. He is out of order, Your Honor, out of order."

"I realize that, Mr. Jackson, but thanks for pointing it out," Judge Beason said sarcastically. "Mr. Bonaventura, sit down—*now*."

The defendant continued his stare at Kat, but finally turned and acknowledged the judge.

"Sit."

Angelo slowly sat down, his face as red as the Tennessee sun during the middle of summer.

He turned and looked at the jury. "I can only tell you the truth. That was not me on that video. I didn't commit those murders. I can only hope you believe what I tell you, because it's the truth."

Rosa looked at the jurors. She couldn't read them. She could only hope the jury based their decision on the evidence that was submitted and not on the insane rantings of a lunatic. She turned her attention to Angelo for one last question. "Again, Mr. Bonaventura, did you kill the two victims in this case, or did you have anyone murder them for you?"

"Absolutely not."

"We have nothing further, Your Honor."

"Cross, Mr. Jackson?"

"No, Your Honor. The state will let the video speak for itself."

"Very well. Mr. Bonaventura, you may step down." The judge turned his attention to the jurors. "Ladies and gentlemen, the court needs to review the jury instructions and has some additional work to complete out of your presence. You are hereby dismissed until one p.m. today, at which time you will listen to the courts instructions and hear closing statements from the attorneys. Please continue to remember my admonition to you."

Rosa turned to Angelo and said, "Meet me in the conference room. We'll discuss where we're going from here."

Angelo and his men walked out of the courtroom and into the hallway. As they did, Rosa looked at Kat and mouthed the words "women's bathroom."

Kat nodded her head affirmatively.

Rosa talked with Marvin for a moment, then noticed Kat had walked out of the room. She walked into the hallway and into the woman's bathroom, which now only contained Kat.

Rosa hurriedly walked to Kat and embraced her.

"You were incredible, absolutely incredible."

Kat smiled. "Will it be enough?"

"We can only hope. Listen, let them provide you with some protection until this is all over, okay?"

"Nope. Don't need it. I've handled situations much more difficult than this one in my life. When you finish tonight, come on out. I'll fix supper, and we'll drink until were drunk."

"Okay, it's your life I guess. Got some great news I'll share with you then. See you tonight."

Rosa hurriedly left the bathroom and walked through the conference room door. She sat down to discuss the proceedings that would follow during the afternoon hours. Angelo was surprisingly upbeat. Maybe he knew something she didn't. After having tried so many cases in her career, she was pretty good at assessing their subsequent outcome. If she were a betting woman, if he was truly optimistic about winning the case after hearing the evidence she just heard, she would bet he was about to be sorely disappointed.

CHAPTER 47

"Well, Rosa, where do we go from here?"

Rosa thought for a moment and said, "What are your thoughts about that video, Angelo? I heard what you said on the stand, but we're alone. You're talking to your attorney now. Is that you and your men or not?"

"It wasn't me." He stood, and then started to pace around the room. "I'm not sure how they did that, but that's not me, and it's not my men. I never killed those people."

"Well, I'm not sure how the jury is going to disregard what they just saw."

Rosa could tell that passive attitude he had exhibited when she walked in the room had disappeared, and in its place was the Angelo she had come to know so well—domineering, controlling, revengeful.

"You know that's an invasion of my privacy, don't you? I'll have you sue the shit out of that bitch once this is over. So what happens next?"

"The judge will read the instructions, both parties will make closing statements and the case will be submitted to the jury. But, Angelo, I'm telling you that video is going to hurt us. If the jury relies on that video, you better have your bags packed, because this isn't going to end well."

Angelo had just turned the corner of the table, walking slowly away from Rosa, but as soon as her statement ended, he wheeled around and slammed his fist on the table immediately in front of Rosa. He leaned over the table, staring at her, the veins on his neck about to hemorrhage, and screamed, "Goddammit. Rosa, that wasn't me in that video. That wasn't me."

Rosa never flinched. She had never been afraid of him, and his dramatic outburst changed nothing in that respect.

She stood up quickly, pushing the chair back with her legs, causing it to fall backward, creating a resounding noise as it hit the floor. She leaned over the table, not inches from his face, slammed her fist down next to his, and said, "Well, goddammit, it sure as hell looks like you. And if I were a betting woman, I would by God say it *is* you."

They stood, both quiet, their eyes locked. No one in the room said a word.

The silence was suddenly broken by a knock on the door.

Rosa turned away from the conflict and walked to the door.

"Ms. Norway, there's been a problem." It was the bailiff. Rosa had known him for years, and knew him well enough to observe he was clearly upset.

"There's been an accident out front with that female witness that just testified. The judge wants to see you right away."

Rosa stood in the doorway, trying to comprehend what he was saying.

"What... what kind of accident? Is she okay?"

"Better go see the judge. I'm not sure. Just better go see the judge."

She turned around and saw Angelo standing there with a grin on his face. He was close enough to the conversation; he no doubt heard every word the bailiff just said.

"Is there a problem, Rosa?"

"You stay here. Don't leave here until I return."

She opened the door, closed it with a resounding thud, and started down the hallway. After a few steps, she turned and walked back to the bailiff. "Don't let them out of that room until I get back. Do you hear me? Do you understand? Do *not* let them leave here before I get back."

"I understand, Ms. Norway. I'll keep them here until you return."

Rosa turned and walked quickly to the judge's chambers. Marvin was standing in front of the judge's desk when Rosa walked in.

"What's going on, judge?" Rosa asked.

Both the judge and Marvin turned toward her as she approached.

Marvin looked at Rosa and said, "Rosa, Kat's been shot. Just as she left the courthouse, someone shot her."

Rosa could feel the blood leave her face.

"Is she okay? Is she badly hurt?"

"We don't know. It just happened. They're waiting for an ambulance now. She's still lying out there."

Rosa turned around and ran to the door. She knew she had to help in any way she could. She pressed the elevator button a couple of times with no success, so she ran to the stairway, kicked off her shoes, which she felt would only hinder her, and ran the flight of steps to street level.

As she walked out the door, she could see a few people gathered around the curb. Law enforcement had traffic stopped in both directions. She ran to the location and squeezed through the circle of people surrounding the form lying with her head and upper torso on the sidewalk, and the rest of her body in the street.

Rosa could hear the distant sound of an ambulance as it approached, but from what she observed, she was concerned it would never arrive in time.

She kneeled down by Kat and could tell the wounds were definitely life threatening. One shot had struck her in the chest, the other in her lower abdomen. There was blood everywhere—on her, on the street, on the sidewalk.

Rosa kneeled down on both knees, near Kat's head, and took her hand. She could tell Kat was in and out of consciousness. Kat looked up at her and smiled.

"The son of a bitch got me. Figured I might... have an issue... with him, but not this soon."

"Don't talk, Kat. Stay still. You're fine. You'll be fine. Just rest. The ambulance is on its way."

"Rosa, Rosa... that video."

"Don't talk, Kat. Yes, you got him. You got him with the video."

"No... No... the note... that video."

Rosa was crying now, just praying to everything that was holy she didn't die.

"Kat, just relax, sweetheart. The ambulance is almost here."

She looked up just as the ambulance crew jumped out of the back of the ambulance.

"Ma'am, move back. Ma'am, move back, please, so we can get to her."

Rosa looked down at Kat and could tell she was now unconscious. She pulled free of her hand and rose to her feet, walking a few steps away so they could place her on the gurney and move her into the back of the ambulance.

As it roared away from the courthouse, Rosa looked down and noticed she had blood on her dress. The sight of the blood snapped her back into reality.

She looked up toward the second floor of the courthouse, the floor where the conference rooms were located. Luckily, the room Angelo was in was on the other side of the building, so if the bailiff did his job, Angelo would have never witnessed any of the activity involving Kat. She would need to change her dress before she confronted him again. She wanted him to have no indication of any kind that she was in any way involved in helping Kat as she lay on the pavement.

Rosa walked back through the courthouse doors and took the steps up to the courtroom floor, retrieving her shoes as she walked. Upon arriving, she hurriedly walked down to the conference room and asked the bailiff if he had allowed anyone to leave. He indicated no one had left the room.

She walked back to the judge's chambers, where Marvin and the judge still remained. They looked at the blood, then Rosa, saying nothing, waiting for her to speak first.

"She was shot. I tried to help her, but I think she's in big trouble. They've taken her to the hospital. I obviously need to change clothes. What time do you wanna reconvene, judge?"

"Do you think we should recess until next week?"

"No. I wanna get this over with. Marvin, you okay with that—at least finish up with closing arguments today?"

"Yes, that's fine with me."

"Judge, I really don't think any of this should be communicated to the jurors by you. I don't want your comments to influence them in any way."

"I agree, Rosa. Why don't you go change your clothes, and let's all grab a bite to eat—maybe reconvene around two. Is that enough time for both of you?"

Both indicated it would be sufficient.

Rosa hurriedly left the courthouse and drove to Mount Juliet for a change of clothing. She grabbed a sandwich from Burger King on her way to Interstate 40, consuming it quickly while driving back to the courthouse.

After parking her vehicle, as she walked back up the courthouse steps, she called the hospital, but, of course, no one would give out any information concerning Kat's condition.

Upon arriving at the conference room, the bailiff informed Rosa that one of the deputies had provided the occupants of the room with a sandwich for lunch. She walked in to a flood of questions from everyone in the room, but Angelo. He never asked a question about what occurred on the street below, because, no doubt, he already knew what happened.

Rosa mentally proceeded through her closing one more time. The judge sent the bailiff, indicating he was ready to finish up.

Presenting her closing statement was simply a blur. She did the best she could under the circumstances. Angelo told her she had done a good job, so at least he was satisfied. The judge sent the jury home, indicating he would submit the case to them tomorrow morning.

Didn't matter much to her when it was submitted. Her thoughts were only of her friend. Of the friend she had only just met a few months ago, but, during that short span, had grown to admire and respect as much as anyone she had ever known.

On the way home, she called the hospital and finally got through to someone who seemed to know the name Kat Rickter.

"Can you tell me her condition? Is she going to be all right?"

"Let me look for a moment. Hold on a second."

Rosa waited for someone to pick up, and after what seemed an eternity, the nurse said, "Hello, hello. Sorry to keep you waiting. You still there?"

"Yes, yes, I'm here. How is she?"

"Ma'am, can you tell me your name please?"

"Yes, of course. I'm Rosa Norway."

"Okay. You're named on her living will. I'm sorry to tell you, but she never made it to the hospital. She died en route."

Rosa terminated the call immediately. She found a rest stop not far down the road and pulled off the heavily traveled interstate. She was crying so hard, she couldn't tell the difference between the road-way and the shoulder. She needed to control her emotions before she drove another mile.

Angelo had taken care of business one more time. She had now lost one of the best friends she ever had at the hands of this animal. She could only hope the jury would take care of business and put the man where he needed to be, or all of Kat's efforts, and even her death, would have been in vain.

CHAPTER 48

They sat quietly while conversation surged all around them. Rosa had met John for a quick cup of coffee at their coffee shop in the Providence Shopping Center south of Mount Juliet.

She had explained, when he called midafternoon and said he wanted to spend some time with her, that it had been a long day and a cup of coffee with him was about all she could handle. He already knew about Kat, as did most of the legal community.

"Now, you didn't actually know her, did you?"

"No, no, I didn't know her, but after her testimony, I was just so very impressed with her. I know her testimony might convict my client, but I was still impressed with the way she handled herself and with what she had done."

"She was a brave woman, I'll give her credit for that."

Rosa looked into space saying nothing, but finally broke her silence when she looked at John and said, "I know Angelo did this. There's no doubt in my mind. She may have said and done enough to get him convicted, but I know how his mind works. In his mind, he was the one that ended up getting the upper hand. He had her murdered."

"Now, wait a minute, you don't know that. From what I understand, she lived a dangerous life. She played a dangerous game, and she played time after time after time. It could have been anyone from any previous case she had been involved in prior to today. You don't know your client did this."

She considered his statements for a moment, until finally looking into her cup of coffee and saying softly, "You're right. I don't. I guess he's innocent until proven guilty. Certainly considering her lifestyle, he deserves the benefit of the doubt when it comes to Kat. She affected a lot of people's lives, and any one of them could have finished her off."

"What's your thoughts on what the jury's going to do?"

"I don't know. I honestly don't know. Looking at it objectively, I'm not sure how they can disregard that video, but as you know, Angelo has always had a way with juries. He always finds a way to get off, and I'm just not sure this will be an exception. Guess we'll know tomorrow."

"Was the video that convincing?"

"Was for me."

"Wonder how long she had that camera filming? Would it have been able to view his other men talking about prior crimes they committed?"

"I honestly don't know. I need to go. It's been a long day, and I'm ready to put my feet up and relax. I'm sorry I'm not very civil tonight, but it's really been a tough day for me."

"I understand."

Trial, Day 13

Wednesday morning came too soon. Instead of relaxing, she spent most of last evening doing the best she could to review a mountain of phone messages and notes. But now it was time to finish up the Bonaventura trial one way or the other, and move on.

They both sat quietly, listening as the judge read the final instructions to the jury. He would shortly submit the case to them, and then would begin the long wait to which she had grown to accept, but not enjoy, especially in cases like this. The purpose was to win—to win the case so your client was satisfied, and you were well paid. This one was all screwed up. If she won, she lost, if she lost, she won.

The judge finished his instructions, and the bailiff took the jury to the jury room to deliberate Angelo's fate. She took him to the conference room and discussed his options based upon all the different scenarios. Angelo was confident they would never convict. He wouldn't listen to options available if he were convicted. To him, that just wasn't going to happen.

The jury was out just a little over an hour. They had listened to evidence for literally weeks, and it apparently hadn't taken but a little over sixty minutes to review all that evidence and come to a unanimous decision.

They stood in front of judge and jury while the judge discussed the results of their deliberation with the jury foreman, but the only word she heard was "guilty."

She wouldn't soon forget Angelo's look of surprise, nor the glare that followed as they cuffed him and walked him out the courtroom door. His men disappeared out the back door of the courtroom. She was certain, based on the video, that they too would soon be arrested for the murder of Stoney and Gail. Didn't matter to her. All that mattered was that Kat's efforts hadn't been in vain. The man that murdered Stoney and Gail had finally been brought to justice.

She knew he would want to appeal, and she would handle it for him. She would present the appropriate basis for appeal to the court of criminal appeals for review. She would try just hard enough to be convincing and appear competent, but not try hard enough to be successful.

His sentencing was scheduled for the middle of next month, so she would have plenty of time to put together a motion for new trial and notice of appeal.

The jury verdict had been rendered some nine hours earlier, and Rosa sat, with Nicki, in a Starbucks on Westend Avenue, discussing the trial, discussing Kat, discussing men.

"So what's going to happen to Angelo?"

"I'm thinking probably the max. Most likely, the judge will order the terms to run consecutively, not concurrently. He'll be there until he dies."

"Exactly what he deserves."

"Finally. But you know, I'm just not sure it was all worth it. We put him away for probably the rest of his life, but we lose someone like Kat. I mean I realize we probably saved a lot of people's lives by convicting Angelo, but we also lost a lot of good in this world as a result of Kat's death."

"It's over. Nothing we can do about any of it. It's over. When is her funeral? I haven't heard."

"Wednesday."

"Wanna go together?"

"Sure."

"Marvin's taking me. Why don't you just meet us at my house, and we can go to the funeral home together."

"How are you and Marvin doing? I haven't had a chance to visit with you at all concerning your relationship."

"Great. Thank you. Thank you for setting us up. You definitely knew what you were doing."

"You know, Kat didn't have much left in the way of family. But I do know most of the Nashville police force will be at the funeral. She was so well respected, not only because she was Mike's wife, but because of how she handled herself in helping to convict a man the police force just couldn't apprehend."

"Is John going?"

"I don't know. I haven't discussed it with him."

"Is everything okay with the two of you?"

Rosa smiled for the first time during the forty-five minutes they had been seated. "Yes, everything's great. He's the only positive in my life since Stoney was murdered. I'm thinking maybe a June or July wedding."

"Wow. That's great. You know, I don't think he and Marvin get along the best. He's never said much about their relationship, but it just doesn't seem to be very good."

"John's not an easy man to get to know. Marvin needs to give their relationship a little more time. John's a person that bears knowing. I can bear witness to that."

"Hey, maybe a double wedding. Whatta ya think?"

Rosa shrugged her shoulders. "Could be. That's certainly something to think about. You and Marvin really that close already?"

Rosa never heard her response. Her mind wondered to conversations by the fire, laughing together after a fourth or fifth glass of wine, parking in the barn, and to her friend—to her friend she would never have the privilege of spending time with again. They had grown so close in such a short time. The thought of never seeing her again was overwhelming.

CHAPTER 49

*L*ate summer in middle Tennessee had been dry. But today, the
September rain that fell was quickly consumed by thirsty soil,
creating little, if any, runoff. Rosa, Marvin, and Nicki walked
in the rain to the funeral home, attending the service, then watched
through a light drizzle, as they carried her body to the hearse. The
weather didn't matter much to Rosa. In fact, it seemed appropriate:
gloomy and dark, consistent with the mood of so many people gathered to bid farewell to a woman many didn't really know personally,
but respected.

A great number of the Nashville Police Department turned out
to honor a woman who had given her life to stop a man no one else
could touch. Rosa did the same. She paid tribute to a friend and
someone she couldn't and wouldn't ever forget.

John didn't make it. He had urgent business that presented itself
about an hour before he was to leave, and called Rosa to cancel. John
told her he really didn't know Kat. It was apparent, even though
he didn't specifically say it, he really didn't appreciate what she had
done. Didn't matter to Rosa. She knew what Kat had done, and she
was exactly where she wanted to be.

Kat appeared to have no family, at least no one that felt close
enough to her to present themselves as family at the funeral. Rosa
had no idea who was in charge of Kat's affairs. As much as Kat was

supposedly worth, she figured some lawyer probably had his hands plunged deeply into the pot by now. That issue was also of no consequence to Rosa. Kat's money never seemed to mean much to her and was never a subject of conversation.

The service ended around three, and Rosa had Marvin drop her off at the office. Her desk was a mess with message piled on message upon message. She felt like throwing a match in the center and watching it all burn. It would take time to get over the feeling of despair she felt with the loss of Kat. She finally concluded, after standing in front of her desk and surveying the mound of messages, that perhaps the easiest way to forget was to just simply dig in.

She sat down and started reading the messages when one specific message caught her attention. It was from an attorney in Lebanon. Don Hyslip had been in practice for years. He handled mostly probate matters, including trusts, living, and testamentary. He was well considered in the community, and he had apparently called to visit with Rosa. She had no cases pending with him, and did not know him socially, so she assumed his call involved a new legal issue and wasn't personal.

He asked her to return the call, but left no information concerning the nature of the business he had with her. The call wasn't the most important one she needed to return, but it was the most intriguing one on her desk. It would be the first one she returned.

"Hi, Don. Rosa Norway. How're you?"

"Well, Rosa. Good to hear from y'all. How are ya today?"

His voice told the tale, at least as to his history, his heredity, his heritage. His thick drawl could have been cut with a dull steak knife.

"I'm fine, Don, fine. I noticed you called. What's going on?"

"Well now, Rosa, truth of the matter is, I need to sit a spell and visit with y'all when you have time. I'd like ya to mosey over and meet with me here in my office. Won't take long, ya know, but

I'd like to see ya as soon as y'all can get here, you know, as long as it doesn't conflict with your schedule."

"What's this about?"

"Well, I'd just rather tell ya in person, Ms. Rosa, if y'all don't mind."

"Is it important? I mean, does this need to be handled quickly, or can it wait until next week or so?"

"Ya know, I just don't think y'all should wait that long. I'll tell you it's about your friend Kat, Kat Rickter. I will tell ya that much."

"I can be there tomorrow morning. What time?"

"Well, I'm kinda slow getting round anymore. How's nine a.m. sound to y'all?"

"See you then."

She terminated the call. What the hell was going on? She didn't mind meeting with him, but his approach to the English language did bother her. As slow and wordy as he was, she hoped she could force him into spitting out more than two words a minute, or her day would consist of nothing but saying hello, and little else. However, that didn't matter much to her. If the meeting involved Kat, she would be there, and stay as long as she could stand talking to Mr. Hyslip or until the clock struck midnight, whichever occurred first.

She walked in his office door at precisely 9:00 a.m. His secretary said he had not yet arrived. He practiced alone and had converted an old house into his office. Everything in his office was old—the furniture, the wall decorations, his secretary.

Rosa heard the door creak as someone entered the reception area. It was Don, walking with his cane and slowly entering the office he had maintained in this same spot for many, many years.

His mop of white hair flew in every direction. He wore a suit that was vintage 1950s, vest included. His multicolored tie was tied in an appropriate knot, but was pulled tight only to within three or four inches of his shirt collar. He walked over to Rosa and said, "Ms. Rosa, Ms. Rosa, so nice to see y'all. Glad you could make it on time."

His breath smelled like old socks, and he had an egg stain on his shirt, directly above the knot in his tie.

"Thanks, Don. I'm anxious to find out what this is all about."

"Follow me, Rosa, and I'll take you back to my office."

Inch by inch he led her down a dark passageway, to the doorway on the right, his office. It was littered with books, briefs, and articles all over his desk and floor. She took the liberty of removing a couple of magazines off one of the chairs before she sat down.

Once he was finally settled in an old rocker-style desk chair, which creaked loudly when he leaned back, he said, "Well, Ms. Rosa, let's get right down to business, shall we?"

Those were the best words Rosa had heard since his initial phone call. Perhaps this conference would end with some time left in the day to do something constructive.

"You knew Ms. Kat, didn't you? I mean, you knew her quite well, didn't you?"

"Yes, I knew her. I'm not sure how *well* I knew her, but I did know her. She was a good friend."

"Yes, Ms. Rosa, she must have been, she must have been." He paused for effect. "You see, I drew her will, and I'm executor of her estate. She left you a little something. Had her will changed about a month ago. She said she was doing somethun dangerous and wanted to get it updated. Now, I guess that was just pretty prophetic, based on her untimely death, wasn't it?"

"She left me something? I don't understand."

"In previous wills, she had donated most of her money to various charities, but she changed that. She left you a half million dollars, Ms. Rosa, a half million, and that's free and clear. If there are taxes to pay, they are to be paid out of the rest of the assets of the estate. The money to you is to be free and clear of any tax. You're a rich woman, Ms. Rosa."

Rosa sat silently, trying to take it all in. She said nothing, finally reaching into her purse, and pulling out a tissue as she started to tear up.

He started to grin and talked just a little faster when he said, "Now, Ms. Rosa, I can help you with that money if you wish. I can help you invest it or place it someplace where it might provide a great return for y'all if you wish."

"That won't be necessary, Don. Thank you. Thank you for telling me."

Rosa got up to leave his office, and as she did, he said, "There's more, Ms. Rosa. Please sit. Let me read you a short provision from her will."

Rosa sat back down as he pulled a four or five-page document from his pile of papers sitting near the front corner of his cluttered desk.

He put on a pair of vintage 1920s spectacles, adjusted them, and said, "Let me read what Article 8 says here in Ms. Kat's will. 'Article 8 I do hereby will, devise and bequeath my home and all surrounding real estate, along with all the contents of the buildings, to my friend Rosa Norway. I know she will enjoy the property as much as I have. I also know she will do her best to preserve its secrets for as long as she lives there.'"

Rosa looked down and again started to cry.

Mr. Hyslip looked over the top of those vintage glasses and said, "Now, Ms. Rosa, what does she mean by that? What does she mean when it says you will 'do your best to preserve its secrets'?"

Rosa wiped a tear away, looked up, and giggled softly.

"Now, Don, if I told you what secrets I needed to preserve, they would no longer be secrets, would they? Just never you mind."

CHAPTER 50

*I*t had been thirty days spent in slow motion. Everything seemed to move at a reduced speed since the end of the trial and the end of Angelo. Rosa worked on his application for a new trial, and on the accompanying brief in support, but not very hard. She had other cases and other issues involving her office practice that needed to be handled. She wanted the application and resulting hearings concerning a new trial to be just good enough to indicate her competence in such matters, but not good enough to prevail. Certainly a fine line and somewhat difficult to do, but she felt it was something she could handle.

He had called her almost every day since his conviction, and she would talk with him about every other time. His men had also contacted her with questions about other business activities, which she would try to answer, but she would soon put a stop to those calls. She wanted nothing more to do with any of the group.

Rosa had traveled to Kat's home a number of times since her funeral. Mostly she just wanted to make sure it was secure. She touched nothing. Other than spoilable items, which she tossed immediately, she left everything as it was the day Kat left her home to testify, her last day alive.

Rosa walked past the fire pit, Kat's words echoing in her mind, remembering all the talks they had while the flames warmed them.

She had no idea how much wine they consumed while sitting there, but to say it was substantial would have been an understatement.

Rosa walked in the barn, then onward to the trees beyond the barn. She remembered Kat's words concerning her final confrontation with Brakus and wondered what tales the property could tell her that Kat hadn't revealed. Kat's secrets were indeed safe. She cried many times as she thought about the loss of her friend, someone who had become so special to her in such a short time.

As Rosa sat, waiting, and having a final cup of coffee, she considered how much her life had changed in such a short time. Nothing seemed quite so important anymore. She had weathered the trauma of Stoney's death, then moved along the best she could. But Kat's death affected her like no other. After her death, life took on a slightly different flavor—everything seemed to move to a different rhythm. The money, like the property, had all been transferred to her. She would take it slow, considering each situation, but she would donate half of it to worthy charities, mostly those that were designed to protect victims of domestic violence. The rest she would put away for a rainy day for both she and John.

Rosa was about to stand and leave when Nicki finally walked through the door of the coffee shop where they normally met when she was in the Mount Juliet neighborhood.

Nicki purchased her cup, and as she approached the table, Rosa said, "Nice you could make it."

"I know, I know, but I needed to see this guy about car insurance, and I couldn't get away from him."

"What was he into, bondage?"

"Ha, ha, ha, that's real funny."

"Wasn't long ago it would have been a legitimate question. How are things between you and Marvin?"

"Great. Couldn't be better. You did good when you hooked us up. We seem to have a lot in common, and he's really the first guy in a long time I'm still involved with a few months after I met him. Setting a record here."

"Good. Glad I could help."

Rosa looked down at her cup and remained quiet.

Nicki was silent for a moment, finally saying softly, "You really miss her, don't you?"

Rosa never looked up. "She was the best. Yes, her death has affected me. She was all that was good in this world. I miss her. I miss our talks. I miss everything about her." She looked up at Nicki and smiled. "Time for me to move on, and I will, as we all have to do, but her death has definitely left its mark."

"What about Angelo? What's the story there? Are you still hearing from him?"

"Oh, sure. I will until all the legal issues are resolved one way or the other. Let's talk about something else. What about you and Marvin? Any future plans, or just playing it day by day?"

"We haven't really discussed the future involving *us*, but we have discussed his job. He and John don't seem to be getting along very well. Marvin can't put his finger on the problem, but just between you and I, he's about had enough. I think he's going to quit and start his own firm."

"Really? John's never mentioned any issues between the two of them. That surprises me."

"For God's sake, don't mention anything to John about it. I think Marvin is going to submit a thirty-day notice next week. He doesn't think the office will have any trouble replacing him, and he's just ready to move on. He isn't happy there, and I have encouraged him to get out and start up his own firm if it's actually the difference between him being happy and enjoying life."

"I agree completely. If it's reached that stage, he definitely needs to move on."

"What about you and John? Set a date yet?"

She hesitated for a moment, and then said, "Not... yet."

Nicki's eyes widened. "So trying to read between the lines here, I'm assuming that means you have finally accepted all this—that you're going to finally take the plunge and marry him, but just haven't set a date yet?"

"Kinda looks that way, Nicki. It just kinda looks that way."

Nicki grabbed her hand and said, "I'm so happy for you, Rosa. Finally! Finally, you're going to take the leap! And such a great guy too. I'm *so* happy for you."

"Well, you'll be right beside me through it all. I want you to be my maid of honor."

"I accept. I doubt Marvin will be his best man, but makes no difference at this point anyway. I'm just so happy for you."

"I think we'll probably just move into Kat's house. I'm definitely not going to sell it. I took him there the other day, and he was excited about the move. He'll have a little ground to play around on, and he didn't seem to particularly care about the commute. It's a wonderful house, well maintained, and big enough for a large family."

"Have you discussed children? What are his thoughts about starting a second family?"

"Yes, we've discussed it. I told him if it was going to happen, it better happen pretty soon. He's ten years older than I am. It's time it happens if it's going to, and we're both aware of that. The plan now is to have at least one."

"With the money you received from Kat's estate and both your incomes, you should be set financially. That helps too."

"He's still paying child support, but he has a good income and so do I. Much of Kat's money will be given to charity, but we'll save a little back for those unexpected issues. It'll all work out fine, but I would give it all up to be able to go visit Kat and sit around her fire pit once a week, I know that."

"She was a special woman, without doubt."

Neither said anything, both obviously lost in their memories of Kat, and the relationship each had with her.

After a few moments of silence, Nicki looked at Rosa and said, "You know your insurance needs really change after you marry. You do know that, don't you?"

Rosa smiled. "One thing about it, Nicki. Insurance needs may change, but you never do. You never, ever change."

CHAPTER 51

*S*he still felt it—the glow, the excitement, the euphoria. Her wedding had been an orgasmic experience! She never thought she would experience the incredible joy she felt as she walked down that aisle, single and alone, then back up that aisle married, and with a lifelong partner. It had been over three months, but she still shut her eyes to remember the joy, the exhilaration she experienced as she mentally walked down that aisle again and again.

Nicki was such a great help to her. She was there whenever she was needed. Marvin hadn't submitted his resignation at the time, and John, at the suggestion of Rosa, had asked him to be an usher. That worked out as well as it could have. It was apparent when the two men were together, there were simmering issues, but nothing that would be obvious to those who didn't know and couldn't recognize the intricacies of the two men. Marvin had only just submitted his letter of resignation, giving John thirty days to find a replacement.

Their honeymoon in the Smokies was an adventure she would never forget for as long as she lived. John was away from work and the pressures it brought with it. He focused on her and her alone, as she did with him. She could only hope their married years passed by as smoothly as the wedding and honeymoon.

They moved all of their possessions to Kat's farm. They had only been there a few weeks, but so far, it was like living a dream.

John loved the open spaces, rather than that continual cramped feeling he endured while living in the middle of the city of Nashville. He didn't seem to mind the commute.

He did, however, retain his townhouse in Nashville. There would most likely be issues concerning the location of his actual residency. Residency in Davidson County was a necessary requirement for the position of district attorney. He would assert a Davidson County residency because of his townhouse, but in the final analysis, he would most likely need to give up the position, and either run for the same office in Wilson County or go into private practice—either option was acceptable. All in all, it had been a good move for both of them.

John had left for the evening. He was reviewing resumes and wanted to find Marvin's replacement as quickly as possible. Rosa had left Kat's office intact. She had closed the double-glass doors when they moved in, and no one had been inside since. Tonight she was alone with little to do, and she had decided this was the night she would look through Kat's personal items in her desk and file cabinets.

The file cabinets actually contained nothing remarkable—mostly financial matters that were now just history since all of her investments had been terminated and the proceeds distributed.

Clad only in a pair of old pajamas, she sat down at Kat's desk, opening the middle drawer, the one immediately under the desktop, and as she did, she looked around, wondering what she should do with the room. Perhaps they could use it as an office for John, and if he didn't want to use the space, maybe an office for her.

Upon pulling the drawer open, the first item she noticed was a sealed envelope with her name on it. She removed it, looking at the remaining contents of the open drawer, but could find nothing else of significance.

She turned the envelope in her hands, but the only information on the envelope was her name. A "note"—no, that wasn't it—"*the note.*" She remembered, as Kat lay dying, she said the words "*the note.*" But she couldn't complete the sentence, and Rosa had no idea what it all meant. Maybe this was the note Kat was talking about.

Rosa carefully opened the envelope, and inside was one sheet of paper. It was addressed to Rosa and was typewritten:

> *Rosa,*
>
> *If you are reading this note, it means I am probably no longer alive. I have always been fully aware of the chances I took becoming involved in the type of work I did, and I knew this job concerning Angelo was particularly dangerous. I knew the risks involved, so don't beat yourself up concluding you had something to do with my ultimate demise. Just have another glass of wine, and wish me the best in my new life, where ever I ended up.*
>
> *There is one more matter which I needed to discuss with you, but not until Angelo's trial had concluded. You had enough on your mind without this additional issue.*
>
> *I gave you all the flash drives I had involving Angelo's office, which were accumulated while we waited to acquire the information we needed concerning Stoney's murder. They are all numbered, except one. It has the letter 'A' on it. You need to go through those drives and find that one. It speaks for itself. Don't hesitate. You need to review it as soon as possible.*

Rosa, you became, in a short time, one of the best friends I ever had. Hopefully, life will turn out better for you than it did for me.

Love Kat

Rosa read the note again. What struck her as much as anything was the urgency it seemed to convey. Obviously, whatever was on that drive was something Kat felt Rosa should view immediately. Rosa saved all the drives. She would never throw anything of that nature away. The night was young. John wouldn't be home for a couple of hours. She needed to get dressed, go to the office, and find that drive.

It took her nearly twenty minutes to throw on some clothes, drive to the office, and locate the small box of flash drives she had placed on the floor of the office safe. She looked quickly through all those in the box, finally locating the drive marked *A*. She shoved it in the port and turned up the sound.

Angelo sat at his desk, shuffling through some paperwork. He continued to do so for over five minutes, causing Rosa to begin wondering what it might be she should be looking for. Her lack of interest quickly changed, and a rather uninteresting situation turned on a dime, when John walked in the room.

Angelo stood and extended his hand. "Johnny, Johnny, my friend, how are you?"

John shook his hand and said, "Whatta you want, Angelo? I need to return to work."

"Sit for a minute, Johnny, just sit for a moment." As they both sat down, Angelo said, "Did you get my payment? I deposited the fifty grand into your Chicago account yesterday. Did you check and make sure it was there?"

"Yes, yes, it's there," he said, clearly agitated. "Now, that's not why you summoned me. Whatta you want?"

"Well, what I really want is for you to get that ignorant fuck Marvin Jackson off my ass. Apparently, he's going to submit evidence he thinks they have on me concerning Stone and Gail, to a grand jury. I need him to get off my ass."

"I can't help you there, Angelo. It's his case. I don't think they'll indict anyway, and even if they do, the evidence just isn't there. But I can't interfere at this point. If you want me to continue to be your man in the district attorney's office, that's fine, but there are some things I just can't do, and this is one of them."

"Okay, okay, I understand. But you're still on board with knocking off Rosa if things don't go okay for me, aren't you? I mean if she learns too much, or I don't feel comfortable with her representing me anymore, and I feel maybe she knows too much, you're still okay with knocking her off, aren't you?"

"Yes, yes, I'll take care of her, just like I did that prick Stone."

"Good, good." Angelo stood and, as he did, so did John.

"I understand your predicament with Marvin what's-his-name, but do what you can to get him off my ass. Maybe I'll try to handle him another way. Just keep up the good work, Johnny, and I'll keep making the deposits."

Angelo extended his hand, and John shook it as he said, "Don't worry about me. I've been there for you a long time, Angelo. You can depend on me."

John turned and walked out the door as the screen went black.

Her face was covered in tears as she leaned back in her chair trying to assess and evaluate what she had just seen. He was on the take, and to make matters worse, he apparently was willing to kill *her,* if need be, once Angelo no longer had a use for her.

She slammed her fist down on the desktop in frustration. She would have never believed this if she hadn't seen the video. Thank

God for her friend Kat, or she would have had no idea until it was too late to do anything about it.

She picked up her phone and punched in Marvin's number. He answered immediately.

"Hi, Rosa. How're you? Haven't seen you in a while. What's going on?"

She couldn't think… she couldn't talk… the words wouldn't come.

"Rosa? Rosa? Is everything okay? Rosa?"

"Marvin…" She did the best she could through the torrent of tears. She heard Marvin stand.

"Rosa, do you need help? What's going on?"

"I just saw one of the other videos, Marvin… from a different day… in Angelo's office. And… and… John was there, Marvin… John was in his office."

He said nothing as he continued to try to assess what she had just said.

Finally, he said, "Oh, I'm sure there's been a mistake. You sure it was him? You actually saw the video?"

"It was him. He's not only taking money, but he told Angelo he would kill me if I got in the way… *kill me if I got in the way. Oh my god, Marvin, what should I do? I don't know what to do…*"

"I *knew* that son of a bitch was on the take," he screamed at her. "I knew it. You stay there. Don't you move 'til I tell you to. You're obviously in grave danger, Rosa. I'll handle this. Don't you leave that office 'til I tell you to."

"Okay, I'll stay here until I hear from you."

Marvin terminated the call, and she pulled out a box of tissues she had in the desk for her clients. During the next twenty minutes, she watched the video again and again. Each time, it helped her accept the fact that it was real, it was not a made-for-TV movie involving someone else's husband. It was the man she married—admitting to murder, admitting to accepting bribes, and admitting he would kill the woman he was now married to if his boss deemed it necessary.

She had just finished watching it one last time when she heard the office door open.

"Rosa, you here? Sweetheart, are you back there?"

It was John. She quickly pulled the drive from her computer and threw it into the back of one of her desk drawers.

She hesitated for a moment, but finally said, "Yes, John, I'm here."

She could hear his steps as he walked back to her office, finally peering around her doorway.

"What're you doing here so late? I thought you were staying home tonight. What're you doing down here?"

"Oh, I just had a few things to finish off, and I thought I'd get them done while it was quiet. Nothing that important, but I thought I'd just finish them off."

He walked in and sat down in front of her desk.

"You look like you've been crying. What happened?"

"Nothing, John, nothing. Just tears of joy. Marrying you and thinking about the marriage, that's all. Just tears of joy."

"Hmmm." He put his hands on the front of her desk and leaned forward.

"You know, I still have a few friends left at the sheriff's office, and one of them just called me. He said Marvin called them and wanted me picked up for questioning. He mentioned you had found a drive or something, a video implicating me taking bribes and murdering Stoney. Do you know anything about that?"

"No. I have no idea what he's talking about. I haven't talked to him tonight."

John leaned back and pulled his jacket away from his belt, displaying a pistol.

"Time to cut to the chase, Rosa. I need that drive, and I need it now."

"I don't know what the hell you're talking about, John. You're starting to scare me."

John got up, pulled the pistol from its holster, and started to pace back and forth in front of her desk.

He never looked at her as he spoke.

"Rosa, you *do* have that drive, and I need it now. It has to be destroyed before they view it. You know that and so do I." He stopped and faced her. "If I have to kill you, I will. I'm not going to prison. I'll never ever go to prison, not for you, not for anyone. Now, I want that drive. Give it to me, or so help me God, I'll shoot you, move you off your chair, and rip up that desk of yours along with your whole office until I find it."

He pointed the pistol at her and cocked it. As he did, a familiar voice echoed down the hallway.

"Rosa, Rosa, you in there? It's Chief Spring. Are you there? Can I come on in?"

John quickly turned toward the doorway, toward the voice originating from the front of the office.

John said, "Stay out. Don't walk down the hallway. Private meeting here. Go away." He turned to Rosa and said, "Who's that?"

Through her tears, she said, "John, that's the chief of police for Mount Juliet. Please, please, put the gun down and give yourself up. We'll work this out, John. Don't be foolish. Put it down."

He started pacing again, brandishing the weapon in one hand and running his fingers through his hair with the other.

"Rosa, we're coming in."

John stopped dead in his tracks. He looked down at Rosa and started to cry. "You know I love you, don't you? I would never ever do anything to hurt you. You know that, don't you?"

She stood. "Yes, John, I believe you. Now please, put the pistol down."

"Fuck, you know I can't do that, Rosa. I love you. Please just believe I would have never ever hurt you." He placed the gun next to his right temple and pulled the trigger.

The shot echoed loudly throughout the office.

Rosa dropped to her chair as she heard Chief Spring yell out, "Rosa, you all right? What's going on in there? We can work this out. Rosa, what's going on?"

She was finally able to tell the chief to come in. As he walked through her office door, she looked down in disbelief—at her intelligent, good-looking husband now lying dead on the floor.

She looked up at Chief Spring as he looked around her office in disbelief and said, "I was going to tell him later tonight he was going to be a father... a father. I'm pregnant. He was going to be a father..."

EPILOGUE

Mount Harper Cemetery
Nine Months Later

S he sat alone, in the middle of an overwhelming number of tomb-
stones. Rosa knew no one buried in this cemetery, except the
one she had come to talk with. Kat's tombstone was small and
inauspicious, but to Rosa, it was a shrine. She came here often. She
would tell Kat her troubles, normally in a nonverbal manner, but
sometimes in a verbal manner if she felt strongly about something
that had happened in her life. This time was different. Today was not
like the other visits. Today she brought Catherine with her, Catherine
"Kat" Norway, all of two months old.

The early autumn sun felt warm on her face. It was a perfect day
for reflection and for a visit to her friend's final resting place.

Rosa buried John in a different cemetery. She didn't want him
in the same resting place as her friend Kat. That just didn't seem
appropriate considering what both stood for during their lives.

She had recently petitioned the court to change her name from
Winstrom back to Norway, and she would do the same for Catherine.
She did not want her daughter or herself to be associated with John

in any respect, especially after, even in death, he was publically disgraced for his involvement with Angelo.

John had, however, done one thing correctly before he died. He let Nicki talk him into purchasing a large life insurance policy, the proceeds of which would now help establish an educational fund for Catherine. Rosa wasn't certain whether it was something he really wanted or something Nicki twisted his arm into buying, but either way, the proceeds had been paid out, which was all that mattered.

She no longer had to worry about Angelo anymore. Apparently, he tried to throw his weight around in prison, and someone stuck a knife in him. He was dead and with his death his motion for new trial and appeal died with him. She had heard by way of the grapevine that his band of thugs, other than the three who were indicted in Stoney's death, had a falling out. Without Angelo's brains, she knew the organization wouldn't last long.

Marvin and Nicki had been married for a little longer than two months. They seemed happy, and Rosa was happy for them. She had started their relationship and smiled to know the union of the two had been successful.

The child had made such a difference in her life. She had slowed her practice to a walk. She couldn't pay full attention to both jobs as a mother and attorney. It was reaching the point where one job or the other would need to take priority. She had already visited with Kat, and had concluded being a mother would, without doubt, take priority. Rosa didn't need the big retainer cases anymore nor did she want them. She had had enough of those kinds of cases with multiple issues and unmanageable clients consuming every hour of her time, both day and night. Those days were over. From now on, she would deal only with the simple cases—simple dissolutions, a few estates, some corporate work, nothing but simple, simple, simple, the rest of her career.

The baby was sleeping. The sun, the flowers, the soft green grass, the peacefulness overwhelmed all her senses.

She tried to recall the name of the guy who called the office this morning. She just couldn't remember. What did his phone message say? She tried, but she just couldn't remember everything it said…

She looked down at Catherine. She would make this child her first priority above all else.

But she continued to try to remember what that note said. Some man had sold a piece of land to someone, over near Knoxville. The purchaser dug up part of the ground while digging a well, and had found a body. As she remembered, not only had they dug up one, but later they had found ten more on the property before they stopped digging. The seller had now been charged with murdering all eleven people, and he wanted her to represent him.

No, no, no, much too difficult. Too much work. Way too involved.

Catherine never cried at night—she was so good.

Damn it, what the hell was that guy's name…?

She stood and waved good-bye to Kat, as she always did. As she walked away, she mumbled, "You know, I might just call that guy to see what the facts really are. It sounds way complicated and much too involved, but I guess it wouldn't hurt to visit with him for a moment and see…"

ABOUT THE AUTHOR

Forever Bound is the sixth novel written and released by J. B. Millhollin. This novel, as is the case with all his prior novels, draws heavily upon his trial experience, which covered a span of over forty years.

He and his wife enjoy life in middle Tennessee, where he continues to write on a daily basis. His next novel, *Redirect*, also focuses upon issues within the courtroom and should be available early next year.

CPSIA information can be obtained
at www.ICGtesting.com
Printed in the USA
LVOW12s0316290617

539750LV00001B/103/P